MW01065915

A BREED APART

By Charlotte Raby

Writers Exchange E-Publishing
http://www.writers-exchange.com
http://www.readerseden.com

A Breed Apart
Copyright 2006 Charlotte Raby
Writers Exchange E-Publishing
PO Box 372
ATHERTON QLD 4883

ISBN: Electronic 1920972838
        Print   9781921314261

Cover Art by: Glenda Tudor

Published Online by Writers Exchange E-Publishing
http://www.writers-exchange.com
http://www.readerseden.com

A BREED APART *Reviews*

Romantic Times 3/4 stars:
"… [this] sensual story is ripe with intriguing conflict between two strong characters. A satisfying read.
—*April Redmon*

Affaire de Coeur 4/6 stars:
"…Ms. Raby gifts us with unique touches…"
~*Heather Nordahl*

Rhapsody Magazine
Ms. Raby's plot clips along at a brisk pace with never a slow moment. She has a sharp eye for detail, and brings a fresh slant to the everyday life of cowboys and ranching.

Her thorough research into the field of veterinary science is commendable, this coming from an owner of livestock who was prepared to jump on any inconsistencies.

Kira and Holt are attractive and appealing. Kira, fiercely independent and head-strong, gives the "I'm-the-man-around-here" Holt a run for his money.

A BREED APART is a fun and sexy read. In her debut novel, Ms. Raby shows she's got what it takes with her clever and humorous take on daily ranch life in the Southwest.
~*Cathy McDavid*, Award Winning Romance Novelist

To Chris: my heart.

Charlotte Raby

Chapter One

A soft breeze carried the crisp odor of cow manure, telling Kira McGovern where to find her new coworkers. Male voices and animal sounds wafted on the dry air, and dust rose up in a cloud in front of the barn's open double doors. She stepped inside, where it was at least ten degrees cooler, and the conglomeration of sounds assaulted her senses. Cowboys bustled around, relaying bales of hay to the loft, cleaning stalls, grooming horses, and yelling commands to one another. In the distance, through the barn's other set of doors was a huge corral, holding several hundred head of lowing cattle, and beyond that, men were branding calves.

Kira caught a man by the arm and asked him where she could find Holt Crockett, the owner's son. Ben, the owner, had hired her to diagnose and treat an illness affecting the majority of his herd and had said Holt was in charge and would give her the details. She was a little nervous, because this was her first job as a professional veterinarian.

The cowboy looked her up and down with a lopsided grin, pointed, then moved on before she could thank him. She looked in the direction he'd indicated and saw a group of men in a corner, one of them standing sideways with his head bent over a clipboard, instructing the others.

A tan cowboy hat topped his caramel colored hair, which curled below his collar. Burnt-caramel stubble darkened his jaw. She couldn't make out the specific details of his face, hidden in shadow. His long-sleeved, white, cotton shirt tapered from square shoulders to his waist, where it disappeared into dirty blue jeans. Knee-length chaps framed his buttocks, and spurs chinked at the heels of his worn boots.

Kira allowed herself to admire the masculine angles of his body as he stood hipshod. Ben's attitude led her to believe Holt was in his early twenties, but this man looked at least thirty, and seasoned by hard work in the desert sun. She figured he was Holt's assistant, but would know how to find him.

She stepped around a wheelbarrow of fresh manure, wondering why men always had to spit where people walked. She approached him and tapped his shoulder. When he turned, he glanced at her, then back to his clipboard, as if dismissing her.

"Treat's in the house, Ma'am," the man hollered above the noise, a toothpick bouncing between his lips. He pointed toward the house and then turned from her, frowning. Apparently not caring whether she overheard him, he said to the others, "Great. Another buckle chaser for Treat tonight. I barely got four hours work out of him yesterday, and he's getting started early today." He looked at his watch and rolled his eyes, laughing sarcastically, then added, "Treat should give out better directions, and maybe even a map down the hall to his bedroom." The men laughed what Kira thought was a dirty locker-room laugh.

Incensed, Kira slapped his shoulder. "Excuse me!"

The man turned to her, an impatient look on his face and pointed toward the house again. Kira shook her head and motioned with her hand for him to bring his head closer to hers. With a patronizing look, he leaned down while the other men watched with interest.

"May I speak to you outside?" She decided she'd put him in his place when she got him away from all the noise and had his full attention. As he stood up, she reminded herself that the best looking men were the worst to get involved with.

He straightened, and his eyes bored into hers, but his mind seemed to be someplace else. Then he blinked, and almost imperceptibly shook his head just once. "Sure."

Kira nodded, then strode out. She heard him following as the other men murmured, and stopped about twenty feet away from the barn, where she turned to confront him. Her voice caught. His eyes shone above high cheekbones and beneath a strong brow, and in the sunlight, they matched the color of his hair exactly. His square chin cradled a dimple that could make a woman swoon.

And she almost did. Her body over-rode her mind, spreading tingles through her chest and making starbursts in her belly. She knew she had to find Holt and escape this man. "I," she began, but it came out in a whisper. Kira swallowed. "Can you tell me where I can find Holt Crockett?"

Blinking, he pressed his lips together, then spoke. "That would be me, ma'am."

Kira stood there a moment, speechless. Holt frowned, then shifted from one foot to the other, hanging his large hands on his hips. The sun pounded her uncovered head, drawing trickles of sweat from her scalp, and glinting off the pearl snaps on Holt's shirt.

Her first-job excitement had turned to dread. A small attraction for this man could grow into a raging desire, and would turn her precariously balanced life into road-kill. But, she had signed a contract.

Kira flipped her hair back from her cheek and held out her hand. "I'm Kira McGovern, your new vet. Ben hired me and said I should see you."

Holt grabbed her hand and froze. "He what?" A violent scowl creased his face.

"I assumed he'd told you," she stammered, her hand slipping from his.

"He damn well didn't." Holt spit out his toothpick. "And we don't need one." He turned and strode toward the house, then stomped inside and slammed the door.

It took a minute for Kira to realize that she'd been fired. But he couldn't do that. He hadn't hired her! She marched after him and whacked the heavy, brass, bull's-head knocker against the door.

The door swung open before she could lower her hand. In front of her stood a loose-jointed, Cheshire-smiling man with shaggy blonde hair, wearing a wrinkled shirt with pearl snaps. Her eyes fell to the huge silver and gold rodeo award belt buckle, studded with several large stones and with 'TC' tooled into the metal. He seemed to be enjoying the argument, which was audible through a closed door behind him.

With feigned enlightenment he said, "Ah, you must be the doctor we're expecting." He stepped back, pulling the door wider. "Please, come in."

Kira stepped inside, deciding she didn't like this person. "I need to speak to Ben," she said, as he swung the front door closed behind her.

"He's busy right now." He smirked at the direction of the argument, then turned back to her. Grinning, he crossed his arms over his chest, and began rocking back and forth from heel to toe, perusing her body. Kira felt as if she were a prime heifer on the block and could barely resist pulling her lips away from her teeth to show him her age and health. Instead, she eased away from him.

"I'm Treat."

"What?" She thought he'd told her he was a treat. To Kira, he sounded just like the men at vet-school, so full of themselves.

"Treat. S'my name." His leather boots creaked as he rocked.

"Nice to meet you." She turned her back on him and examined some Indian pottery on the wall, groaning inwardly.

"And a treat's what I could give you," he added, in a conspiratorial tone.

She smirked at him over her shoulder. "Sounds like a lot of empty calories to me." Kira heard his creaking pause, then continue. She smiled to herself, moving her attention to another wall. But her smile didn't last long. She needed this job.

Kira's sister and brother-in-law, Cleo and John, had died three months ago in a car accident on the way to her graduation. Yesterday, she'd been in court fighting for custody of her niece, Zoe. Cleo had left Zoe's custody to Kira, which outraged John's parents and triggered the fight. The court was concerned that Kira hadn't found a job or permanent residence yet.

Truthfully, Kira had been so depressed about her sister, she hadn't even looked for a job. She'd survived on the remains of her school loans, while adjusting to instant motherhood. But the judge had given her two months to prove herself and keep Zoe.

After her case had been heard, Ben, who was there with his attorneys for a case, had introduced himself and offered her a job. Besides the perfect timing, Ben was just as desperate as she was. He couldn't afford to pay her right now, so he'd proposed that she would receive a hefty ten percent of the ranch, including room and board and a fully stocked veterinary trailer to start her own business if she was successful in diagnosing the cattle disease.

If Kira failed, she would walk away with nothing. And she couldn't lose Zoe. It was what Cleo and John had wanted, and Kira loved Zoe as her own daughter.

Her shoulder muscles tensed as she remembered the pain and stress of the last few months. At least, Treat silently watched her now. She looked at the closed door and wondered what was going on in there.

* * *

Holt leaned his hands on the front edge of Ben's desk. "What you're doing is just plain wrong." Holt glared at his father, sitting behind his mammoth desk. "How can you so easily give away a piece of the ranch? Of ...our family heritage?"

"Son, you have to understand that I'm thinking of the future--"

"I'm the future of this ranch." Holt jabbed his thumb into his chest. "Me and Treat." He knew his younger brother listened outside the door.

Of course, Holt never thought his brother would be a part of the ranch. Treat was more interested in women and rodeos, and had already promised he'd sell his share when he got it. Which was good. Holt couldn't imagine working side by side with him; they'd been adversaries since childhood.

"Hell, Dad, I'm thirty-two years old. It's time you stepped down and let me handle it." Holt began pacing in front of the desk.

"Damn it." Ben Crockett slammed his fist onto the desk pad. "I told you, you're not ready to take over yet."

Holt halted and faced his father. "You said I was in charge. What does that mean, then?"

"It means what it means. You're in charge. For now. We'll see how you do, and if necessary, we'll try Treat." He waved his arm at the door. "You're still so damned pig-headed."

"But Treat's a screw-up," Holt mumbled under his breath.

"You and Treat are so different from one another. I don't know how I could have spawned the both of you."

Holt flinched. When he was thirteen years old, he'd heard the men talking about his mother getting into trouble with Hiram Bogie, the neighboring rancher, and then marrying Ben. He would never forget the fear and shock he'd felt back then. He'd

11

hidden behind some bales of hay, and cried nearly all day.

It was easy to question; Holt had been born about nine months after his parents were married. Plus, Ben seemed to favor his younger brother, appearing more proud of Treat's accomplishments than Holt's.

It worried him so much, that for the last nineteen years he'd worked like hell to be the best. He wanted Ben to know that he was worthy, and there was no way he'd let anyone take ownership of even one cowpie. This ranch was a part of him, belonged to him. He loved it and he'd earned it.

Holt began pacing again, his mind racing. He didn't need a vet. He was sure he'd figured out the problem already, and could take care of this on his own. And once he did, that gold-digging vet could take a hike.

"Eventually you'll see the wisdom of investing a piece of the ranch in a good vet," he heard Ben say.

Holt flared his nostrils, trying to control his breathing. He opened his hands, beseeching. "I just need some time."

"We don't have it, son." They studied each other. "Do you know where I was yesterday?"

"No."

"At the courthouse." Ben paused, and Holt's interest perked. Why hadn't his father told him? It was just like Ben to leave him out of important things. "Our creditors caught wind of our trouble and have called in our loans. The lawyers got it delayed."

"Well, then...we have time." Maybe he could turn this around. "I know I can handle this on my own. I can-- "

"No, Holt. It's a done deal." Ben raised his right brow. "You'd better catch her before she gets too far. And bring her in here so I can fix things up with her."

Holt stood a moment more, willing himself to stay calm. He couldn't believe this was happening. He turned, strode to the door, and jerked it open, almost knocking Kira down.

She'd probably heard everything that just happened between he and his father. Backing up, he stood aside and motioned for her to enter. She nodded and walked in, while he waited for her to take a seat in front of the big desk. Hell, he may resent her, but that didn't mean he wouldn't show manners--in the house, anyway. His mother wouldn't stand for anything less. Besides, if he was going to have to work with her, he may as well enjoy the scenery. She did have one hell of a backside.

Treat followed to the door and leaned against the jamb, arms crossed, grinning. He looked to Holt like he'd been having fun with the doctor. Besides being an obvious gold digger, maybe she really was a buckle chaser. Holt stared at his father's back, as he stood with his hands clasped behind him, looking out the window through wooden shades.

Turning, he looked at Holt a moment, then Kira. "Kira, please accept my apologies."

Holt felt her tension. She was wound up like a pig's tail.

13

Ben dipped his head and chuckled. "I thought I'd told Holt about your arrival, but I guess that I forgot. Just a part of gettin' old."

Holt grimaced at his father's lie. He'd figure out a way to beat this. Holt pulled out a toothpick from his pocket to substitute for the cigarette he really needed, unwrapped it, and ground it between his molars.

"Holt is in charge of this ranch." Ben stopped and gave his son a meaningful glance. "Fortunately, we've come to an understanding, and we'll be keeping you on."

Kira smiled, then said, "That's good to hear, Ben. Thank you." Holt had expected her to castigate them both for not having their act together. Maybe she was a little afraid of Ben, he mused. If so, maybe he could intimidate her himself. Then she might quit this job before messing things up for him.

Ben stopped pacing at the center of the desk and faced them both. "Mrs. Crockett and I are leaving this afternoon for Barbados. He held up his hand as if warding off any argument. Now, wed planned this trip a year and half ago, and there's no refund if I cancel. It was supposed to be a month long, but with all these problems, we'll only stay about a week."

From the corner of his eye, Holt saw Kira look from Ben to him and he smirked. Treat gave a soft guttural laugh. Holt knew Treat was going to pursue her into his bed. Of course, she'd be a major step up for his brother.

Whatever his feelings on the matter, this woman did have class and looks. If it weren't for his situation, Holt might try to have a go at her himself. But this was war. If Treat was successful in his wooing, Holt could use that to embarrass her. She'd lose the respect of the rest of the men and have to leave.

Ben sat at the desk again and arranged papers. "I trust that by the time we return, you both will be working together smoothly and our cattle situation will be almost resolved."

He seemed to believe that his words had fixed the problem and that everyone finally agreed with one another. Holt hated that.

"There." Ben wiped his hands in the air. "Now, I've got a plane to catch."

Kira jumped to her feet as he walked past her. "But-- "

Ben paused. "Oh, Kira, meet my other son-- "

Kira turned. "We've met." She looked at all three men as if they were insane.

She looked like she was feeling trapped. And really, she was. She was closed in by him, a man who didn't want her here; Treat, who wanted her in one place only; and Ben, who wasn't going to be here himself. It was perfect. Before the day was out, he'd have this little filly broken and trained. Holt leaned back in his chair and enjoyed Treat's moves for the first time.

Treat stood away from the door jamb, squaring his shoulders. "Not officially," he said, with a challenging grin.

"Treat's our rodeo champ, Kira." Ben slapped his son's back. "He's put the family on the map!" Ben beamed and Holt snorted.

Kira stepped behind Holt and approached Treat with her hand extended. "Nice to meet you." She smiled briefly.

Holt watched as Treat's eager hand grabbed hers and held it several seconds too long, then he frowned when Kira wiped her hand on her jeans.

Ben nodded his approval. "Well, good luck then. See you next week." He disappeared down the long hallway, leaving Kira standing between the two brothers.

She stood motionless. Treat relaxed against the door jamb again, looking at her as if she were naked.

Holt watched all this with amusement, and then rose. "We'd better get started."

"Absolutely." Keeping her eyes on Treat, she moved toward the door. When Treat refused to budge, she stared at him until finally, he winked and sauntered away. Cocky as ever, true, but Holt had to admit Treat got a reaction--and was always successful. Maybe he'd watch closely and get himself a little action in town - after the ranch was in the black again.

* * *

Kira veered off from their path to the barn and surprised Holt when she approached a motorcycle, rummaged through the storage compartment, and pulled out a doctor's bag and a pistol. What kind of a woman rode a motorcycle? Holt kept walking, and didn't acknowledge her when she caught up with him. He hid his pleasure at the fact that she almost had to run to keep up with his long stride.

16

"I assume you can ride a horse." Holt motioned to some hands and told them to saddle up Betsy for her.

"I've ridden a few times."

As he bridled and saddled a brown and white Quarter horse, an old cowboy, white wisps of hair jutting from under his hat, brought her a spotted Appaloosa mare. Random braids decorated its long black mane.

He was sure she'd just lied. Didn't matter. He'd see the truth soon enough, and then she'd have another strike against her, the first one being merely her presence. Not to mention the fact that she was too small to be a large-animal vet, and too good-looking. She'd have her men falling off their horses and roping each other instead of the cows. That was more than enough to convince him she didn't belong here. Holt slid his rifle into its sheath on his horse. "Shorty, tell Treat I want him to ride the south fence starting today." He looked at her and realized she was missing an important piece of gear. "And loan her your hat," he added with disgust.

"That's okay, Shorty." She turned to Holt. "I can get by for one day without it."

Holt looped a coil of rope over his saddle horn and began checking the cinch. "Ms. McGovern, while you're on this ranch, I'm responsible for you. You won't be as valuable to my father with a sunburn, let alone heat stroke." He turned to Shorty. "Shorty, I know it's a lot to ask, but if you don't mind."

Shorty nodded then, with a grimace, lifted the black felt off his head and handed it to her. He turned away and averted his eyes. To a cowboy, it

17

was bad luck for anyone else to handle your hat, and Holt thought it was damned inconsiderate of her to have not brought her own.

Kira smiled her thanks and donned the hat. Holt noticed she was careful to hold it by the front and back of the brim so as not to crunch the creases in the crown.

"Thank you," she said to Shorty, then turned to him and smiled.

He busied himself by tying canteens to the saddles and rechecking the cinches for the third time, trying not to stare.

She looked Bea-utiful.

When he first met her, he'd assumed she was here for Treat, even though she wasn't his type. Treat's type of woman was drenched in perfume, with stiff, curled hair and lots of make-up.

His mother had always told Holt that he was a man for details, and he'd sure noticed some on Kira. Her eyes were a blue-black that lit up in the sunshine like the neon sign down at Julio's. Tiny almond-colored freckles across her nose and cheeks led his eyes to her bow-tie lips.

And when he had leaned over her in the barn that first time they'd met, her soft, shoulder-length black hair caressed his nose, filling his head with sweetness. Time seemed to have stopped, and he watched as pinpoints of glistening perspiration had slid past the opening of her shirt. A silver ball on a silver chain snuggled between her breasts, something he had instantly imagined himself doing.

All right, so she was something to look at, which he'd already noted was part of the problem. But she

18

made him remember how long it'd been since he'd had a female in his bed. His experience with pretty faces was that there were never enough brains behind them. And this pretty face was a threat, besides. Just the thought of what she could do to his life dwindled any desire he might otherwise have felt. Or so he tried to tell himself.

"Let's go."

He walked his horse out of the barn, mounted, and gently spurred the animal into a walk. A few moments later, he heard the doctor's horse galloping up behind him and her butt slapping the saddle. The slapping sound slowed and subsided as she caught up with him. Holt sighed; it was going to be a long ride.

Holt's mind worked, going over the situation. He had to accept his father's decision about hiring her, and he had to work with her. But he didn't have to actually help her. He didn't have to make it easy for her. She'd have to pull her weight just like every other hand on the ranch. Holt grinned inwardly, as a plan began to form in his mind. By the end of today, this little snippet of a woman would be calling it quits. He'd cure the cattle without anyone's help, and he'd end up with the ranch--all of it. Hope surged in his veins like good whiskey. He smiled and turned his horse south, through rugged terrain toward the holding corral.

Chapter Two

Two hours later, after plowing through prickly scrub brush and traversing arroyos, rocky ravines and mesas, they reached the corral. Holt hadn't responded much to her attempts at conversation. Why should he waste his words or time? He dismounted and waited for Kira to do so. She slowly lifted her right leg over Betsy's back and to the ground, and then pulled her left foot from the stirrup. She walked stiff-legged, rubbing her rear-end. *Well, a saddle-sore ass does not a cowgirl make*, he thought, turning away to hide his grin. He walked his horse to the aluminum shade overhang.

She joined him in the shade. "I was wondering why we took horses out here instead of a truck, or ATVs, and now I know." She lifted Shorty's hat off her head and wiped her brow with her cotton-clad forearm.

"Most of the ranch is like this." He dropped the reins of his horse and took the top off a barrel of water. Holt felt her watching him as he held a large ladle of water under his horse's nose, allowing the animal to drink. He repeated the procedure for Kira's horse. That's all the water he'd give them right now. He loved them, but sometimes they weren't too bright. They'd end up drinking until they made themselves sick. The horses snorted and twitched their tails to keep the flies away, then nosed each other and moved further into the shade. Holt stroked each beast's neck and nose, and then unsaddled them, slinging the saddles and blankets over the fence.

Next, he untied the half-gallon canteen from his saddle and twisted off the cap. He almost handed it to Kira first, but instead took a deep swig of the water, mentally shaking himself. He wouldn't think of her as a woman. She was a hand who just happened to be female. Everyone was equal on the ranch during working hours. He'd worked with cowgirls before, but a cowboy never had to worry about their frailty. He handed the canteen to her, wondering if she was too delicate to drink after him. To his surprise, she took it and gulped.

"Ah." Water dripped down her chin, and she laughed as she wiped her mouth.

He suddenly wanted to laugh, too, but caught himself and scowled instead.

She handed the canteen back. "Thanks."

Holt took it and tied it back onto his saddle, then turned and gave her his most intimidating glare-nod combination. She just smiled and untied her doctor's bag from her saddle, then walked to the corral.

Holt turned his attention to the cows. These were some of the sickest. They were his test cattle, the animals he was examining, experimenting on. If he could get something to work on these cows, then he'd apply it to the rest of the herd. He came here every day, before and after the other ranch work was done, to check on them and try extracts of herbs and grasses he'd cooked up and distilled over a burner in his bedroom.

Most were lying in shaded areas, but they were too quiet. His heart ached when he looked at them.

He would help them. Somehow. He just hoped they could hold on until then. Holt followed Kira to the fence, and put his elbows and one foot on the rungs, unintentionally mirroring her pose.

"So, how long have the cattle been sick?"

"About four weeks." Holt grabbed another toothpick from his pocket, savagely unwrapped it, and popped it into his mouth. He was trying to quit smoking, even though all the cowboys he knew smoked. He wouldn't admit it to anyone, but after seventeen years of stogies, he could feel himself not getting enough breath when he got real physical on the ranch. He told the guys it was because he wanted to taste good for the women--as if he had any. He carried an unopened can of chew in his pocket to detract attention away from his lack of smokes.

Kira set her bag down. "Where are the rest of the sick ones?"

"Sectioned off on a corner of the property, away from the well cattle."

"Good." Kira knelt and opened her bag. "What are their symptoms?"

Holt noticed that she hadn't looked at him since they started talking, and hoped he was starting to get to her. "Weight loss. Depression. Diarrhea ... and abortion." Holt heard his voice grow more tense with each word.

Kira nodded. "Could be one of several diseases."

Tell me something I don't know, he thought, rolling his eyes.

She pulled on a pair of Latex gloves and tied on a surgical mask, then handed up a pair of gloves and a mask to him. "Here. Until we're sure about what it is."

Holt looked at her kneeling on the ground, rummaging through her bag. Her large, white, cotton shirt that billowed around her when they'd first started out was now wet with sweat. It clung to her back and waist. He could see the color of her flesh and the narrow band of her bra. This woman had no fat on her body, but she did have wide hips that angled into a narrow waist. Her jeans hugged the upside down heart-shape of her butt, and before he could stop himself, he envisioned their bodies entwined, slick with sweat. He shook his head and noticed that Kira now stood in front of him. Somehow, he now held the mask and gloves.

Expressionless, she turned and walked to the holding chute with her bag. She set the bag back onto the ground, took out a small cardboard-covered notebook and began writing inside it.

"I don't think it's contagious to humans." He followed her, stuffing the items into his front pocket, his jeans tighter than they were moments ago. He bit down on his toothpick, and then pushed it to the other side of his mouth with his tongue.

"What's the abortion rate?" She paused, her pen poised above the page, waiting for his answer.

"'Bout sixty percent." He mashed the end of his toothpick into splinters. How could he have imagined making love to this dry, unfeeling cow pie? She scribbled. "Mortality rate?"

"None."

"Yet." She wrote again. "How many sick?"

"Four thousand. One third," he growled.

She looked up and her blue eyes reflected his own heartbreak over the suffering of his animals, then something in her gaze hardened and she went back to scratching on the pad with her pencil.

He felt his anger surge at the moment she showed emotion toward his animals. What was wrong with him? Why did he care whether she showed feelings toward his animals or not? Man, he had to get a grip.

Kira slapped her book closed, slipped it back into her bag and stood up. "Let's get started." She moved to the fence. "See if you can get me that one, there." She pointed. "After you put on your gloves and mask."

He looked to the animal she indicated, then back to Kira. Control of this situation was shifting, and he didn't like it one bit. "I'll get you that one instead." He pointed to another animal. "And I don't need these." He pulled the mask and gloves from his pocket and held them out to her.

"I might test that one later, but first, I want the other one. And yes, you do."

Her defiant stance and level gaze made him wonder if it would be worth it to argue. With a quick nod, he slipped the things on and entered the corral. He knew she'd expect his men to wear these things, and they wouldn't want to if he didn't. If he were to give the illusion of working with her, then he might as well start now. He moved toward the end of the corral and picked up a large wooden gate. He held the gate in front of himself and slowly moved it toward the animal she wanted, chanting "Ho now, ho," in a deep voice to calm the group. The cow labored to get up, and then Holt maneuvered her into a funnel shaped fence. Next, he forced her into the squeeze chute and head gate to keep her stationary for the examination. He nodded to Kira to let her know it was okay.

Kira hung a stethoscope around her neck and approached the cow. She looked into her eyes, mouth, nose and ears. She examined its hooves and joints, and felt its abdomen. She listened to its heart and lungs. "I'm going to take her temperature, then I'll need your help to get some samples."

Holt grew sullen. She seemed to know a little something about animals. But it didn't matter. Book smarts was one thing, stamina and strength for ranch work were different. Besides, he was still sure what the disease was, and what treatment was required. But, he'd given his word to his father, so he'd see this thing through.

"Fever." Kira shook out the thermometer as she walked back to her bag. She took out several small vials and a syringe. With the syringe, she took a blood sample. She then filled one vial with the bovine's saliva. She picked up two more vials and stood up, handing one to Holt. "I need fecal and urine samples."

Holt took it and stood next to her at the side rear of the animal, feeling his anger begin to burn clear up into his brain. He shouldn't be taking orders from anyone. Especially a woman.

"Do you own a helicopter?" she asked after several seconds of silence.

"No."

"I thought all modern ranches used them." She looked at him with those damned eyes, over the edge of her mask.

"Not this one." He stared straight ahead, still holding his vial at the back-end of the cow. It wasn't her damn business that he couldn't afford one. He wanted one, but this sickness with his cattle had blown his budget all the way into the next county. And now his budget had to handle this woman's expenses.

She seemed to get the hint and gave up. Finally, the animal obliged, and Kira and Holt collected their samples. She labeled the vials and placed them into her bag with several cold packs.

"I want samples from three more animals."

Holt rolled his eyes. How much more effort was he going to allow himself to put out? He hesitated.

"Come here." She pinned him with her gaze.

He questioned her through squinted eyes, frowning.

"Please. Let me show you what I've found."

Well, since she'd said please. Just a few more seconds of this nonsense, though, and he just might burst. They both knelt at the cow's hooves.

"See these erosions of the mucous membranes where the claw joins the skin? She probably has them in her forestomachs and intestines, too. We'll assume she does, until I do an internal examination or an autopsy on a dead animal."

They stood, and Kira showed him the erosions in the animal's mouth and nose.

"These lesions, combined with the fever and other symptoms, make me think your cattle have

Bovine Virus Diarrhea or Mucosal-Disease Complex. Either way, it's caused by the same organism."

"That's what I've thought all along." He felt triumphant. "You're just wasting everyone's time here, Doctor." He crossed his arms and gloated.

Kira crossed her arms, too. "How would you treat it, then?"

"Push fluids and nutrition and hope they recover, but I can salvage the ones that don't. And I can vaccinate the well animals."

"What if it's something else?" she countered. "Are you really going to treat your whole herd based on a guess?"

Holt uncrossed his arms. "Listen, lady, I'm in the middle of branding babies, rounding up other animals from the range to brand, and I've gotta get ready to take them to market. I don't have time to dally."

She forged on. "If you treat the wrong illness, you've just stressed your cattle for nothing. Less may survive, and you'll still have to treat the correct disease, stressing the same animals all over again. You'll also expose the vaccinated animals to a disease they're not immune to. How might that affect your trip to market?"

At the moment, he didn't have a comeback, so he just gave her his angry stare. She smiled.

"I suggest I collect samples from three other animals," she repeated. "And run some tests. In the meantime, we can vaccinate a few animals and put them with the sick ones. If they don't get sick, and the tests come back positive, then I'd advise a mass vaccination for the well bovines."

He started shaking his head in the middle of her statement. "I don't think we should just ignore all the sick animals until your experiment proves what I already know." He saw her bite her bottom lip, eyeing him. "Look at them, for Christ- sakes!" He swung his arm toward the cows and raised his voice. These were his animals, his pride. His joy. He wouldn't just go along with this without a fight, no matter what his father thought. "Some of them don't look like they're going to make it much longer unless we act now."

She looked at the animals and back to him, scrutinizing him. "Okay," she began, flaring the fingers of both hands, palms down. "We give the fluids and nutritive shots to the ones that are in the apparent late stages of the disease--the ones exhibiting extreme dehydration and weakness. That way, we're acting now for the ones that need it now. It buys us time and we don't unnecessarily stress the others. That's as far as I go."

Holt's anger diffused only slightly; he couldn't think of an argument. But if he at least went along with this idea, then Ben would figure he was cooperating. And this was not a major breakthrough. Almost a no-brainer.

"Fine." He went back into the corral to get another animal.

Holt brought Kira three more cows of her choice, and she examined them. By the time they were done, the day was shot. The sun rested on the horizon, suffusing the sky with pinks, oranges, and reds.

"I'm glad that's done." She packed her bag and snapped it shut.

Holt nodded. He reached into his pocket for his last flavorless toothpick. Maybe soaking them in whiskey would help. Whiskey was good for a lot of ailments, and right now, he sure was ailing. Trying to make this woman back down and quit was going to take more concentration. She could think, not just recite facts from books. Had a bit of moxie, too.

"Well, today was a short day." He led the horses out from the overhang, and handed Betsy's reins to her. "Our days start before sun up and don't end until well after sun down. We all eat breakfast together, and I expect you to eat with us before starting out." He mounted up and waited for her to mount Betsy. "Don't want you wilting on me from lack of energy." When he was sure he had her full attention, he continued. "It'll be late when we get back tonight, but we'll have to put in some planning time."

Her eyes reflected a sort of deep weariness. Holt looked at the shadows beneath her eyes and swore he did not feel guilty. Strangely, his thumbs itched to stroke the tender skin there, and he chastised himself. He hardened his heart with determination, reined his mare toward the direction of home and spurred her on.

* * *

They returned to the ranch at about ten in the evening, and then spent an hour making plans for the next day. Kira was whipped, but refused to show even the slightest hint of it to Holt. She was sure he'd be pleased if she couldn't hack it. Maybe she wasn't cut out for this kind of work. Her muscles were screaming and would be twice as sore tomorrow. Besides the physical rigors of the job, Holt made her tense, stressed out. How much of that could she take? And she missed Zoe. But she'd probably have to push hard like this for a while, until she got things under control here. Then, she'd be able to back off and spend more time at home.

She mulled it over as she dragged herself to her motorcycle and swung her leg over it. There was virtually no activity outside. Men's voices, punctuated with high-pitched clinks and clangs of dishes, came from around the house somewhere, reminding her that she was starving. From another direction, she heard more voices and horses snorting. She couldn't see where the sounds were coming from, and couldn't guess how far away they were, but it calmed her, made her feel alone - the good kind of alone that lets you know you're strong and able. Kira took a deep breath and exhaled, feeling better.

She was due back at ten tomorrow, after dropping off her samples at a lab, and buying fluid bags and shots. But Holt expected her to be here at five each morning thereafter. Kira shook her head and prepared to start her engine.

"Nice mount." Gravel crunched behind her.

Kira startled and looked back. It was Treat, again. "Thanks." She faced forward and started the engine.

He came in front of her and straddled the front wheel, holding on to the handlebars. "Your bike purrs. I could make you purr, too."

Kira looked first at his proprietary grip on her bike, then at him. Spotlights from the house lit up

30

one side of his smug face. He was so sure of success. "I told you. I'm on a diet." She looked at his hands and back to him, indicating she wanted him to let loose.

"Why don't you curl up with me tonight? I've been known to please the most finicky of felines."

Kira laughed. She couldn't help it. Maybe she was just so tired she was punchy, but it just really struck her as funny. And what was even funnier was that the poor guy was so surprised, he stood with his mouth half open. She laughed even harder and couldn't stop.

Kira backed her bike away from him. "Like I said...no treats for me." She opened the throttle, turned the front wheel to the left, and whipped the back wheel around, spraying Treat's shins with gravel and sand, then sped away.

* * *

Candace, her roommate, met her at the door of their rented two-bedroom house.

"Is she asleep?" Kira knew Zoe was down for the night at this hour, but hoped anyway.

"Yes, she's been asleep forever." Candace swung the door wider for Kira as she entered. "What took you so long?" She closed the door and followed Kira into the family room. Kira dropped her helmet onto the couch and carried her doctor's bag into the kitchen.

"What's that?" she asked Candace, looking at an artfully decorated but quite lumpy looking cake, before opening the refrigerator and pulling out a soda. An electric cooler sat, plugged in, next to the refrigerator. Kira opened it and put the whole doctor's bag in, then dropped the lid.

Candace smiled proudly. "That's my latest creation. Strawberry Pineapple Peanutty Bomb." She took two plates from the cupboard. "I waited for you so we could test it together." Her kinky blond ringlets quivered. Her huge smile and gray eyes beamed.

Kira turned and smiled. "That'd be great." She slid into a kitchen chair and rested her face in one hand as Candace pulled a knife through the thing and served it. Candace was Kira's best friend from high school, and a recent, albeit unemployed, graduate of the Randy Milner School of Pastry Design. They'd graduated high school together, but while Kira went directly to college and then veterinary school, Candace tested out various options - not the least of which were several long-term disastrous relationships with walking egos, who only wanted Candace for her ornamentation value. Now, while looking for her dream job, Candace worked as Zoe's live-in nanny, sans paycheck. Kira couldn't afford to pay her yet, but soon, she hopefully would be able to, and also planned to help her start her own pastry business.

Kira dug into the concoction without thinking, and stuffed it into her mouth. This was ritual now, and it helped her unwind at the end of the day and keep her mind off Cleo. She chewed, knowing Candace covertly watched her reaction.

Surprised, Kira said, "This is really delicious, Candace!" Kira put another bite into her mouth. "The peanuts really combine well with the fruit. You're getting good at this."

Candace giggled. "Do you really think so?" She began eating, too.

"I really think so. You should enter it into a contest."

"Oh, I don't know." Candace fussed with the folds in her napkin.

Candace examined the weave of the napkin for a few moments. "Well, if you think it's good enough."

"It is. Go for it."

She set down the wrinkled cloth with finality. "Okay. I will."

"Good for you!"

They sat in silence for a while. "So," Candace said. "Answer my question."

Puzzled, Kira looked at her, then remembered. "Oh. What took me so long?" She put her fork down and leaned on her elbows. "Well." She sighed. "What took me so long is a stubborn, blockheaded cowboy. First his father offered me the job, then the blockhead fired me, and then his father rehired me. Then I had to deal with his crappy attitude all day, and I swear he undressed me with his eyes a time or two." Kira leaned back in her chair. "I thought I was going to have to shoot him or something," she added with a sarcastic grin.

"Hmm. Doesn't sound so bad," Candace said, picking up their plates. "I thought all cowboys were like that."

Kira looked at her friend, aghast. "Like what? Sordid? Blockheaded? Confrontational?"

"No, silly." Candace giggled. "Animalistic. Down to earth. Independent. Loyal." Candace cleared the table, and giggled more. "But especially animalistic. I think that's sexy."

How her friend got those adjectives out of what she'd just said, she would never know. He was sexy, in an animalistic sort of way, but not because of the way he acted. As a matter of fact, if he had just stood there and not opened his mouth, she could have actually fantasized about him. "Well, whatever he is, he should just stay out of my way so I can do my job." Kira got up and headed for her and Zoe's bedroom. "I have a deadline, remember."

"Yeah, I remember." She sobered and followed Kira. "So, what are you going to do?"

"Don't know yet. Blockhead is so territorial. I think he wants to own the entire ranch himself." Kira was able to put those pieces together from what she'd heard of Ben and Holt's muffled argument that day. "I'm going to win this job, though. Then we can live on the ranch."

Candace touched Kira's arm. "I know you'll get the job, Kira. You've always gotten everything you ever went after."

Kira tilted her head to the side. "Blockhead could make us miserable."

"I'm sure he's not as bad as you think."

"Huh. Just wait 'till you meet him. And his brother." She paused at her closed bedroom door. "If I do get the job though, Zoe and I won't have to share a bedroom anymore."

"Good," Candace whispered. "Then the poor thing won't have to suffer your snoring anymore."

"I don't snore." Kira exchanged grins with Candace, then quietly entered the bedroom.

Standing at the crib, Kira stared at her beautiful baby. Zoe had fallen asleep with the fingers of one hand tangled in the dark curls at the back of her head. She intermittently moved her jaw up and down, dreaming about sucking, and murmured in her singsong voice. The humidifier sighed on the dresser.

Zoe was the image of her mother. Tears welled in Kira's eyes. Jupiter could orbit through the jagged rip in her heart and she wouldn't notice.

Was it even still beating? How could she go on? How could she not? If she stopped moving, she'd have to think about it, and she wouldn't survive that. Kira kissed her fingertips and touched them to Zoe's forehead, then untangled the baby's fingers from her hair.

* * *

Kira showed up at the ranch at ten the next day, driving Candace's van loaded down with the fluid bags and nutritive shots needed for the animals, and other things they'd need later. She and Holt had discussed building a dozen or so head gates so all his men could round up and treat the animals. Half the men would be out in the field, getting everything ready. The men knew how to give shots, but she would have to teach them how to apply intravenous lines. Kira hoped to make serious progress, and make it through the week without a confrontation with Holt.

"You're late," Holt accused, the moment she stepped from the van. He stared at her with tight lips.

Kira looked at her watch and blinked at him. "It's ten-o-two." She walked to the back of the van and opened the door. Holt followed her and motioned to his men to come unload the supplies.

He lugged a box out of the van. "Ranches run on schedules and if everyone threw it off by a few minutes, then we'd never get anything done." The men piled up at the back of the van and began relaying the boxes to two four-wheel drive trucks.

"I'm not late. Two minutes could be the difference in a watch setting." She grabbed a box and walked over to one of the trucks. Shorty met her at the lowered tailgate and helped her push it toward the back. "I remembered my hat today, Shorty."

"I'm glad, but I would'a let you borrow mine again." He smiled. "If'n I had to."

She laughed. "Well, you won't." She pulled a small packet out of her front jeans pocket. "And to thank you, I got you this." Kira handed him the packet and watched him unwrap the anaconda-skin hatband she'd bought in town this morning. Kira understood cowboy superstitions, and she appreciated that Shorty had been so gracious when she'd borrowed his hat yesterday. The other men admired the gift as they dumped boxes into the truck bed.

Holt came up behind her, then followed her to the van. "Well," he continued, "set your watch to mine. I can't keep people on who hold us back."

She bent over another box and said over her shoulder, "Your father hired me, not you." Well, that was immature. Why was she letting this guy get to her?

He took the box from her. "My father's gone, and I'm in charge. I doubt he'd fault me for firing someone who couldn't show up on time."

"I'm on time," she growled.

She stopped. What was happening to her? She had never behaved this way before. What kind of an impression was she making? And better yet, why did his opinion matter so much? Kira looked around. All the men had stopped working and stared at her and Holt.

Holt looked around also, and tucked his chin. He dumped the box on the tailgate and sauntered back to Kira. "Come over here." He walked a short distance away.

She followed, and when Holt stopped and turned around, she assumed an open stance, trying to diffuse his anger. He glared at the men over his shoulder, which spurred them into action, then turned back to her.

"Look. We don't need to be acting this way, but you are really getting under my skin, woman." He seethed his anger through thinned lips, his dimple almost disappeared from his chin.

"I'm sorry," she said, conciliatory. "I just want to do my job, and I need a little room to do it." She began to cross her arms, and stopped, forcing them to her sides.

"I want you to do your job, too, and I need you here on time."

She looked at him, incredulous. "I was here--" She crossed her arms. "May I get back to work, Boss?" Kira saw a fire flare in his eyes.

"Look. I don't have a choice about you right now, but I expect you here early every day, and we're going to work until past sundown every day. And you need to be here for dinner, too, so we can plan afterwards." He brushed past her.

Kira turned. "I can't." She cringed inside, cursing her tongue.

Holt stopped in mid-stride and slowly turned around. "What?"

Her arms were still crossed, and, beyond thinking about body language, she had spread her feet apart in the dirt.

Holt's tone was soft, deadly. "If you abandon this job when your presence is required, you won't be coming back. I'll report you to the veterinary board, and I'll make sure that no other rancher hires you. The contract you signed stated that you would be here for all pertinent ranch activities."

Kira gave Holt a stony look. "Maybe we should stop wasting time arguing and get to it. We can talk about this later."

"And we will."

Chapter Three

Kira forced herself to walk calmly to one of the loaded trucks and climbed inside, shutting the door softly. She concentrated on slowing her breathing, as she waited for Shorty to close the tailgate and tie down the boxes. She was going to have to find a way to spend time with Zoe. Apparently it had been weighing on her mind more heavily than she'd thought, and now she'd messed up things with Holt. But, if she was never around Zoe, what was the point? And John's parents would have more ammo against her. She tapped her fingers on the window frame.

Shorty slid behind the wheel, a wise expression on his face, and shut the door. Holt and most of the other cowboys mounted their horses and took off en masse. The remaining two hands got into the other truck and drove away. Shorty followed them out of the ranch and into the desert.

He leaned over the steering wheel like a vulture as he drove, staring through the windshield. His craggled nose hooked over a wide-mouthed, yellow-toothed grin. Kira was sure that his chin and nose would some day meet. His short, stick-thin legs tapered into an almost non-existent butt, which had a barrel shaped torso stuck on top. Shorty spit a long, thin stream of saliva-drenched chew out his window, probably through the wide gap between his front teeth, then wiped his mouth on the back of this hand.

"So," she started. "I'd like it if you'd call me Kira." She noticed he'd slipped the hatband onto his black felt, which meant they'd become friends.

Shorty grinned, almost closing the nose-chin gap and nodded. "Kira. Sharp tongue's good on a woman. Gets through to a man. Sometimes."

"But not always?" she asked.

"You got creativity in ya. That's what's drivin' your tongue. But it's like this, see." He spat again.

Kira had't known he had more of the stuff in his mouth, and had to swallow hard to kill an urge to puke.

"It's like this," he repeated. "Men are like the animals, see?"

Like the animals? Ha! This certainly was not news to her.

"Some's bulls, some's horses." He looked at her with faded eyes floating in wrinkles, then looked back through the windshield. "Now, you don't do the same thing to get a bull to do your biddin' as you would with a horse, see? Bovines, they need a little nudging and guidance all the time. But a horse, now he's the smartest animal on the ranch. He needs somethin' different. See?" He smiled, looking as proud to Kira as if he'd just summarized all of macromolecular biology.

Kira had no idea what Shorty was talking about. "Uh...yeah."

"I know'd these boys since they was little."

"Ah." She nodded. "So, what tool should I use?"

"Like I said. You got creativity in ya."

"Meaning, figure it out for myself?

"Brains, too."

40

"Hmm. Thanks."

He chortled and maneuvered the truck across a rocky, dry creek bed, then looked at her. Then, with a grunt, Shorty turned his attention back to his driving.

Maybe he had something. Words weren't going to work on Holt the way they did on Treat. Fighting with him wasn't getting her anywhere. It was apparent that he was a man who respected action, but he also seemed to like things to go exactly his way. Yet, she needed to have the freedom to think and work for herself, and she needed time with Zoe. Somehow, she'd have to give Holt what he needed in order to get what she needed. But what? And how?

Two hours later, they'd arrived at the designated area. The trucks had traveled the perimeter of the ranch to get to a far corner where the cattle were being held, but the cowboys had already rested their horses, and completed building the chutes and head gates, looking eager to begin.

Kira passed out the gloves and masks, then taught the men--initially in one large group--how to administer the intravenous bags. The forty men broke off into groups of two at each of the twelve newly-built head gates, with four men carrying supplies from the trucks, and the last twelve on horseback, rounding up and guiding the animals into the head gates for treatment. The riders didn't wear the masks and gloves, since they weren't getting as close to the animals.

Kira walked to each group of men and assisted on their first animal. By the time she'd made it through each group, the first group was ready for the next animal, which she supervised as the men tried it themselves. She had fun meeting all of the men, and joking around with them. One of the men clowned around, trying to make her laugh.

"What's your handle, cowboy?" She smiled behind her mask.

"Oh, people just call me Dave, Ma'am," he answered, suddenly acting bashful.

"No name like Shorty, or Stretch, or Skinny?" The other men laughed at him, and someone pushed his hat over his eyes.

He pushed his hat back up. "No, Ma'am."

Kira rolled her eyes. "I thought all cowboys had nicknames." She looked at them standing around her, and most of them shrugged. "Well, maybe I watched too much television when I was a kid," she said back to the first man, "but I'm going to call you Funny Bone, because you tickle mine." She laughed.

Funny Bone's friends agreed, slapping him on the back and trying out his new name. He smiled, looked down at his feet, and then said, "Thank you, Ma'am."

"And will you guys call me Kira?"

"Yes, Ma'am," they replied in unison.

Kira laughed again, as she walked away. "If you guys need any more help, or any new names, let me know. I'll be making the rounds."

By the time she'd supervised each group, Kira had christened several more cowboys with new names. She named a tall man Stretch, a thin man Skinny, a blonde man Whitey, a hairy man Rug, and a burly man Grisly. It was when she was on this naming roll that Treat rode up on a mare, stopping his horse close to where she stood at the last head gate.

"Hey, Beautiful," he oozed, as if her rebuff last night had never happened.

Kira looked at Treat and smiled. "Well...hello, Trick." The others guffawed conservatively.

Treat blinked as his face stiffened and turned red. "My name is Treat." He pulled his horse's reins. The horse stomped and backed up a few feet.

Kira shrugged and relaxed her hands on her hips with the tips of her gloved fingers tucked inside her front jeans pockets. She peered up at him, warming to the subject "Hmm. Well, suit yourself. Trick or Treat. It's really the same either way."

Unable to control themselves any longer, the other men whooped and hollered. Some of them slapped their hats on their thighs, others murmured "trick or treat". Treat jerked his eyes from man to man, then dug his heels into the horse's sides and galloped toward the herd.

Kira turned to the group and shrugged. She laughed again, then walked back to the two trucks for a drink of water, wiping her brow with a bandanna. Holt rode up on his horse, dismounted, and met her at the water jug.

"How are things going?"

His civility surprised her. "Very well. Looks like we'll get about half treated today, the rest tomorrow." Kira removed her gloves and filled up a little paper cup with water. "How are things going with you?"

"Not bad." Holt seemed fidgety. "Seems like you're getting on all right with the men." He grabbed a cup and filled it at the jug.

Kira smiled, wondering what was going on in that head of his. "Yeah. They're a good bunch of guys.

Fun to work with." She drank another cup of water, then crushed it in her fist. "Well, I'd better get back." She tossed her cup into a bag hanging from the tailgate, and Holt nodded. Then he touched her arm. Barely. If there had been a wind that day, she would have thought it was the breeze softly pushing her shirtsleeve against her skin. She stopped and looked at him, surprised, this time, by his gentleness.

"I, uh...I wanted to apologize for this morning." He looked her in the eye, but from under his lowered hat brim.

"You do?"

"Yeah, well." He fumbled with his leather gloves a second, and then seemed to catch himself. He put his hands on his hips and stood hip shod. "I had no call to get on you like that."

"Well, thanks." She waited to see if there was more.

"I better get back." He tipped his hat to her, then mounted quickly and rode away.

She would never have guessed Holt had anything like that inside him. It was something to ponder. But later.

The noise from the cattle, and the dust they kicked up, left Kira exhausted toward the end of the day. Her muscles had finally loosened up, thanks to all her manhandling of bovines. Holt may have apologized, but he still drove her as hard as anyone else and sometimes, she thought, maybe even a little harder. It led her to conclude that if she could just hold her tongue, she'd win him over with her skill and hard work. The men had started asking for her opinion on the disease. They were concerned about having to wear the masks and gloves.

"So, we're really just being cautious until we know what it is. Just like with the way we'll all clean up at the end of the day, which we'll talk over later." Kira saw that the men believed her. Having earned their respect meant she'd proven to them that she was tough enough for ranch work, as well as smart enough to solve problems. She thought it would take longer, and felt pleased.

"Hey, good job, Sweet Pea." Treat snaked his arm around her shoulders.

Kira sighed, then turned and stepped aside to get out from under his arm. She then faced him, cringing inside. "Now, how'd you know that was my flower?" she asked him sweetly. She wanted to catch him off guard again, which was surprisingly simple. Kira had categorized Treat as a bovine instead of a horse.

"I'm just that good, Darlin'," he drawled.

"You know, I've been thinking." Her voice was low and deep. He grinned, and she knew she had him. "I kind of like the Halloween theme for your name. You know, Trick-or-treat?" His grin fell. The other men snickered. "Yeah. I like it so much, I think your name should be Halloween from now on." Kira turned to the others. "What do you guys think?" Of course, she received immense agreement on all sides, along with a few grunts, whoops, hollers, and more snickers.

"Okay then." Kira looked around her feet. "Where's my scepter? Oh, here it is." She pulled a long, dry, yellow weed from the ground and tapped Treat's shoulder. "I hereby dub thee Halloween, now and forever." She bowed her head and swept her arms wide.

Again, at a loss for words, Treat squinted in confusion, then picked up a box of supplies and walked toward the truck. He looked back a few times as he went, shaking his head.

"Well," she infused a royal tone in her voice, wiping her hands together, "my work here is done." She bowed once more, to everyone's laughter. Then they all began the task of clearing the area and packing the trucks. Just as she turned toward the truck with a box in her arms, she caught Holt watching her from behind a group of men, close enough to have heard everything that just happened. For the second time that day, he nodded and touched the tip of his hat.

* * *

Tired and hungry, they dragged themselves into the ranch at eight that night. As she and Holt had discussed, the shower stalls in the bunkhouse had been closed off from the living quarters and bottles of antibiotic wash left in each stall. Until the disease was diagnosed, everyone would have to disinfect bodies and clothes each night. The men would enter the showers at one end, dropping their clothes into a bag, and would exit at the other, entering the bunk section where they could dress into clean clothes. Kira would know if her initial diagnosis was correct, and if they'd have to continue with the gloves, masks, and showers, tomorrow, when the lab faxed the test results to Ben's office.

46

Kira showered before the men and went to the barn to check on Treat's mare. She'd learned from Grisly--Halloween's friend (she was amazed he had a friend)--that his mare was ready to foal any day now. If she was going to be the ranch vet, she needed to have her hands into everything that was going on.

Treat was in the stall, stroking the horse's nose, murmuring softly and hand-feeding her oats, oblivious to the other horses munching hay in the surrounding stalls. Apparently, he'd left the group early and already cleaned up, because he wore fresh clothes and his hair was wet and combed back. Kira noticed a wood plaque nailed to the stall gate, and it looked like a kid had burned the word 'Maggie' into its surface.

Treat reached up and scratched the mare's left ear. "You're gonna be okay," he said against Maggie's neck. The horse snorted at Kira's presence, and he looked up, startled. He stiffened, and stepped back from the animal. "She's ready to drop soon." Looking at the horse, he ran his palm down the curvature of her huge belly.

Kira pretended that she'd not witnessed his private moment with Maggie and moved forward. "Certainly looks like it." Kira scratched both of Maggie's ears, and examined her eyes. "Hey, Maggie," she cooed to the horse. She stroked Maggie's face then lifted her lips to examine her gums and teeth. "You're beautiful, aren't you?" Kira continued her calming dialogue as she moved to Maggie's side and lightly palpated her belly. Kira felt Treat's tension ease as he rubbed Maggie's nose and watched Kira's examination.

47

"What do you think?"

"Looks like she's been eating well," Kira said. "Have you had a vet giving her boosters?"

"Yes. Until he retired." He flashed his all too familiar come-on grin, slid his hand down Maggie's neck and slipped closer to Kira. Heat and cologne radiated from his body.

She ignored him. "She seems awfully big, and I'm feeling something strange. Did the other vet do a scan to check for multiple fetuses?"

That stopped him, and he tensed. "No. And what do you mean 'something strange'?"

Panic rose in his voice, so she held up her hands. "Don't freak, Halloween. I think she might be having twins. If your previous vet had checked, he could have eliminated one of them to make it safer for her and the foal."

"Oh, man," he growled. "I'll hunt him down and kill him if anything happens to Maggie." His face became grotesque with anger.

"Don't get overly worried, okay?" She tried to calm him, but apparently aggravated him even more. "Leave someone here with her when we're gone so they can come get me--"

"Us."

Kira stared at him. "So they can come get *us* from the range."

"And my name's Treat, damn it." He stormed out of the barn leaving Kira awash in the sounds of at least sixty horses snorting, munching, and swishing.

She stayed a while, brushing down Betsy and picking the gunk out of her hooves.

"Dinner's ready."

48

Kira twirled around, dropping the pick, almost falling on her butt. "How long have you been standing there?"

Holt shrugged and eased toward his own horse, handing the mare a sugar cube. "I came to remind you that we need to plan some more after dinner, which is ready."

Kira saw him measure her reaction, examining every minute detail, probably even her pupil dilation. Keeping her face passive, Kira returned his stare. She was hungry, and she couldn't survive on Candace's desserts, no matter how delicious. And, of course, if she stayed, she wouldn't have to argue with Holt about it.

God, he was sexy in the waning light. The sunset colors filtered through the open door and loft, warming his skin and eyes with a soft glow. It made her feel jittery inside. Kira shook off the sensation. She was under a lot of stress and had just finished her second day of major physical exertion. Maybe stress was the reason she began having thoughts about Holt... thoughts of wrestling him in the hay ... of his long-fingered, callused hands on her breasts ... she gulped.

"Lead the way." She still wondered how long he'd been watching her.

* * *

His first thoughts when he'd found her in the barn had focused solely on her jean-clad rear end. But, from there, his gaze took in the rest of her and his brain quickly became a secondary organ. Alarmed

49

by his growing desire, he blurted out the only thing his hobbled brain could conjure up.

He was starting to doubt Treat would bed her. The woman wouldn't stand still long enough, nor let his brother sweet-talk her. But she was sure doing some sweet-talking herself. In one day, she had his entire payroll falling all over themselves to chew a little fat with her. She had a smile for everybody, and something personal to say to each one of them. Well, except for him. She even seemed to enjoy dealing with Treat. Of course, she was giving him hell, but Holt liked that. He'd never before seen a woman resist his brother.

Holt took stock of the last two days. She'd somehow got him to compromise on what to do with the cattle. She'd made friends with everybody. She worked like a dog, right alongside his men, sweating, and even bleeding--all without complaint-- and she'd handled his brother's advances without losing her stride.

The worst part was she seemed to know what she was talking about, and didn't mind telling him so. Holt scowled at his growing admiration. This wasn't part of the plan.

Holt glanced at her and watched the warm evening breeze lift her hair from her neck. He hoped she didn't think his apology earlier had changed anything. The only reason he did it was because he'd thought of his mother and her expectations.

He waited for her to seat herself at the table in the dining hall, and then sat next to her. The room was just off the kitchen of the main house, and contained three rows of picnic-style tables, running

50

about twenty-four feet long. Large bowls of beans--cowboys love beans--were placed at the end of each row, with big ladle handles sticking out. Then large platters of beef--cowboys love beef--were set at the other end of the rows. In addition, there were baskets of bread and butter, and dishes of potatoes and carrots, green beans and corn. Cowboys ate big.

"Hello, Brother," Treat slurred. He looked at Kira, sitting next to Holt, then sat across from her. The others scooted over to make room, greeting him with nods, but not missing a bite.

"Treat." Holt knew what Treat meant, by the way he emphasized the word *brother*. Treat had heard the same scuttlebutt that Holt had when they were kids, and hadn't let it rest since, calling him all kinds of names that meant they weren't really full brothers. Holt would have thought he'd be used to the jabs by now.

"That's not his name, anymore."

Holt smiled at Treat, mentally thanking the doctor, nodding his appreciation to her. "That's right. What is it now? Ghost? Ghoul?"

She laughed at his joke, and his chest swelled. "No. It's Halloween, but those were good guesses."

Her smile shook him to the core.

"Ha ha." Treat grabbed a couple of rolls from a basket and began buttering them. "And what should we call you, Holt? How about half bree--"

"Treat--" Holt felt ready to spring, wanting to fly over the table if he had to, just to shut him up for once.

"What's the matter? Won't let your little brother play?"

Grisly nudged Treat as if to tell him to knock it off. Treat just nudged him back. The rowdy voices of the men dwindled until only the sound of silverware on plates filled the room. Holt knew that most of the men here speculated on his parentage, or at least had heard the rumors.

He tried to maintain control, but stared at Treat, waiting for him to make the first move, just push a little further. He could see Treat gauging him, taunting. It was going to happen sooner or later, he figured, and he could feel his tension rising, the pressure building. Holt narrowed his eyes, wishing he could strangle Treat with his thoughts.

"Who wants pie?" Lupe yelled, coming through the swinging kitchen doors, bearing a huge, round tray stacked with wedges of blueberry pie.

The room was still too quiet. "I do!" Kira yelled back. "But, may I have two pieces? I worked like a man today, so I have a man's appetite."

Lupe laughed and moved toward Kira. The tension in the room evaporated, and the other men made their bids for pie, too. Again, Holt was grateful to Kira. He looked down at his plate, ashamed of his temper. Out of the corner of his eye, he saw Kira rearranging her dirty dishes to make room.

"Sí, Señorita," Lupe said, placing two plates in front of her. "Uno. Dos." She paused. "Tres?"

Everyone laughed. "No, gracias. You better let me start with this. And would you happen to have whipped cream?"

"Oh, sí." Lupe served all the pie and returned with whipped cream. Holt and Treat watched as she smothered both pieces in the stuff.

"You're not really going to eat all that pie, are you?" Holt asked.

She looked at him as if he were an idiot, and then shoved the first huge bite into her mouth. "Of course." She spoke despite full cheeks. "Why would you doubt it?"

He just shook his head and smiled at her. What a pig! He ate his pie more slowly than he ever had before, because he was so busy watching her demolish her two pieces. She scraped her fork across both plates to gather every smear of pie filling and whipped cream. He didn't know why, but he loved to watch her eat like that, so unselfconsciously, and then realized she did just about everything that way. Would she be that way in bed, too?

"Ah. That was wonderful." Kira held her stomach with both hands. "I think it's good that I'm driving the van. My stomach would tip me over on the bike." She smiled at Holt and got up. "Well, you want to get started?"

Holt couldn't seem to do anything but stare at her. He knew he had a lopsided grin on his face. Maybe he *was* an idiot.

They took only a few minutes to plan out the next day, and then he followed her out and found himself opening the van door for her.

"We have to talk about the hours you're expecting, you know."

"I know." He shut the door and stood back. "Think on it, and I will, too. We'll come up with something tomorrow." He shook his head. If he wasn't an idiot, then he was high on something, and if he weren't careful, he'd screw up his own plans of

53

getting rid of her. Holt watched Kira back up and drive off. He heard Treat's footsteps behind him.

"Don't get your hopes up. She's headed for my bed."

Holt crossed his arms and stared after the van. "No. She's not." He chuckled. "Goodnight ... Halloween." He looked at Treat and walked to the house.

* * *

"So, did you think about it?" he asked her the next day. She looked good. Better than in his torturous dreams last night. He noticed she wore new jeans and had bought them long this time--like a real cowgirl. As they walked, whoever saw her, called out to her. She waved and smiled.

"Yeah, I thought about it." She sipped the cup of coffee he handed her as they walked to the dining hall.

"And?"

She stopped and turned to him, taking a deep breath. "Holt, I do need less time here. Or maybe, different time."

Holt tried not to be curious. Was she married, or living with someone? "Ideas?" He took a drink of his black coffee.

"I think that breakfast and dinner are not pertinent ranch activities."

He felt his anger flair, but let her continue.

"I think that if extra time outside of actual ranching is required of me, I'd like to skip breakfast and work during that time instead. I could use the

54

office in the house." She held her cup with both hands.

Holt didn't like being called on the dinner thing. He forced himself to pause, working hard on taking time to think before speaking or acting. He cleared his throat. "I only wanted you at dinner so we could plan for today." Actually, he'd only been busting her chops. "But after the way you ate yesterday, I know you'll need to eat a lot before starting out."

She blushed softly but continued looking straight at him. He stared back at her a moment and heard the words come out before he could catch them back. "How about this? We could have our planning sessions with breakfast in the office."

"Okay." She sounded surprised and a little suspicious. "Thanks." Her skepticism hurt his pride, yet he had set out to be uncooperative, and he still had his goals.

They resumed their walk toward the now loud and aromatic part of the house. "We'll be doing some castrating and de-horning today, so we won't have as many men out treating cattle."

"Any calf pulling?"

"Nope. Don't have to. We don't use growth hormones--that's one thing my father and I agree on--and we always start out a virgin cow with a smaller-breed bull to give her a smaller first calf." Suddenly, he felt awkward, and his collar felt tight. He cleared his throat again and thought he caught her grinning at him. "So, when did you say we'll receive the lab results?"

"Today, hopefully. I gave them your fax number from Ben's business card."

They stopped at the open doors, and Holt let her enter first. "I'll keep someone here and have them ride out with it as soon as it arrives. As a matter of fact..." He touched her arm like he did yesterday; he liked it... "If you want, you can stay and help with the other stuff around here instead." That would be good for him. It'd let him spend more time with the cattle, give him a chance to refocus.

"No, I'll work with the sick cattle today. I'll have plenty of opportunity to castrate."

"Talking about what you're trying to do to me?" Treat interrupted them from behind, then hung his arm around her shoulders.

Holt ground his teeth.

"Trying to?" She lifted his arm from her shoulders and dropped it, while Holt chortled.

"Man, you are one tough bi--"

"Treat." He put his palm on Treat's chest. "I want you to stay and work with the calves today."

Scowling, Treat knocked his hand away, then entered the dining room.

"You have such a way with him," Holt said, feeling strangely happy.

"All in a day's work, Boss."

"Call me Holt." When she looked at him again with surprise, he added, "Please."

"Then, call me Kira." She grinned at him sideways before entering the dining hall.

Breakfast was fast, as usual, but that didn't mean they all didn't eat tons. Holt knew they'd be starving before lunch was hauled out to them. The men called Treat Halloween, much to Holt's amusement, and

Treat continued to insist they call him by his given name.

Holt was only a little disappointed that Kira was coming along. She seemed to brighten up everyone's day. Even Shorty, who never talked much had become a regular chatterbox. Holt felt a pang of envy. He'd never been able to work like that with the men, and they sure worked smoothly with her.

"Okay. Let's be careful today, guys," he warned, after they'd all arrived at the site. "We're not as many as we were yesterday." Everyone mounted up and road out. They only had a couple men cutting today, including Holt. Kira walked out to the head gates and began working with a small team.

A couple hours later, Holt saw Kira at the water jug, and sitting on a stallion next to her was Treat. Angry that Treat had disobeyed him, Holt delivered a cow to the head gate, then raced his horse over to them.

"Halloween, what the hell are you doing here?" Holt rode closely to his brother to get him to back away from Kira. He didn't like the stallion standing so near her. The horse was known to be a little cagey.

"I got bored and decided to come out to where the action is." He smiled down at Kira, who continued drinking from her cup, ignoring Treat. Holt's gut relaxed a bit.

"You can't tell me there wasn't enough action to keep you busy at the corrals." Treat just shrugged. "I needed you there."

"You're just trying to keep our new vet to yourself, brother. I know it when I see it."

Kira looked up at Holt, with a vaguely amused look on her face.

"Think what you want. Since you're here, you might as well help cut."

Treat winked at Kira, and then road away on his beautiful, prancing black stallion. That horse had a bigger ego than Treat, Holt mused, watching the horse dance with his head held high, its tail even higher. He shook his head and turned to Kira. "Sorry about that."

"It's okay. I can handle him."

Holt watched her wipe water from her mouth with the back of her hand, then sweat from her forehead with her sleeve, and felt strong urges rise up in his gut and groin.

She turned and replaced the rubber gloves to her hands and the mask to her face. "See you out there." She walked back toward the last head gate.

Holt dragged his gaze from her and headed toward the first head gate to check on his men.

The day passed quickly, but Holt kept his eye on his brother, and every time he approached Kira, Holt found an excuse to ride up and goad him back to work. He could feel Treat's frustration building for keeping him away and because of Kira's lack of interest. Trouble was brewing. He could feel it.

At quitting time Holt rode past Kira to call in the men. She was on her way to the trucks, and nodded to him when he tapped the edge of his hat with his forefinger. It seemed they'd found a better balance with each other, thankfully.

"Look out!" someone yelled.

Holt turned in his saddle to see what was happening. Several men were waving their hats as they ran past him. Holt's prized Brahma rammed into the fence--a part that Treat should have had repaired last week-- knocking it down. The angry bull chased after Treat's stallion as he continued to whoop and holler at the bull, causing the animal to charge and stop, then change directions and charge and stop again.

Holt reined his horse around and spurred her into a gallop. Treat was always getting himself into trouble, but this time he'd gone too far. Treat loved to tease that bull, and so did that damn stallion. Holt cursed as he heard the lowing of the cattle increase. The Brahma was rousing the sick animals, agitating them.

Suddenly, the bull charged past Treat and ran toward a group of his men. The men scattered, running for the closest set of chutes and head gates. Still the animal continued to change directions, unable to decide which target to attack. After altering his path several more times, the bull pushed forward with determination. He was headed right toward Kira.

Chapter Four

Everything seemed to move in slow motion. Kira had been further from the chutes and head gates than the others, and was still running for shelter. The men at the head gates tensed and their voices rose from all directions. She'd never make it in time.

Other riders, coming in from the herd were too far away to help. Holt rounded his horse toward Kira and spurred the mare. As he tore at the distance separating them, he saw that Kira also realized she couldn't outrun the bull. She turned and stood her ground, facing the rushing beast, fists at her sides, panting.

Good girl, he thought. Bulls had poor eyesight and her best bet was to freeze and hope he'd miss her. He was a monster at twenty times her size, and if he hit her, she'd be dead. Holt's tongue turned to tumble weed as he urged his mount to go faster. The bull screamed and grunted. Its muscles rippled and jerked with each strong stride. Dust flew around him and settled on his shiny, sweating hide. This bull wanted blood.

Some of the men left their safety and ran out, attempting to distract the animal away from Kira. Holt was afraid they'd anger the bull more, but the Brahma had made up its mind and hadn't lost sight of her.

Holt traveled at a perpendicular path to the animal. If he could get to Kira first, he could grab her and hopefully swing her onto his saddle behind him. And that was only if Kira knew what she had to do. Holt's vision sharpened as he focused solely on Kira.

He would beat the bull to her, but it was going to be damn close.

"Kira!" At first he thought she hadn't heard, but a second later, she turned her head and made eye contact. Holt leaned over and stuck out his left arm. Kira nodded and braced herself. With one last look at the bull, she aimed her left arm for Holt's midsection and jumped. Holt grabbed her armpit, swinging her behind him.

The bull lowered his head to gore the horse, and Holt's mare kicked backwards, twisting its rear-end away from danger. Holt almost dropped Kira over the other side, but she seized the back of his collar, ripping it, and dug her nails into his gut. She righted herself, then wrapped her arms around his waist, squeezing the breath out of him. He jabbed his heels into the mare, leaving the bull in a cloud of dust.

By this time, the men reached the area and took turns distracting the animal until the other riders took over and forced him back across the fallen fence. They made a hasty repair, as the bull grew bored and finally trotted away.

Holt slowed his mare to a walk to calm her. Hell, to calm himself and Kira, too. They were quite a distance from the trucks and work area. The horse's slower rhythm eased his heartbeat. After a few minutes, he stopped and pried Kira's hands from his stomach, which stung where she'd torn his skin. He swung his leg over the mare's head and slid to the ground. Dazed, she turned, her arms out, and Holt gently lowered her from the saddle.

He barely got her to the ground before her knees buckled. She fell forward into his arms and Holt kneeled with her, holding her between his legs, her head on his shoulder. She was trembling.

He stroked her hair. "You're okay now."

She looked up, and in her eyes, he saw a shattering emotion. She grabbed the silver ball under her shirt. The chain around her neck strained against her dirt-smudged skin, and all he could think of as they stared at each other was that she was more beautiful than any other creature alive.

"I could hear his breath," she choked out, haltingly. "I could see his nostrils spraying."

With each word, Holt felt and heard her terror increase. He squeezed her upper arms.

"I felt his feet pounding the ground...oh, God..." She sobbed and searched his eyes.

"Shh, you're safe, baby, you're safe." Before he could think, he pressed his lips to hers. She tensed a second, then kissed him back. Their kiss intensified as he emptied the desperation he'd felt in trying to save her onto her warm, soft lips. She opened to him, and he held her tightly as the kiss deepened.

Slowly, they parted, and looked into each other's eyes. Then, she leaned over his thigh and puked.

Holt really needed a cigarette.

When she finished, Holt held her, and she rested against his chest, breathing slowly, but gripping his sleeve. He heard sounds of the trucks and saw the men driving out to them. When they arrived, he picked her up in his arms and laid her on a blanket one of the men had spread on an opened tailgate. The other men ran up and gathered around them, trying to catch a glimpse of Kira.

"Thanks, Dave."

"Uh...it's Funnybone, Holt."

He nodded. Even now, at a time like this, he saw her effects on his men. He wet his bandanna from the water jug and wiped her face. She seemed confused, but when she saw Holt's face, she sat up and clutched at him. Holt held her to his chest and rocked her, murmuring to her like he would to calm his horse. Let them talk or make fun of him. He'd bust everyone of 'em if they did. Holt squeezed her to him until she loosened her hold.

Treat, the last one to arrive, rode up on the stallion, and Holt wondered when he was going to stop screwing up. Each time, the outcome was worse--except for Treat--he was always lucky. Holt lay Kira back down and met Treat before he got too close with the stallion.

"Jesus Christ, Treat! How the hell could you have let that happen?" Holt had only heard of seeing red until just now. He was surprised at how quickly his anger rose to the surface, and gave up on restraint.

"Dammit, Holt, it's not my fault. Maggie's out until she foals, so I had to ride Mack, and he's as hot as a three dollar pistol." Treat stayed mounted, struggling to control the frenzied, stomping animal. "One fine mare shakes it across my path and I'm done for," he yelled.

"Don't blame this on a randy stallion, Treat. I saw you messing with the bull, trying to get a rise out of him. If you would have done like I told you earlier, you wouldn't even be on a horse right now."

"Yeah? Well, this wouldn't have happened at all if you could manage the ranch better." Treat spit at Holt's feet, just missing his boots.

That was it. That was the limit of the crap Holt was going to take, brother, or not.

"Come down off that horse," he growled, stalking toward him.

Treat stayed put. The horse reared at Holt's angry approach. Fearless, Holt grabbed the reins and jerked the horse down. With immense effort, he held the horse steady. "I said get down." It sounded deadly to him, and he felt deadly. Treat would pay.

His brother faltered, looking at the men watching, then back to Holt. "All right. You want it, you got it." He lunged from the saddle, knocking Holt down.

The reins slid through Holts fist, yet he reflexively gripped the ends as Treat landed on him, causing the horse to trample them both. Holt felt a sharp pain in his ribs; light exploded in his head. He released the reins and the spooked horse ran away from the fighting men.

Treat got the first punch in, then rolled on top of Holt, slamming his right fist into Holt's left eye, before ramming both fists into his stomach and ribs. Holt shot his left arm up to block the next punch, and pushed his right hand against Treat's face, shoving him over.

Holt rolled to the top and did as much damage as he could, concentrating on Treat's face, thinking that Pretty Boy might not be so pretty when this was over. Treat brought his legs up and caught Holt around his head then jerked him backwards. Holt toppled away; they both gained their feet.

"I am going to tear you up," Holt told him.

"Try me. You're nothin' but a dirty bastard," he said through a sneer.

Something inside Holt snapped. He'd taken it from this man he'd called brother, so many times, for so many years, he'd lost count. And he would not take it again.

He attacked Treat with a mammoth vengeance. Holt surprised him, knocking him back to the ground, and pounded both his fists into his face, not even aiming anymore, but glorying in the wet, smacking sounds. He knew there was blood, and reveled in it. Guttural snarls that he didn't recognize as his own filled his head.

At first, the men let it happen, but now, they pulled Holt off. Treat got to his feet, unsteady, and then fell to his knees. His face was smashed, tissues swollen, broken open, bleeding. He shrugged off the help they offered, laughing, blood dripping from his mouth.

"Still a bastard. Always will be." Holt wanted him again, but they restrained him. He struggled, and Treat continued to taunt.

"This is disgusting."

Holt turned, and with his good eye, saw Kira, hands on her hips, looking beautiful.

"You both are," she added.

He was glad to see her. "You're feeling better?" He smiled against the pain in his jaw.

She gave him that same 'you're an idiot' look he got from her last night. "Is this worth it?" she asked, with a swoop of her hand.

Holt looked at his brother. He felt his own pain, and knew he probably had at least a couple cracked ribs from the horse, an eye that wouldn't heal for a month. His brother might have to be in bed for a while. Holt straightened, grew serious. The men let loose of his arms and Treat shut his mouth.

"Yeah. It was worth it." He brought his swollen lips together and tried to whistle for his mare. She came to him and he mounted her. "It really was."

Kira just looked at him and shook her head. He didn't care if she thought he was rotten. Treat may be more hurt than he was this time, but she didn't know what he'd put up with over the years. He watched as several men helped his brother to one of the trucks and lowered him inside.

Holt scanned the land. His land. He felt proud, strong, and full of a wild energy. If someone had told him he'd feel this great after beating the crap out of Treat, he would have done it a long time ago. But now he needed something. He looked around at everyone milling about, checking on Treat, and putting things into the trucks. Then his eyes came to rest on Kira.

Holt wouldn't deny himself. He wanted her, and even after today he'd have her. Holt nudged his horse in her direction. In the distance he saw a rider coming fast. It had to be the lab results, and Holt was glad they'd be getting on with their work. The others turned and watched the approaching rider. Dirt flew at them when he halted his mount a few feet away.

Holt turned to him. "Jim, what is it?"

"I'm Grizly, Holt --what happened to you?" Then he saw Treat. "Jeez O'peach."

Treat hobbled over to a mare grazing by the truck and picked up her reins. "Is it Maggie?"

"Yeah."

"Let's go, Kira." It sounded muffled through his swollen lips and cheeks.

Holt watched as Treat spit blood, then forced himself onto the back of the horse. Kira winced, sucking air between her teeth. She looked at Holt accusingly. Yes, he had behaved like a brute today, and he felt like a new man.

Kira mounted a mare that Skinny brought to her and rode it over to Grisly and Halloween. Kira looked to Holt again. He nodded. "We'll talk later."

"All right. Let's pack up and head back," he said to the others. Then, he turned to the battered man on horseback. "Good luck with Maggie, Halloween." And he meant it.

As the small group turned away, his brother mumbled, "My name's Treat. Damn it."

The others watched them go before turning to the task of cleaning up and gathering the supplies. None of the men would look Holt in the eye. Except Shorty. Shorty leaned against the truck and examined him.

"What?" Holt shot out.

"Yesterday, I would'a said a horse. But today, I see somethin' of a bovine-nature." Shorty stood away from the truck and got inside, slamming the door.

Well, what the hell was that supposed to mean? Perplexin' old man. Holt decided he wasn't sticking around until they cleaned up. He felt a little peaked, and thought he should get back and call the doctor. For Treat.

Without saying good-bye, or receiving any acknowledgment from the men, Holt rode out.

* * *

They didn't talk on the way back. After a while, once Kira felt assured that Treat wouldn't fall off his horse, she allowed herself to think about Holt. She was beginning to figure out what was between these brothers. Holt wasn't a full-blooded Crockett. But even though it seemed Treat had it coming, it wasn't right for Holt to pummel him like that.

She shuddered, suddenly serious. Holt had saved her life. She'd been knocked down by a giant bull before, but in a contained situation. Kira knew she'd never forget the look of that two-ton stack of steel charging toward her, nor the feel of her arms around Holt's solid chest, her body pressed against his wide, hard back.

And the kiss. Now that was interesting, wasn't it? Here he was giving her a hard time, and he goes and plants a luscious one right on her lips. And it was delicious. Kira felt a rush of womanly power. *I am woman, hear me roar.*

* * *

"Thank God for shoulder-length surgical gloves." Kira turned her head and grimaced as she pushed her hand and then her arm into the horse's birth canal. When they had arrived, Maggie was lying on her side, with one of the unborn foal's hind legs protruding. They'd gotten there just in time.

Breathing through her mouth, Kira pushed the leg back into the birth canal and felt her way up to Maggie's cervix. Treat and Grisly leaned against the stall rails, watching. A minute later, Treat slid down into the hay, pressing a rag to the roughest part of his face and lip. His bleeding had stopped, but he still looked terrible. She would have tended to him first, but Maggie's situation had been more urgent.

Grisly gave an un-macho groan and turned his head. Later, when she was alone, she'd laugh at the memory of this big, burly cowboy blanching at something so natural.

She moved her hand along the inside of the horse's cervix, stretching it open. "Maggie's not as dilated as she should be." Kira pushed the foal's leg back into the womb and groped for its head. All the manuals she'd read on birthing said turning a foal was tricky and usually shouldn't be attempted, but she had no other choice at this point. Maggie couldn't give birth to a backwards foal. Kira paused in her movements as a crushing contraction started, peaked, then ebbed.

The end-of-day heat clung in the air, making her thirsty. Kira put all her muscle into working against the dam's contractions and jerking hind legs. Maggie squealed and threw back her ears, and the men moved in to help hold her.

Sweat dripped onto Kira's right eyelid and she shrugged it off on her shoulder. Wisps of her hair pasted themselves onto her brow and cheeks. Warm air wafted in, pushing the aroma of fresh hay through the slats of Maggie's stall, doing nothing to cool Kira's body.

"Okay, I can feel its head. It's coming along now. And there are two foals." She slowly removed her arm from the horse and began to roll down her glove.

Grisly tossed her a towel.

"Thanks." She caught it and did a cursory wipe. "There's nothing to do now but wait." She hung the towel over the stall and looked at Treat, rooted to the ground. He stared at Maggie.

"Halloween--" She stopped at his sharp look. "You have to be calm for Maggie's sake." He looked back at his mare. "You know she'll sense your unease," Kira continued. "Besides, you need attention now. Let's get cleaned up and meet at the bunkhouse."

Treat ended up needing some butterfly tape on his cheek, and five stitches on the inner corner of his eyebrow. The rest was just a mess that would need time. His face was already purple, but Kira applied ice to stop any further swelling.

"You're doing a pretty good job on Treat, there," Grisly said, looking over her shoulder.

"Well, men are like animals." They chuckled, and Treat sniffed. "Why don't you rest here, while Grisly and I go back out to Maggie?"

Treat pulled himself up clumsily. "No way. I'm going."

Kira rolled her eyes. "Just don't fall on your face." She stood up, scraping back her chair, and walked toward the door. At the barn they watched for any difficulties in the birth. Two hours later, Maggie gave a final push, and her first new colt gushed onto the ground.

"She did it," Kira said in awe. "And he's beautiful. What's his name, Halloween?"

He sighed, as if the stress of the world whooshed from his lungs. "Jack."

She and Grisly looked at each other and Grisly gave a quick grunt. "He looks like a Jack," she agreed.

"Congratulations," Grisly said.

Treat looked at his friend and nodded, then squatted by Maggie's chest. He stroked her, and Maggie swung her head up to look at him, then laid it back down.

The foal struggled around the stall, trying to stand.

Kira opened her doctor's bag and rummaged through it. "I'm sure you know all of this." She pulled out a small bottle and looked up at him. "Treat his navel stump with this antiseptic solution." She handed it to him, and he put it in his shirt pocket. She tilted her head. Was he getting any of this?

"Swab it once a day for at least five days." Kira waited for acknowledgment, but didn't get any. She handed him a package of swabs from her bag, which he stuffed into his pocket with the bottle.

Kira noticed Maggie's stomach muscles contracting again. "She's getting ready to deliver the second one."

Treat backed up to give his pet some room. Moments later, another foal emerged, and eventually slid out onto the hay.

But something was wrong. This colt didn't immediately attempt to stand, or search for Maggie's teat. It just laid there, the sound of its shallow breaths filling the silence.

Treat exhaled, shook his head, and pulled himself up slowly, looking at it. "You're gonna to have to

71

take care of this. I can't do it." He limped out of the stall. Grisly squeezed Treat's shoulder as he went by, then followed him out of the barn.

Like Treat and Grisly, Kira saw that the second colt had Contracted Foal Syndrome - the foal's spine was curved. He'd have to be put down. She grabbed a bottle and syringe from her bag and put them in her back pocket.

Kira knelt next to the newborn and wrapped him up into a piece of burlap that had been hanging over the rails. Maggie turned her head and licked at her baby, showing the whites of her eyes. Tears pooled in Kira's eyes as she stood and walked to a corner of the barn, out of Maggie's sight.

"I'm sorry, baby." She stayed with the foal, stroking it, softly humming, until it was gone. Kira's throat tightened and she let herself cry. She cried for everything that was lost: her sister and Zoe's mother, the things she'd never get to do with her sister, and Maggie's newborn foal. The pain of losing her sister suddenly felt as fresh, as constricting, as the day she'd received the news of her death.

Kira grabbed her necklace--Cleo's locket--and silently cursed the unknown forces in life that had taken her sister. If she hadn't left the state to go to vet school, Cleo and John and Zoe wouldn't have been on that road on the way to her graduation. Cleo and John wouldn't be dead.

She pushed away from the stall as she forced the feelings down. She had to keep moving.

"Come on," she said to herself, sniffing. "You have a cowboy to console." She shook her head hard and took a deep breath.

Kira stopped just outside and saw Treat and Grizly, arms propped on the top rail of the corral, each with one foot resting on the bottom rung. Treat chewed a dry blade of grass, and stared off into the darkening sky.

Kira walked to them and put her hands into her front pockets. "It's done."

Finally, he met her eyes. He nodded, and then squinted toward the barn. "Where is he?"

"He's still in the barn, but I'll take care of it, Treat."

"Jack's a real fine colt, Treat," Grisly said.

He nodded, then looked away again, thinking. He glanced at Grisly, then at her, holding her gaze a moment. Then he said, as if it were an after thought, "The name's Halloween." He slid his hands and foot off the fence and walked toward the ranch house.

Kira and Grizly watched him go. She gave Grizly a small smile and leaned on the fence to look at the sunset. It was full of fuchsia, neon-orange, and deepening purple. The cicadas began chirping their high-pitched melody, which draped like gauze over the occasional stomps and low grunts of the cattle.

Kira's sorrows blended with her surroundings, quieting, then stilling in her heart. She reminded herself that although there was pain, there was always hope, too. And right now, she hoped she wouldn't see Holt until tomorrow. But his show of violence frightened her. Holt had become an animal, unaware of his surroundings, as he bludgeoned Treat into bloody submission. She could well imagine that it came from anger that had been pent up for years. Kira hadn't truly believed that parents could favor one child over another, but she saw it with her own eyes in Ben's office that first day.

Now she understood Holt's ambition. It was all he had. Her disgust at the brothers' display of aggression lessened. But, she reminded herself, Holt's anguish wasn't an excuse. She felt wary of him, and wondered what would happen if she ever pushed him to the brink as Treat had.

"Good evening." It was as if her thoughts had summoned him. Kira braced herself and turned. Holt was already cleaned up, his hair dry, indicating that he'd been back a while. He nodded at Grisly, and Grisly nodded his greeting as he prepared to leave. It was obvious Holt wanted to talk with her alone.

"Be seein' you at dinner, Kira?"

"I doubt it, Grisly. See you tomorrow." She watched his back a moment as he walked away then returned her attention to Holt. "Hi."

"Hi," he said again.

They looked at each other a moment, and it seemed that Holt felt as awkward as she did.

"How are your ribs? You should let me take a look at them."

He looked as though he was about to protest, but then nodded.

Kira picked up her doctor's bag, and as they walked back toward the house, she felt a strange uneasiness between them. When he opened the front door for her and she passed him, she breathed in his scent. He had a warm, skin smell, and she fought against wanting to bury her nose on his chest for more.

Suddenly, Kira realized the danger of her situation. The memory of his kiss was still fresh on her lips, and Holt exuded a raw animalism that showed even in his posture, his walk. And, what if he was still feeling violent?

Kira walked past him again as she entered the office. He stared at her - that same intense, single-minded stare he'd given her in the barn when they'd first met.

She motioned toward the coffee table in front of the couch. "Why don't you sit here?" The couch and table were joined by two armchairs on either side, in front of a fireplace at the other end of the office. It was cozy. "Actually, maybe you should sit over on the desk." She turned to go back and he grabbed her arm.

Chapter Five

"This is fine."

She looked at her arm in his grasp and slowly removed it. "Okay." She set her bag on the table and Kira watched him sit, but he never took his eyes from her face. She stared into that gaze a moment, wary.

"Take off your shirt," she heard herself say. She forced herself to break eye contact when he began to unbutton, and opened her bag to rummage around for some wide tape. Even though she wasn't looking, she knew he still watched her. Then, he jerked a bit and took a sharp breath. She bobbed her head up and put her hands on him.

"You shouldn't have ridden back. You might have caused more damage." She moved her hands gently around his ribs, first one side, and then the other, her face so close to his she could feel the warmth from his skin and breath on her cheeks.

"I wanted to get back quickly."

"Well, you certainly made time. No one else is back yet." She felt a swollen lump along his side. She jerked her eyes down and noticed four long gouges across his stomach.

"What happened here?" she asked, lightly prodding them with her fingers. Holt's abdominal muscles clenched beneath her touch.

"You've got quite a grip," he said with a smirk, as if he was feeling no pain.

Kira looked at him with surprise, then she remembered how she'd almost flown off Holt's horse as they'd escaped the bull. Kira didn't like where her thoughts were leading her, so she backed away. But he grabbed her upper arms and slowly pulled her up toward him.

"You need to have your ribs wrapped." She pulled away and moved to her bag as fast as she could. "You have a couple cracked ribs on the left." She took out the roll of stiff material and some scissors, and then turned back to him. His expression seemed knowing, purposeful.

Pretending he didn't have a face, she unwound a length of the tape and knelt between his thighs. Kira tried not to touch him, but several times the insides of her upper arms grazed him as she wound the tape around one side, and reached around him to grab it on the other. She found herself praying that this would be over soon, but at the same time that it would last several hours. He winced again.

"Sorry."

"I'm fine."

"There," she said, cutting the tape from the roll. "One more thing." She dabbed some disinfectant on the scratches, and before she was able to stop herself, imagined those scratches on his back. She looked up again, and Holt looked as if he'd been thinking the same thing.

She tore her eyes away and capped the medicine. "Be careful."

"I will." He started to stand up and Kira realized that unless she wanted his crotch in her face, she'd better stand quickly as well. She jumped up and teetered backwards. He caught her and held her to him a moment.

She took a step back, wondering why she ever thought that the female held the sexual power over men. She'd better say something.

"I wonder what happened to that fax we were supposed to get today?" She dropped her eyes to his bare chest and casually pulled her arms from his grasp. She strolled out of the cozy alcove toward the business end of the office.

"It's here." He bent and retrieved his shirt, grunting.

Kira saw he was having trouble. "Here." She walked back to him. "Let me help." She took his shirt and held it behind him. "How'd you get this on before?" she asked.

"Wasn't easy, but now it's impossible with this tape around me."

She pulled it onto his shoulders and then moved away. "Where is the fax? When did it come?"

He motioned to the desk, grimacing as he attempted to button his shirt. She approached the desk and picked up the small, messy group of papers. They weren't in order yet, so she laid them out top to bottom until she had a neat stack, then held it up to read.

By then, Holt stood beside her, his shirt hanging open, exposing his carved chest and stomach muscles. Kira couldn't keep her eyes from roaming past the bottom of the first page to the strip of whiskey colored hair disappearing at the waistband of his jeans.

"What does it say?" he asked. His voice was husky, but with pain or lust, Kira couldn't tell. She pulled her gaze back to the page and forced herself to concentrate.

"Well, let's see." She made her way to the other side of the desk, putting distance between them, hoping he wouldn't follow, then sat in the big chair, and placed the first page on the desk. Holt sat across from her and Kira leaned her elbows on the desk. "Damn."

"What is it?" He started to lean forward, groaned, then leaned back.

"It's not BVD."

"It has to be. They must have screwed up at the lab."

The anger in his voice reminded Kira to be careful. "I don't think so. Looks like everything is in order here." She paged through the report once again, just to make sure. "The tests were pretty simple, so it has to be right." She looked up from the papers, and jerked back. Holt was now leaning over her, glaring at the report.

"Then maybe you screwed up." His voice was low as he raised his eyes to meet hers.

She stood up and leaned over the desk into his face, incensed. "I can't believe you would even suggest that." She glowered at him. "You were there and saw me take the samples. You saw me put them on ice packs." Kira became very still. "You know I did it correctly." She straightened and waited for a response.

Holt merely narrowed his eyes and grunted, which antagonized her more.

"You're just angry because you were wrong. Without me, you'd be treating the wrong thing."

Holt's face hardened, and he began to stalk around the desk toward her. He looked seriously determined to do...Kira didn't know what. Alarmed, Kira tried to pretend she wasn't afraid, and circled the desk the other way, keeping the furniture between them. She was very much afraid that she'd pushed him too far, which wouldn't be far at all for a man in his state.

"If you take another step toward me, I'll scream." She tried to keep her voice from rising into hysteria.

Holt blinked. "You think I would hurt you?"

"Well..." She tried not to gesture too much. "You're coming after me around this desk, and all I can do is wonder what you might do if you catch me."

"I--I wasn't going to hurt you." He looked down, and shook is head. "The truth is, I don't know what I was going to do." Holt raised his head and looked at her. He pressed his lips together. "I'm sorry."

Kira was unsure how to respond. She stood away from the edge of the desk but couldn't relax. She'd been under way too much stress lately. "All right." Her words came out slowly.

Holt continued looking at her and she thought she should say something. "I'm sorry I goaded you about being wrong and needing me here."

Holt waived his hand in the air then wrapped his arm around his ribs.

"Don't --" Kira resisted the impulse to rush to his side. "Well, I guess we should call it a night, then." She moved with caution around the front of the desk.

Holt took a step toward her, but she forced herself to walk smoothly to the door, grabbing her bag on the way. Holt reached the door with her and opened it. She gave him a polite smile, and took her first steps over the threshold.

Holt gently took her arm and turned her back toward him. "I am sorry, Kira."

She squeezed his forearm, above the hand holding the doorknob. He looked down quickly, then back up. She wanted to assure him that she'd accepted his apology, but she couldn't get a word out. Facing him, his hand on one of her arms and her hand on one of his, their bodies were close enough she could feel his heat.

She looked into those caramel eyes and saw that he'd felt it, too. His gaze softened. Holt pushed the door shut, his muscles shifting under her hand as he released the doorknob. As the latch clicked behind her he wrapped his hand over her forearm, sliding it up, grazing the side of her breast.

He looked at her several seconds more, as if waiting for her to protest, but all she could do was hope he'd kiss her. Holt pulled her against his chest and hesitated only a moment more, then dipped and tilted his head to meet her already parted lips.

He molded his mouth to hers, then slowly, reverently, gained entry with his tongue, exploring as if this kiss held a new discovery. This was the only kiss she was meant to experience; it felt so comfortable, familiar. So right.

Holt's hand slid from the back of her head to her left breast, where his tentative strokes became sure. Kira wanted his hand on her skin, and as if hearing

81

her thoughts, Holt reached for her shirt buttons. Kira rubbed her hands along his back, every sensation of moving, working muscles burning into her mind.

She lifted his shirttail up to touch his skin at the same time Holt slipped his hand under her bra and cupped her breast. They both paused and gasped at the new sensation.

Holt lowered her to the floor and lay partially on her. Bright flashes of color exploded behind Kira's eyelids as he broke the kiss and moved his lips over her neck, rubbing his smooth cheek against hers, as if marking her. Kira bent her head back to allow him greater access, and moaned softly.

Holt hummed in answer and brought his lips further down, to the center of her neck, then rubbed his face between her breasts, against her bra. He slid his hand under the band, to the back, and unhooked it. Kira sighed in relief, and Holt murmured. He lifted her bra away, moved her necklace to the side, and cupped both breasts, burying his face between them again, kissing her everywhere.

"You're so beautiful. You taste so good." He trailed desperate kisses along her neck, her cheeks, and her lips.

She wove her fingers through his hair. "Mm."

Holt returned to her lips and tugged on the button on her jeans, dragging Kira from her delirium.

She grabbed his wrist, and Holt's hand froze. He lifted his head, his eyes glazed and dark, his lips flushed, damp.

She hadn't been with a man in ages, and she'd promised herself that the next man she'd sleep with would be the one she'd marry. He would cherish her. Love her.

She wanted Holt so badly, but neither one of them were making any promises. Kira took his hand from her waistband and brought it up to her lips, kissing his rough knuckles. Holt took his hand and leaned above her on both elbows.

"What's wrong?"

"I'm not ready."

He nodded. "I can wait." He bent his head and gave her a small peck on her lips, then smiled.

Outside the office, the front door swung open and slammed against the inner wall, causing them to flinch. "What the--?" Holt asked, rolling to his side and wincing at the effort.

They heard Ben, hollering.

"Oh, man," Holt said, and tried to get up. He held his hand out to Kira. She took it, but let go when he winced again.

"What's he doing here? He's not due back for days." Just a few days ago, she didn't want him to leave, and now, how she wished he were still gone. She fumbled with her buttons, deciding not to waste time re-hooking her bra. Holt rose slowly.

"I don't know. I feel like an idiot, trying to cover ourselves like a couple of kids." He struggled with his shirt buttons.

Kira tried to straighten her hair.

They heard his voice booming closer to the closed office door. "Where is Holt?" Ben yelled.

Kira helped Holt finish the last of his buttons and turned to face the door. She and Holt stood at attention just as the door flew open.

"What in Sam Hill is going on here?" Ben stood in the doorway and looked around his office, then at Holt and Kira.

"What happened? Where's Mom?" Holt looked around his father toward the entry.

"She's fine." Ben moved into the room and made his way to the big chair behind the desk, examining them. "She had a feeling something was wrong and wanted to get back."

He eased himself into the chair, put his feet up on the desk, crossed his hands in his lap, and tilted his face up toward them.

"Oh." Holt motioned around the room. "Well, as you can see, everything is fine. Kira and I are working well together as you predicted, and we're close to resolution."

Kira resisted looking at him in disbelief.

"I saw Treat at the bunkhouse." The corners of Ben's mouth tightened, turning down.

"Oh." Holt lowered himself into one of the armchairs.

Ben indicated the other chair. "Kira, why don't you have a seat?"

Kira smiled disarmingly and sat. "How was your trip, Ben?" She crossed her legs, trying to appear nonchalant. "I've heard Barbados is wonderful this time of year."

"Oh, it was wonderful. The beach was beautiful, the food great. Catherine and I truly enjoyed it." He smiled, and Kira hoped she'd loosened him up a bit for Holt. "I'm just sorry I had to cut it short." Ben glared at his son. "Did you think I wouldn't notice your injuries, Holt?"

"No, sir." He held his father's steady gaze.

Ben studied his son a moment, and then turned back to Kira. "So, Kira, tell me how your first few days on the Crockett Ranch have been. What have you accomplished?"

Kira explained quickly that she and Holt had agreed to hydrate the sickest cattle, the BVD tests were negative, Maggie had foaled, and the colt's name was Jack. She didn't elaborate about the deformed twin colt, leaving that for her weekly written report.

Kira also left out, of course, all of the other details about Treat trying to pick her up, Holt giving her a hard time, the bull almost killing her thanks to Treat, Holt saving her life, and of course, what just happened with Holt on the office carpet.

"So," she continued, "I need to run some other tests, and perform an internal exam on one of the animals, preferably a recently deceased one, to investigate further. At the least, I'd like to take some tissue and bone samples."

Ben looked at Holt, who nodded in confirmation, then looked back to her. "What's your timeline? What do you need?"

"Well, I've made some notes in my book." Kira got up and retrieved her bag from the floor. She pulled out the book and opened it, then paged through it until she found the spot. "Here's a list of lab equipment and supplies I would need." She put the book on the desk and turned it around so he could see it. Ben took his feet off the desk and reached for the book. When he looked down, Kira glanced at Holt, who watched her with a questioning look. She shrugged at him and turned back to Ben.

Ben pushed the book back to her. "Holt, take care of this. I think we can borrow or rent most of this stuff. Also, find a place here where she can work." He leaned back into his chair again.

"All right." Holt reached for the book, and she slid it across the desk to him. Just then, Kira heard brisk footsteps in the foyer. Catherine entered the office and made a beeline over to Holt. "There you are. Hi, Kira." She smiled at Kira before looking back to Holt. "What happened?" She gingerly took Holt's face in one hand and turned it to the light.

"I...I fell off my horse today. Cutting." His eyes slid over to Kira and she raised an eyebrow.

"That's just what Treat said." His mother clucked and cooed. "Well, looks like it'll heal anyway." She released his face, and Holt looked sheepishly at her. "You boys should be more careful."

"I know, Mom." Squeezing her hand, he smiled kindly at her. "I'm sorry to upset you."

Kira felt her warmth toward Holt grow; Holt loved his mother.

"Well." She looked to her husband.

"Well," Ben said, too.

"I guess dinner's on. Will you be joining us, Kira?" Catherine asked.

Kira stood and watched as Holt stood slowly, but without any outward sign of pain. He was a good faker. She also noticed Ben observing his son, an odd expression on his face. "No, thank you, Catherine. I really need to get going." Kira glanced at Holt.

"Oh. Well, that's too bad."

Ben rose and came around the desk to his wife's side. "Well, then, Kira, we'll see you tomorrow." He tipped his hat to her and Kira nodded. "Son." Ben took Catherine's elbow and they left the office, closing the door behind them.

"Sure you don't want to stay?" Holt asked, pulling her toward him with a grimace.

"I really need to get home," she said, as he brought her tightly against his body. Kira held her hands at his elbows, resting her forearms on his. "And I just remembered something I have to do in the barn."

"Oh, that's right." He released her and took her hand in his. "I'll help you." He led her from the office and out the front door.

"What do you mean, 'that's right'?" she asked, following him down the steps.

"I mean, I know about the other foal."

"How?" She pulled on his hand but let him tug her forward.

"I just do," he said, squeezing her hand. "Come on."

They went to the barn and found the foal, still covered in the burlap, the way she'd left him. Kira felt very sad, all over again, and plopped down in the hay.

"Come on," he coaxed. Holt lowered himself to her, with a slight groan, and put his arm around her. "You had to do it."

"I know." She tried to keep the tears from her voice. Fortunately, it was dark enough in the barn, she didn't think he could see them shimmering in her eyes. She leaned her head into his shoulder, glad for the comfort. They sat there for a while, and Kira let

Holt rock her and stroke her hair until she started to feel better.

"So." He eased her a few inches away and looked down at her. "It seems by your lists and notes that you'd thought those tests would come back negative."

She shrugged. "I try to plan ahead, that's all."

"Well, I guess we'll have to go with your plans."

"That's what I was hired for, right?" She cocked her head.

He got up. "Yeah. That's right. Come on, let's get this foal into the truck. I'll have one of the guys take care of it tomorrow."

At her insistence, Holt grudgingly let Kira carry the foal through the barn to one of the work trucks, where she delicately laid it into the truck-bed. They stood together for a moment, silent, looking at it, and then Holt squeezed her shoulder. "I'll walk you to your bike."

Kira unlocked her helmet from the side of her bike and lifted it over her head, but Holt grabbed her arm, lowering it. She brought the helmet to her hip and cradled it in the crook of her arm.

"About tonight."

"I know." She crinkled her eyebrows. "Look, people do stupid things, sometimes, when they're under a lot of stress. And...and I'm sorry. Okay?"

He made an incredulous sound. "You think that came from stress?"

"Well, obviously. But I don't mean just you. I've been going through a lot lately, and --"

"I want you, Kira."

It took a few seconds for Kira to assimilate what he said. She realized Holt was waiting for her to say something. "Well...I wanted you, too, back in the office."

Holt chuckled again, and cupped her jaw with his right hand. "Well, obviously," he said, using her tone. "But I used present tense just now."

She knew her face had turned day-glow red. How could she have lost control of her professionalism, allowing her passions to take over like that? Thankfully, the house spotlights were at her back, illuminating Holt's face instead. At his triumphant grin, she shook her head. "Boy, you Crockett men just go right after what you want."

Holt frowned. "I'm nothing like my brother."

Kira swung her leg over her bike and sat down. "Listen. Everything about this is dead wrong and you know it. In the morning, everything will look different, and you'll be glad nothing happened."

Again, he made an incredulous noise. "First, it's stress, and now it's nothing. I wouldn't call that nothing."

Kira sighed. "Okay, nothing more, then."

He reached out to touch her face again, eyeing her. Kira lifted her chin away from his grasp, so he crossed his arms. "The way I see it, the only thing wrong with this situation, besides the fact that you're not willing to follow your desires, is that I'm keeping the whole ranch no matter what. You wont be able to handle that if we get involved."

"Your desires do seem to be mutually exclusive." She readied her helmet to put onto her head.

"But--" He pulled her arms down again.

Kira sighed and rolled the helmet to her hips once more. "But what?"

"It might not be wise to just walk away from this."

She narrowed her eyes. "Walk away from what? There's nothing to walk away *from*."

"Oh, I see. Well, I'm not afraid to see where this may lead," he drawled.

"I'm not afraid, because I can't be afraid of something that doesn't exist," she drawled back. "Besides," she continued in her regular tone, "when I get part of the ranch, you won't be able to handle it." She shook her head and raised her helmet again, only to be blocked by Holt's hands.

"That won't happen, because I'll get the whole ranch. So, really," he shrugged, "you'd have to decide if you could handle it."

She tried to hold her tongue, but it didn't work. "You will not end up with it all, because I'll own some of it. And you're on." She pulled her helmet onto her head with defiance. "I'm not afraid to see where this leads us, either. This isn't an attraction, it's--it's impulse under duress."

Kira stood, hit the ignition button, then paused and the engine roared. Kira had to tell him about Zoe. She flipped up the visor on her helmet.

"There is something else." Her voice was soft.

"What's that?"

"My sister passed away and I'm raising her baby." She gauged his reaction: Holt's brows furrowed, but he didn't flinch from her gaze. "Think about it."

He nodded, crossed his arms and nodded again.

Once she was well away from the ranch, her heartbeat slowed. What had she just gotten herself into? She was dead-tired, crazy-stressed, and she knew, just knew, this would be a mistake.

* * *

A baby? Holt watched her go, questioning his sanity. Until today, he'd never wanted a woman the way he wanted Kira. He was in pain he needed her so badly, and the pain wasn't in his ribs. But, a baby? Holt didn't believe in non-biological parenthood. It hadn't worked in his situation, and he surely didn't want to repeat it and damage some other poor kid. He would get attached to Kira, and when she failed to get part of his ranch, he wouldn't want to let her go.

Holt's heart warmed as he remembered the way she'd handled his pesky brother. And the feeling of her in his arms after the bull had charged her. He'd watched her in the barn tonight, putting down the deformed foal. When Kira had begun to cry, it was all he could do to stay hidden, to not go to her and hold her. And at that moment, his heart had melted. He'd have done anything for her.

He sighed and shook his head. A nagging voice inside his head taunted him. *Now, who's afraid?* it asked. He kicked the dirt with the toe of his boot, put his hands on his hips and looked up at the stars, then turned around and went into the house.

Chapter Six

The next morning, Kira rode out with Shorty, as usual. Only half the men showed up to finish hydrating the cattle, and Holt wasn't with them. She wondered if he'd decided to avoid her today. Or, what if he'd decided to let her work this problem alone? she wondered, with a sinking feeling. Kira wasn't so sure she wanted to work it solo, now, and went through the day trying not to frown.

Even though Treat was there, he didn't serve up the usual diversions. He'd come to accept his new name and the fact that she wasn't interested in him. He did, however, tease that damn bull again. Apparently, he felt safer doing it, now that the fence was reinforced.

Fortunately, the bull wasn't interested in him either. Kira assigned a few more nicknames to the men, which was good for a few laughs. But it just wasn't the same without catching glimpses of Holt. She imagined him riding shirtless, his muscles flexing in unison with the mare's. Kira was torturing herself, she knew, and without him around, the work felt harder, the sun hotter. She cursed that damn cowboy.

With fewer men, it took until three o'clock to finish, and Kira resented Holt for that. The least he could have done was tell her what was going on. She dragged her tired, sweaty body to the truck, and then fumed on the ride back, planning on confronting Holt when she returned to the ranch.

When she and Shorty finally pulled up to the house, Holt came out looking clean and refreshed. How dare he! She glared at him through the windshield, but he smiled and touched his hat brim. Kira got out, slammed the truck door, and stomped toward him.

"Holt," she began, still covering the distance between them. "Why--"

"I'm glad you're back. I have something to show you." Holt took her elbow and guided her around the house, greeting the men on the way.

Kira jerked her arm away, still angry and a little self conscious about being so dirty and stinky. "Where are we going?"

"It's a surprise. Come on." He tugged her along.

When they reached the back of the house, Holt kept going. Kira pulled away from him again, but he continued walking. She stood there a moment as he headed toward the bunkhouse. What could he possibly want to show her in there? He knew she'd have to shower in the bunkhouse, and usually did before the men, but she'd be damned if he was going to be in there with her. Holt stopped and turned around. He motioned with his arm for her to keep following. Kira put her hands on her hips and glared at him. Holt shrugged, then turned and disappeared around the corner of the bunkhouse.

She followed him to the corner of the building and cautiously peeked around it. He wasn't there, but little dirt puffs hovered a few inches off the ground at the next corner, which had to have come from his boots. She followed a little faster, the thought of being alone with him dissipating her anger.

"Aha!" she yelled, as she threw herself around the corner. He wasn't there. Kira looked around. He stood several hundred yards away, in front of a small building that looked like a freshly painted, but very old, wooden tool shed. With his hands on his hips, he looked as proud as Candace was of her creations. Kira made her way toward him.

"What is this?" she asked.

"This is your lab." He took her hand and turned toward the building. "Come on." Holt stepped up two wooden steps and jerked opened a plank door set in the middle of the plank wall. "Be careful of this door. It gets a little stuck sometimes." He pulled her inside with him.

The drone of a window air-conditioning unit was the first thing Kira noticed, but a split second later it hit her. Holt had converted a tool shed into a primitive, but functional one-room laboratory for her. It had two sinks, and counters running along the adjacent wall on the left. Past that, on the left wall, she saw a small bathroom, including a shower. Just past that was a narrow closet with a muslin cloth hanging on a rung, pushed to the side.

She scanned the wall facing her. A raggedy looking loveseat fit perfectly between two small bookshelves. Her gaze passed over it then darted back. She imagined herself and Holt entwined on the cushions, before she could force herself to continue her inventory.

The wall to the right and adjacent had counters, and sitting on them was all of the equipment she'd requested: microscopes, boxes of glass slides, petri dishes, bottles of liquid and powder chemicals, a small battery-operated, circular bone saw, notebooks, and other things. Underneath one of the counters were a tiny refrigerator and several stools with wheels. By the door was a water cooler with paper cups.

Kira looked at it all again, in wonder. "You did this? Today?"

"Yep." Pride rang in his voice and outlined his stance.

"So, this is where half of the men and you disappeared to."

"Is this how you're thanking me? You're complaining that I left you short-handed?"

"Well, you did." Kira tried to look mad. "But, thank you." She gazed around for the third time, noticing new details. "I am impressed."

"That's better." He stepped toward her. "But...is that all I get?"

Kira looked at his teasing face, knowing he wanted a kiss. "How about my undying gratitude?" she smirked and leaned back against one of the counter tops, propping herself up on her elbows.

Holt moved closer. "How about this?" he asked, and planted a hand on either side of her. He leaned against her and lowered his head toward her upturned face.

"Wow! This is great, Holt," Grizzly yelled from outside. Holt jumped back from her and turned toward the door, holding his ribs and grimacing. Kira heard Grizzly's feet hit the steps. They met Grisly at the door. Several men who had worked in the field that day gathered outside, admiring the other men's handiwork. Kira and Holt stepped down and joined the group.

"So, you just ran electricity and plumbing from the bunk house, huh?" Funnybone stood over a recently disturbed strip of dirt leading from the base of the bunkhouse to the base of the lab. "Who's idea was that?"

"Mine," Holt answered, a little too gruffly.

Kira smiled to herself and turned back to Holt. "I'm even more impressed now. You seem to be a jack of all trades."

"I know some things." He narrowed his eyes and grinned.

The men broke up and headed to their bunkhouse to shower, leaving Kira alone with Holt again. "So, I take it that shower actually works?" She nodded toward the lab.

"Of course it works." He emphasized his words.

Kira laughed. "Just checking." She started away, then turned back to him. "Towels?"

"I've thought of everything," he assured her. "I dare you to find something wrong."

"We'll see." She danced up the two steps and slammed the door, locking it behind her.

Indeed, he had thought of everything. Even her duffel bag of clothes was waiting for her. The towels looked new and smelled freshly washed. Body lotion sat on the sink, and a dish of citrus potpourri adorned the back of the toilet. What had he done, raided his mother's supplies? Studied a woman's magazine?

This was a very good reason to be avoided for a day. She liked that he'd labored all day making something for her, thinking about her. Of course, Ben had told him to find a place for her to work, but this was above and beyond that. Wasn't it?

She allowed herself a moment to imagine sharing her life with Holt, and Holt being the best father ever for Zoe, to pretend that this wasn't just some exciting way for them both to avoid conflict, alleviate stress. But it couldn't be serious, couldn't last.

Kira shook her head at herself in the mirror for worrying about something that wasn't really real. She rolled her eyes and undressed, looking forward to her first unhurried shower since being on the ranch.

Twenty minutes later, Kira bounded down the steps with a contented sigh. She was heading home early today, and tomorrow she'd bring her books and everything else from home that could be used in the lab. But today, and for the rest of tonight, she was going to be one-on-one with a certain little baby. Kira's mood soared; she'd be home before the sunset!

"Hey."

Kira twirled around at Holt's voice. "You scared me."

"Sorry." His lips curled in a smirk. "So, how was it?" A toothpick hung from his lip.

"Great, of course."

"Of course." He looked at her a second. "You taking off already?"

"Yep." She slid both hands into her back pockets.

"Well, that's a good idea. It'll give you time to pack."

"Pack?"

"Yeah. I talked it over with my father and we've decided it'd be best if you moved into the guesthouse while you work on a diagnosis. It'd give you more time. Plenty of room for you and your baby."

"When?"

"Tomorrow if you can," he said, with a quick nod.

"Wow." She raked her hand through her hair. "Um, Okay." Plans and lists started running through her mind. Then she remembered Candace. "Oh...I have a roommate, and--"

"It's a three bedroom house, Kira. Furnished."

"So...?"

Holt shrugged. "It's your business." He paused, cocked his head, and pulled the toothpick out of his mouth. "It's not a man is it?"

Kira laughed. "Definitely not." She propped her hands on her hips. "Besides, another man would get in the way of our...experiment. Right?"

"Definitely." Humor lit his eyes, and he flicked the toothpick to the ground.

"Right." She started to feel awkward.

Holt appeared to have noticed her discomfort and smiled faintly. He closed the distance between them and stood in front of her, his face looming above hers. Kira took a deep breath and tried to stay calm, while Holt cradled her face in his hands and bent his head to hers. His kiss was soft and full of promise.

"See you tomorrow, then," he said as he continued to hold her face.

"Right," she whispered, concentrating on remaining upright.

"Call me if you need help with anything."

"Okay."

When he released her, she backed away a few steps, as steadily as possible, then turned and walked away.

Holt forced himself to stand his ground and watch her go. When she was showering, he'd leaned against the outside of her lab, and it was torture, imagining her nude body slick with soapy water, her hands skimming across her soft skin. Holt rummaged his pockets for another toothpick. With Kira around, he'd need to keep a huge supply handy.

Since he wouldn't be able to sleep tonight, he would take some of his herbs and extracts to the testing corral. He'd take his spotlight so he could work late, and his bedroll, just in case he actually could get some sleep. Tomorrow, he'd be able to tell if the few well animals they'd placed with the sick ones were coming down with the illness.

Within the hour, Holt trotted away from the ranch, his bedroll bouncing on his horse's rump, the containers of his concocted substances clinking in his saddlebags.

He rode in just before sunset and scanned the group of sick cows. They seemed to be holding their own, he thought, as he removed everything from his saddlebags, then let his horse roam loose. Tonight, he was going to give the animals concentrated extract of blackberry leaves and Echinacea, hoping the combination would ease their symptoms and boost their immune systems. Native American healers had used Echinacea to help ward off infections, and Holt thought it might work on animals, too. This was his last idea.

He planned to give each cow a few drops on their tongues tonight, and again every few hours until morning. But he wouldn't treat the animals that had been placed here a few days ago, because he didn't want to affect the results of that test--whether they'd get sick or not. Even though he worried that the well cattle would get sick, he still held out hope that Kira's tests had somehow been flawed. Holt looked out over the animals again, wishing this was all just a bad dream, then tucked two containers of extracts into his front pocket and entered the corral.

By the time Holt had administered the first treatment, it was just starting to get dark. He washed up and threw his bedroll onto the ground. Lupe had packed him some cold steak, rolls and corn on the cob. He imagined the most beautiful woman in the world was sitting across from him. Kira.

Holt snorted -- stress! Did the woman not know herself any better than that?

Holt wanted nothing more than to be alone with her right now, to make her belong to him. Suddenly surprised by the strength of his feelings, he gulped from his canteen. It wasn't stress. It clearly was that she was an attractive woman, and he hadn't been with anyone for a long time. And she was attracted to him, thank God.

When Kira had told him she had a roommate, he'd almost choked. An overwhelming sense of propriety had made every muscle in his body tense. He finished his meal and grabbed his spotlight. Hell, he didn't want to own her, but he damn sure knew that he'd have to have her heart. And her body, of course.

A few hours before dawn, Holt checked that his pistol was snug by his side, and then laid back, his hands folded underneath his head. The stars were so plentiful out in the middle of nowhere like this. He breathed deeply, gazing at the Milky Way. He found it hard to comprehend that he could see it, diffuse and glowing across the night sky, and yet be a part of it, too. When he looked at it, he felt so insignificant. It made Holt feel that all of his problems and worries didn't matter nearly as much as it seemed. After all, who would remember him or his problems in a hundred years? Then again, maybe in a hundred years, he'd be up there with the stars looking down, seeing how his efforts had changed things.

But he wondered whom he'd be with besides his mother. Would he have a father, any other siblings? Would he have to struggle as hard up there to belong, as he did down here? Or would he just be stardust? Life would be easier that way.

Holt closed his eyes and listened to the night. The fragrant desert air made him think of Kira, and he was glad that he'd be seeing a lot more of her now.

* * *

"Just a few more feet'll do it." Kira hung her head out of the passenger's window to make sure Candace backed the van up to the guesthouse in a straight line. Zoe giggled from the back seat and threw her stuffed doll to the floor. The guesthouse was easy to find, and placed well enough away from the back of the main house to ensure privacy.

"How's that?" Candace asked.

101

Kira brought her head back in. "Perfect." She unlatched her seat belt and opened the door. "It'll be good to be done with this move."

Between this job and being with Zoe as much as possible, Kira was beginning to feel the strain. She was so tired, and had begun losing sleep lately, finding herself waking up in the middle of the night thinking about her sister. She'd lie there for hours, willing herself to relax and go back to sleep, until finally, from pure exhaustion, she'd drop off for another hour or two. Kira didn't know how much more she could take. Most of the time, instead of relaxing, she'd cry. She was weakest to the onslaught of her sister's memory at that time of night, when everything was quiet, when she didn't have anything or anyone demanding her thoughts and actions, keeping her from facing her loss.

But now, Kira had to squeeze back the emotions. "Will you get Zoe for me while I go find someone to let us in?"

"Sure." Candace gave her a worried look before climbing between the two front seats and unbuckling the baby.

Kira took only three steps and was greeted by Ben. "Good morning!"

Ben quickly made it the rest of the distance in spite of a stiff walk.

"Are you feeling okay?" Kira shook his outstretched hand. "You look like you're in a little pain."

"Oh, it's just old age, I'm afraid. It creeps up on me sometimes, especially in the mornings."

They walked the little distance back to the van. Candace appeared from around the back of the vehicle with Zoe on her hip and her best and biggest smile on her face. Kira smiled at her. "Ben, this is Candace Dressler and this is Zoe. Candace, this is Ben Crockett."

Candace adjusted Zoe on her hip, and then reached for Ben's hand. "Nice to meet you, Ben."

Ben shook her hand and then wiggled Zoe's fingers, his eyes twinkling. "I'm delighted to meet you, and I hope you'll all be happy here."

Ben motioned toward the guesthouse. "I guess I should give you these keys and show you around."

Kira was impressed with the outside of the house. Its Territorial arches, beams, and rustic plaster were only enhanced by the desert. Bird of Paradise bushes lined the outside of a short wall, the orange flowers a sharp contrast against the white plaster. Terra cotta Mexican tiles, imbedded in sand, created the floor of a small, courtyard entry. Wrought iron patio furniture and hanging plants completed the look. When Ben swung open the carved front door and stood aside, her first glimpse of the interior took her breath away.

Candace oohed and ahed as they entered the foyer. It was just as beautifully decorated as the main house. Two, white, overstuffed couches rested on thick carpet. Modern art statuettes sat on polished wood furniture all over the room, accenting American Indian artifacts along the walls.

Kira felt strange accepting such hospitality. "Are you sure you want us to stay here, Ben? I mean, this is just so..." Kira was at a rare loss for words. She hated it when that happened.

Ben laughed. "I'm sure. But Holt is very sure. It was his idea. Didn't he tell you?"

Holt's idea? Candace nudged her.

"Yes," Kira said. "I didn't mean to seem unappreciative. It's just that, I'm your vet, and," Kira held out her open palms, "this house is fit for royalty."

"Well," Ben said, starting to laugh fitfully, "You solve my problem, you will be royalty." He handed over the keys. "I'll send over some men to unload your things. Just tell them where you want everything."

Candace switched Zoe to the other hip as they made their way back to the front door. "Oh, great! I love to order men around."

"Now, she's my kind of woman." Catherine appeared in the doorway and joined them.

Ben wrapped his arm around Catherine's shoulders and introduced her to Candace.

Catherine shook Candace's hand, and then turned to Kira. "Kira, we're so glad you've decided to stay with us. I think it'll help ensure your success."

"Thank you. I was just telling Ben I wasn't sure if we should stay in such a wonderful home."

"Oh, pshaw! This place just sits around empty most of the time, so we're glad it's getting some use. Please, make yourselves at home." Catherine squeezed Kira's shoulder, and turned to Zoe. "Now, who might this be?" She spoke in that universal baby-pitch Kira heard from everyone who spoke to babies, and Zoe smiled.

Everyone seemed to fall in love with her. She always smiled, always seemed so confident and happy. Most of the credit went to Candace for that, and Kira felt a rush of gratitude.

"This is Zoe." Kira grabbed Zoe's waving hand and noticed her voice rise to the high range, too.

The three women began cooing and playing with the baby, huddled in a cluster. Ben cleared his throat. "Well, I'll let you four ladies get acquainted and I'll send over the men." Kira had to admit that this situation was already making her feel better, more in control of her life. Although being here would definitely help her work, she didn't buy that as Holt's main reason for it.

He wanted her. She wanted him. Stress.

"Hello?" Treat appeared in the doorway. He knocked on the doorframe, then noticed Candace and froze.

"Oh, hello, dear." Catherine approached her son and pulled him inside, shutting the door. "We were just getting acquainted." She motioned to Candace. "This is Candace Dressler and Zoe. Candace, this is my son, Treat."

Kira looked at Candace, expecting her to react as her usually bubbly self, shoving her hand into his and shaking it with exuberance. But she didn't. With her head tipped down, she was actually looking at him through fluttering lashes. Slowly, she raised her hand toward him and smiled as if she'd never seen a man before.

"Hello."

Treat took her hand almost as slowly as she offered it. "Hi. Call me Halloween." He turned her hand and bent his head, pressing his lips to her knuckles.

105

"Call me Candy." She didn't even giggle. And Candace never asked Kira to call her Candy. Great, Kira thought with a smirk. Now I'll be hearing the words Halloween Candy every day. She looked between them and saw that Catherine seemed just as perplexed. They smiled at each other and Kira shrugged.

"Yes, well." Catherine cleared her throat. "Are the men ready to help unload?"

"Hmm? Oh. Yeah." Treat released Candace's hand but continued staring at her. "We'll get started now."

They all turned toward the door, and found Holt with his hand on the doorknob.

"Hi. We didn't hear you come in," Kira said.

"Hi, son," Catherine chimed. "You're just in time to help the girls move in."

Kira moved toward Candace and Zoe. "Holt, this is my friend." She was about to introduce her when he interrupted.

"Candace. I know." He touched the brim of his hat. "Nice to meet you." He took a quick look at the baby. "Let's get to work, Halloween." Holt turned and walked out. Through the door, Kira saw him go to the van and open the back doors. Several men arrived and began unloading and handing boxes to others. Kira met Candace's questioning eyes and arched one brow.

Holt looked like he hadn't slept last night and was wearing the same clothes from yesterday. "Well...." she turned to Catherine. "Thank you again for letting us use your guest house. I promise we'll leave it in exactly the same condition."

106

Catherine smiled and moved toward the door. "I'm hoping you won't be leaving." Treat grinned at Candace and went out to help the others. "There would be no reason to," Catherine said, taking Kira's hand between her own. "Once you diagnose the disease and become our full-time veterinarian."

"That's what I keep telling her," Candace said.

"See? My kind of woman. Listen to your friend, Kira." Catherine let go of Kira's hand after a brief squeeze and turned to leave. "I'll let you get settled, and have Lupe bring you some dinner tonight. Of course, you're always welcome to join us in the hall, if you'd prefer."

They thanked Catherine again and said good-bye, and then Candace greeted the first of the men to arrive at the door with their things and began directing the action.

After an hour of ordering the men around, then unpacking for a couple more hours, Kira and Candace had everything under control. Kira kissed Zoe and went to her lab, lugging a box of textbooks and reference manuals. She needed to get more samples and start working, but before she could do that, she'd have to unpack this box, and start reading as much as she could about diseases that looked like BVD. Kira plopped the box onto the counter top, pulled out the first manual, and settled in.

Chapter Seven

The next morning brought a beautiful sunrise, and some humidity, with the first heat of the day. It was already in the high seventies and Kira was starting to dread the summer. Riding outside in 118 degree heat, if she was still working here then, was going to be torture.

Kira and Holt had agreed to meet first thing, to ride out to the holding corral for more samples. She'd beat him to the barn and began saddling up Betsy, as she listened to the stillness of the morning: horses stirring from sleep, the last of the night's crickets chirping, a few hooves stomping. And the morning air smelled so sweet. Dew brought out the scents of sage, mesquite, and greasewood shrubs, and every other bush and plant in the area. It always salved her wounds, especially after rough nights.

She'd had plenty to keep her mind busy during the days -- Holt was a source of distraction as well, keeping her heart tingling, but her nights were still painful, with her sister's face filling her dreams. Sometimes, the dreams seemed so real that when Kira woke up, she'd forgotten about her death.

She forced herself to focus on what she might see today at the corral, what she had to do until this thing was done. She wondered how the illness had advanced in the sickest ones, but was afraid to find out. Before this was over, they'd lose some cattle. Kira just hoped she'd come up with the solution before they lost too many.

"Morning," Holt called behind her.

She turned her head and smiled, but continued tying her doctor's bag onto the back of the saddle. "Morning."

"Looks like you're eager to get going." Holt lifted his saddle off the rack and carried it over to his mare, that nickered and tossed her head in greeting.

"I woke up pretty early today, and thought I might as well get started. Got some food from the kitchen for breakfast and lunch." She patted her saddlebags.

Holt looked at her. "Must have been pretty early. You look haggard."

"Thanks a lot." She gave him a sideways glance.

"Sorry. What's wrong?"

"Nothing." Kira pretended to be busy with her gear. "I just wake up early sometimes."

"Hmm," he said, in doubting tone.

Kira walked Betsy out into the new light and mounted her. She looked back, waiting for Holt to join her. Sometimes Kira felt the bad kind of alone, disjointed from the rest of the world.

"You're frowning." Sitting atop his horse next to her, his forearm rested on his saddle horn.

"Am I?" Kira tried to relax her face and smile.

"I know just what you need." He gently spurred his animal and moved forward. "Come on."

"I'll just bet you do," she said.

"It's not like that. You'll see." He led her away slowly.

After consuming four pastries and a thermos of coffee on horseback, Holt reined in his horse. They stood at a low point, just below a gentle rise in the terrain. "Okay. Dismount here."

Holt spoke quietly, making Kira feel as if she shouldn't speak. She dismounted and joined him next to his horse. Holt pulled her reins from her hand and dropped both sets to the ground, then took her hand and led her up the incline.

When they reached the top, she gasped. Holt had brought her to a wide, far-reaching vista, completely covered in wildflowers of every color and type imaginable. Kira sighed at the sight of so many pinks, whites, yellows, oranges, reds, and purples. The entire vista spread into rocky landscapes, all surrounded by an immense, dark purple mountain range.

"It's the most beautiful thing I've ever seen." Her voice cracked as she tried not to cry. She looked at him and he searched her eyes, then looked back out across the waving sea of color.

"Sometimes I take different routes to get a new view of things." He breathed deeply, his nose pointed toward the sky. "This place has something. It's--"

"-- miles and miles of nobody," she finished for him.

He looked at her, surprised. "Yeah..."

"And of nothing...and everything."

"Exactly."

Kira looked at him and smiled. He knew exactly how this place made her feel. "I wish I knew what some of those flowers are."

Holt grabbed her hand. "I'll tell you." He pulled her down the other side of the rise into the knee-deep plants, urging her to run, until they stood like an island in the middle of it all. Kira laughed, trying to catch her breath.

"It smells so good." She squeezed his hand. "You've given me something special. Thank you."

"You're welcome. Point something out. I'll tell you what it is."

Kira looked around. "That one." She indicated a bunch of white flowers with six long petals each, which looked like stars.

"Easy. Those are Desert Lilies." He put his hands on his hips. "Next?"

Again, she looked around then pointed. "Those."

"Ah..." Holt bent down and picked one of the flowers with the thousand, tiny, cream-colored petals tipped in fuchsia. "This is one of my favorites." Holt tucked its stem behind her ear and stroked his fingertips along her jaw. "Desert Thistle."

Holt moved toward her, taking both of her hands.

Kira tilted her face to meet his, and as he lightly touched his lips to hers, Kira had never felt more beautiful or desirable. Gently, he pressed closer. His tongue stroked her mouth and lips with reverence, and he lowered them to the ground.

Kira leaned into his embrace, wrapping her arms around his waist. It felt as if every cell of her body had begun screaming for its own intimate contact with this man. Holt hugged her tightly, deepening their kiss. Kira returned Holt's pressure with her arms, and he moaned. He laid her onto the ground and covered her body with his, bringing his right hand to her breast, moving his lips to her jaw and under her ear, trailing sweet kisses as he buried his face in the crook of her neck.

111

Kira ran her fingers through his hair and held him to her. Holt moved his face lower, nuzzled her breasts for several moments, then brought his lips back to hers. Holt softened his lips, then lifted his head.

She opened her eyes, pained by his withdrawal. He smiled down at her, and she smiled back, feeling drugged with arousal.

"Your beautiful face is surrounded by Colorado Four O'clock."

Kira shifted her eyes to the left and then the right. Indeed, her entire head lay on a pile of small, round, fuchsia flowers. "Is that like five o'clock shadow?" Holt chuckled, and Kira pulled his head back down to kiss him.

Holt kissed her back and raised his head again. "No, but one of us could be wearing it if we continue in this vein." He snuggled her other ear.

Kira draped her arms loosely around his neck. "You're right. We should get going." But, boy, did she want to stay right where she was.

"Yeah. I've detained you long enough."

She smiled. "This is the kind of detention I can get into. Much better than detention hall in school."

Holt gave her one last, brief kiss, then stood and pulled her up. "You never spent any time in detention hall."

"Oh, yes, I did." Indignant, she brushed off the back of her jeans and shirt. "You think I'm a goodie two-shoes, but I assure you that that is just an unfortunate outer cloak I've had to live with my whole life."

Holt took her hand and rolled his eyes at her, smiling. "Unfortunate outer cloak?" Holt's shrill whistle brought his mare running, with Kira's mare tagging along.

"Yes." Kira straightened her hair and made sure her Desert Thistle was still in place.

"What did you do, then?" He sent her a challenging glare.

"I'm not sure I should divulge that," she said, trying to sound snotty. She pivoted and walked to her horse.

Without taking a step, Holt reached out and took his mare's reins. Kira mounted up and trotted her horse over to Holt who was already astride his mount.

"Oh, please. Shock me with your badness."

Kira sighed heavily. "I forged a letter to get a friend out of a test."

Holt gasped in mock horror. "Oh, heavens!" he screamed in falsetto.

"Stop," she laughed, swiping at him. "It was a big deal, at the time."

"For you, I'm sure it was." Holt smirked and reined his horse around.

"All right, then. What did you do to earn detention? I know you couldn't have avoided it. " Kira kicked her horse into a trot to catch up.

"Oh." He sucked air between his teeth. "It might be way too much for your sensibilities."

"Oh, please," she said, in her deepest, most disgusted sounding voice.

"I'll only tell you the most minor thing, then," Holt said, looking at her from the sides of his eyes.

113

"What?"

"I..." Holt paused. "Well, I set off a few firecrackers in class."

Kira laughed. "Is that all? Big deal," she hooted. She did think it was a bad thing to do, but wasn't going to let Holt know that.

It was Holt's turn to feel indignant. "Well, the teacher was so shocked by it that she had to go to the hospital for her heart."

"Oh. That is kind of serious."

"Yeah."

"I don't want to know any more," she said, looking forward.

"I knew you wouldn't." After several seconds, he added, "Goodie two-shoes."

* * *

"So, what the hell was your problem yesterday at the guest house?" Treat tossed his hat onto the rack and grabbed a beer from the refrigerator. "I've stayed clear of you since..." Treat looked around to make sure they were alone. "Since our fight."

"My problem was that I couldn't believe you'd come on to Kira's friend. Why don't you just stick with your type?" Holt had his feet stretched out on the coffee table in the living room, drinking his own beer. Dinner would be ready soon, and he took this rare opportunity to put his feet up, sitting motionless, except for the required bending of his arm to bring the beer to his lips.

Treat sucked at his beer, gulping several times before replying. "You're so full of it."

"I'm sorry. I can't understand your mumbling through that swollen jaw." Holt leaned his head back and closed his scratchy eyes.

Treat faced his brother and enunciated. "I said, you're lying."

Holt brought the lip of his beer bottle to his mouth, then let the cold, fizzing liquid fill his mouth. He held it on his tongue a few seconds, then swallowed. "I don't know what you're talking about."

"Get real. It was that kid."

Holt flexed his jaw and squeezed the bottle in his hand. Seeing the kid in the flesh today had set him off balance. He hadn't known he'd been so obvious.

"Maybe you shouldn't be coming on to Candy's friend."

Just then they heard the clanging of the dinner bell and both rose, heading toward the door. Holt moved out ahead of Treat, but as he passed, heard him say, "I guess it'll be a new family tradition, raising some other man's mistake."

Holt whirled around, enraged. Treat backed up a step. Holt grabbed his brother's collar, twisting it around his fist. "First off, you don't know a damn thing about Kira or that baby. So, don't say another word about it. To anyone." Holt lifted up on Treat's collar, and yanked Treat's face closer to his. "And second, if you think you're getting to me with that illegitimate crap, think again. I'm still the acting foreman and our mother's first born."

Holt released his grip on Treat's shirt and shoved him back with the knuckles of his fist. Treat breathed deeply through his nose, making Holt think he might

115

have to fight him again, but Treat stood there, feet apart, face expressionless, and eyes full of fury.

Holt headed towards the dining hall.

When he arrived, most of the other men were already there, so Holt found a space at the end of one of the tables, and a few minutes later, Treat sat across from him. Their parents had already seated themselves a little further down at the same table. Lupe and another server wheeled out the huge vats of vegetables and meat, and everyone dug in.

A moment later, Kira walked in with the baby, followed by Candace carrying a folded high chair. Holt wiped his mouth and jumped up, taking the chair from Candace. "Hi. Perfect timing." He tried not to look at Zoe. When he'd been alone with Kira today, he'd forced the baby from his thoughts, but now that was impossible.

"Is there room for us at the end here?" Kira asked. "It'd be easier."

"Sure. I'm glad you came." He'd missed her this afternoon when they'd parted to tend to their own jobs. Holt unfolded the high chair and Kira hugged Zoe, then put her into the chair and secured the straps. Candace locked the tray in place.

Holt slid down the bench. Kira sat next to him, and Candace sat next to Treat, who became oblivious to all else. Holt pretended interest in his meal.

Kira was so wrapped up in the child that she made only feeble attempts to talk to him or anyone else. He began to feel tense and crowded, closed-in. Sweat beaded on his forehead. He must be giving himself a heart attack.

He felt ridiculous letting a little baby do this to him, but he had to get away, get some air. "Excuse me." He wiped his mouth and laid his napkin onto his plate.

Kira and Candace looked at him, and then Kira moved off the bench, letting Holt slide out. He'd explain himself to Kira...later.

Once he made it to the corral, he leaned his head back and breathed, letting the cool air calm him. He blinked his eyes a few times to clear his head, then went to his room to pack all of his extracts and herbs. He couldn't face Kira tonight, not after his sweaty flight from her. He then went to the kitchen and packed enough dry food to last two weeks. After leaving instructions in the office for Shorty, Holt packed his gear onto his horse and rode out.

* * *

That night, Kira lay in bed with her eyes closed, fuming. She couldn't believe Holt. It was obvious what was going on here. He hadn't seemed to mind when she'd mentioned Zoe, but Holt had grown more distant each time he'd been around her. She opened her eyes and sighed, nowhere close to sleep.

She sat up, swung her feet to the floor and paced around her bed, her arms wrapped loosely around her waist. What was he so afraid of? Maybe, for him, there was a connection between Holt's situation and the fact that Zoe was another man's child. Or maybe he just didn't like kids. Kira crawled back into bed, feeling let down. She realized now that she had actually wanted something between herself and Holt,

117

even it was some manifestation of stress making her want him. But, he wasn't the man she'd thought he was.

The next morning, after a measly bit of sleep, Kira dragged herself out of bed to start the slow process of preparing slides and growing cultures. On the way to her lab she asked Shorty if he'd seen Holt, thinking that it'd be best to talk to him, get it all out into the open. Shorty told her, with a look of sympathy, that he wasn't sure where Holt was or when he was coming back.

The sympathy was the toughest thing to swallow. Apparently, everyone knew what was up, or thought they did. The men seemed to be walking around her as if she was a delicate cake that might cave in at any moment.

Okay, he'd run away. Like a little boy. But she was going to take it like a woman. Kira stomped up the stairs to her lab and slammed the door. She took one of the plush purple towels that Holt had so kindly provided, folded it three times, pushed her face into it, and screamed.

* * *

"May I come in?" Candace asked from the doorway, Zoe on her hip.

Kira lifted her head from her microscope and laid her pen onto her notebook. "Sure. I could use a break."

Candace shut the door behind her. "That little window unit keeps it pretty cool in here."

118

Zoe reached out for her, and Kira pulled her close. "Hi, baby." Kira kissed Zoe's fat cheeks, and nuzzled her neck, making her giggle. She turned to Candace. "Yeah, it's nice. I'm getting used to the constant humming. It actually helps block outside sounds."

"Good." Candace looked down at Kira's papers and books. "Um, I was wondering..."

"What?"

"Since you usually take a couple hours with us at lunch time, what would you think if I left Zoe with you, and I went on a picnic with Halloween?"

Kira grinned. "I think that'd be a good idea. You need a break, too."

Candace grinned back. "What if it takes...more than a couple hours?"

"I have a feeling it might." Kira looked at the mess of work she'd accomplished the last five days of Holt's absence. She'd worked in her lab from sunup to sundown. "You know, I could use a longer break." Kira stood. "Why don't you go ahead, but if you could be back in about four hours, I'd appreciate it."

Candace hugged Kira and Zoe. "Thanks."

They walked back to the guesthouse, arm in arm. Candace's ringlets shimmered in the sunlight, more golden than Kira remembered them, and her smile and giggle sparkled. She was really falling for Treat, and Kira hoped it would turn out all right.

Kira helped Candace pack a lunch and then watched her leave on horseback with Treat on his mare and Candace on another. Kira had almost told them about the wildflower vista she'd shared with Holt, but just couldn't bring herself to do it.

119

She turned from the kitchen window and walked toward the highchair. "It's just you and me, girlie." Kira kissed Zoe, and made 'pfbpfbt' sounds on her belly, making her squeal. "How about some lunch, cutie pie?"

* * *

Holt woke up on the fifth morning away feeling exhausted and defeated. He'd tried everything he could think of to save these animals. And he wasn't sure he'd gotten anywhere.

He walked over to one of the animals and helped her drink some water. When he moved to the next animal, she stood there as if she didn't see him. Holt leaned down and peered into her eyes. Suddenly, the creature's forelegs buckled.

With a shout, Holt dropped the water bucket and kneeled beside her. She struggled to get up, but he could see that most of the struggle was mental. This cow could no more raise herself up again than Holt could save her. He started to shake.

She lowered the rest of her body to the ground, then collapsed onto her side. Dust puffed up around her, and settled onto Holt's body. He moved to her head to be with her.

She looked tired. Her last breaths came in wheezy pants for several more minutes, until finally, she just didn't take another.

Stunned, he sat there, trying to believe what he saw. His eyes had filled with tears, but he fought them off and got to his feet.

This was his fault. Holt stood over the cow with his hands clenched, seeing the truth. He'd allowed this to go too far. Holt now saw that saving these animals, keeping the ranch running, was far more important than losing ten percent to an outsider. Sure, Kira would be a very rich woman someday, but he'd still have a livelihood, and so would the rest of his family.

Allowing one more look at her, Holt turned and ran to his horse, hoping it wasn't too late to save the ranch.

Chapter Eight

Holt stood outside the arcadia door, watching Kira feed Zoe. She smiled at the baby as she talked to her, perhaps encouraging her to eat. A thick orange goo covered Zoe's face, and Holt half smiled before catching himself.

For five days and four nights, he'd thought about what he might or might not be feeling about himself, his situation, and Kira, and he still didn't have any answers.

All he knew was that it felt somehow wrong to be away from Kira. So here he was, watching her with her baby, remembering all the feelings that Zoe's existence in Kira's life had dredged up. Abruptly, he reached up and knocked on the glass door.

Kira jerked her head to the side and when she saw him, jumped up with her hand over her heart. He'd scared her, probably because he looked like half mangled vulture meat. The baby waved her arms in the air, in his general direction, while the orange food oozed down her fingers. Kira walked to the door, hesitated, then unlatched it and slid it open the width of her face.

He nodded once. "Hi."

Kira looked at him from head to toe. "Hi." She wasn't cutting him any slack.

"Uh, something's happened, and...we need to talk."

She looked back at Zoe, then turned to him again. "We needed to talk days ago, but I'm listening."

"I haven't been working to further your efforts here and I'm sorry." He waited for a reply but she gave him her unwavering attention. "I'd like to join forces with you. So we can beat this thing, if that's still okay with you. But, I need to know now if we're together on this, because someone's got to go back out there with me today."

The way Kira looked at him made him think she would say no.

"What's happened?" Not even the passionate anger he'd heard from her the first few days colored her voice now.

He dropped his gaze, and his head followed. He noticed he had manure on his boots, and reflexively tapped the toe of one boot against the wall, then looked up. "One of the cows at the test corral died today." She appraised him, squinting her eyes. "I won't fight you anymore. I want to be part of decisions, and help with whatever I can."

"Hm. What can you contribute?"

Holt pushed his hat up an inch. "Let me show you something?"

"Candace won't be back for a while, so I can't leave the ranch."

"It's in my room." She looked at him like he was attempting some juvenile tactic. "I'm serious."

Kira exhaled, still scrutinizing him. "I have to clean up Zoe. It'll take a couple minutes. Why don't you disinfect in the bunkhouse and I'll meet you at the main house." She slid the door shut in his face, latched it, then walked away.

Okay, okay. He deserved this and more, and he was willing to shoulder it all, because he'd hurt her.

Kira had probably figured out immediately why he'd left that night. But he wasn't going to bring it up. It was better left untouched, and the wedge he'd put between them was better left in place. Even though he wanted--needed--to be near her, she didn't need him messing up her life. He turned and made his way to the bunkhouse. He knew first-hand how a child that didn't belong to both parents would feel and would be raised, always second best, never good enough. Holt couldn't allow himself to hurt Zoe like he'd been hurt.

On his way to the main house, his path converged with Kira's, and they walked in silence the rest of the way. When they entered, Catherine came around the corner to see who it was.

"Holt!" She hugged him. "Where have you been? And hi, Kira."

She always had a smile for Kira, Holt noticed.

Kira returned her smile. "Hi, Catherine."

"Working at the test corral," he replied, using the boot-puller by the door. "I'm sorry if I worried you, but I had some things to take care of."

"Well, I'm just glad you're okay. How are the animals?" Catherine took Zoe's pudgy hand and bobbed it up and down.

"Not too good, Mom. One died today."

"Oh, I'm so sorry." She looked at Kira and then back to him. "Well, we had to be prepared for anything while you both were working this out."

Her statement made him feel guilty. If she only knew, she'd be disappointed in him. He was disappointed in himself enough for the whole family.

124

"Yeah, well. I brought Kira to show her some things in my room."

"Okay. Well, have either of you had lunch?"

"No," Holt answered for both of them. Kira looked at him, but didn't say anything. He figured she hadn't eaten, because there was no lunch plate next to her when she was feeding Zoe.

"Well, when you're done, why don't we eat together?"

"Sounds great, Mom. Thanks." He smiled at her and walked down the hall with Kira and Zoe following.

Holt held open his bedroom door for her and Kira entered without a word. She stopped abruptly and looked around. The room was large, and along one side were three desks with several apparatuses sitting on them. Some of his stuff was pretty old, and he felt embarrassed, knowing that Kira had probably worked with new, more advanced equipment.

"I know it looks almost prehistoric," he began. "But, I've been working on trying to find a treatment." He moved past her and glanced at her face. She looked up at him with raised eyebrows, her silence making him sweat. Holt held up a small pad of paper. "I've jotted down the things I've tried. Mostly extracts of herbs and other plants."

Kira took the pad from him. Holt noticed that the baby had fallen asleep on her shoulder and she walked around the room as she read his notes, then stopped and faced him.

"I can see why you would try some of these things. You had some good ideas."

He nodded, surprised by her positive words. "Thanks."

"What effects did you see?" She handed the pad back to him, then with a gentleness that made his throat ache, she walked over to his queen-sized bed and laid the sleeping baby in the middle of his mattress. She untucked his pillows from the thin bedspread and put one on either side of Zoe, then caressed her cheek before turning back to him.

"I...there were no effects."

"How do you know? Did you have a control group in the corral?"

"Control? No. But I didn't treat the well cattle that we put in when you first got here." At least he'd done that right, he thought.

"Hmm. You should have treated half of the well animals." She crossed her arms. "And, of course, you should have only treated half of the sick cattle to see whether these extracts had an effect after infection."

He was an idiot. Now he'd never know if what he'd been trying truly got him nowhere or not.

Kira sighed and let her arms drop. "Okay, listen. If we're going to work together there has to be no more competition between us. You have to tell me everything you've already done." She'd started pacing, and Holt followed her with his eyes. She was speaking quietly so as not to wake Zoe, but with enough emphasis to tell him she meant business.

"Okay."

"And anything else we do will be done as a team, not individually. We have to keep some control on this thing so we know why something's changed, or why it hasn't."

126

He nodded. "Anything else?"

She stopped pacing in front of him and leveled her gaze at him. "Yes. Whatever was between us before you left is over." Her chin trembled.

"All right." It was exactly the way he wanted it, too, so why did he feel like he did when that cow died this morning? Probably just from eating dried foods all week.

"Hungry?" He motioned toward the door.

"Yes." Kira went to the bed and slowly lifted the baby.

"Do you want to leave her here for now?"

"I don't want her to wake up in a strange place and not see me." Kira walked past Holt, and down the hall without a second glance. Holt shut the door and followed, feeling a strange emptiness inside that definitely was not hunger.

Catherine had set the table and put food down for the three of them. While Holt sat, Catherine helped Kira lay some of the couch cushions onto the floor for Zoe.

"I know we could have gone to the dining hall for lunch, but I thought it'd be nice just the three of us."

"It's real nice, Mom." He hoped this would help make up for worrying her.

Kira and Catherine small-talked through lunch, and Holt found he couldn't bring himself to participate, unless they spoke to him directly. Of course, Kira didn't speak to him at all.

"You know, Holt's been so glad that you joined us," his mother said.

Holt shot his head up and looked at her.

Kira raised her eyebrows. "Oh?"

127

He looked at Kira as she forked a chunk of crab salad into her mouth.

"Yes. He said working closely with you would help us cure the cattle as fast as possible."

"He said that?" Kira asked, as if it were very interesting.

"Well, not exactly, but - "

"Mom, I'm sure Kira doesn't want to hear all of this." He looked from his mother to Kira, who smiled at him. There was judgment in her eyes.

"Well, I'm just so glad you two have such a nice working relationship."

Kira looked at him and said, "Hmm." She swung the word up and then down, nodding her head as she did so.

Holt swallowed a rock of fear. They looked at each other a moment, then Kira opened her mouth to speak, and drew in a slow, deep breath.

"Well, Holt is a great partner, and I'm sure we'll know what's made the cattle sick in a couple of weeks." She put another bite into her mouth and smiled at Catherine.

Holt hoped his exhalation of relief wasn't audible. He felt grateful to Kira, and embarrassed at being caught in a lie to his mother.

After lunch, on the way out, he asked, "Why did you do that?"

Kira kept walking and didn't look at him. "Why would I want to hurt your mother?"

Holt stopped, feeling as though he'd been slapped. She continued on to the guesthouse, the still sleeping baby in her arms. She marched up the steps, opened the door, and shut it without so much as a backwards glance.

For the next hour, Holt met with the men and found out what had been accomplished while he was gone. He worked out their plan for the next several days, and was even civil to Treat, who'd just arrived on the scene and seemed to be in a better mood than Holt could ever remember.

"What are you so happy about?" Holt asked him, finishing up some notes on his clipboard.

"Nothin'."

To Holt he looked like he'd just won the lottery, so it had to be about some woman.

"Sorry to hear about that cow out at the far corral," Treat said.

"Thanks." Holt didn't trust the sincerity in Treat's voice.

"Maybe if you'd helped Kira right away, it wouldn't have happened." Treat's face held none of the usual challenge.

"You're right."

Treat's eyes widened slightly.

"I just hope I'm not too late." Holt tossed the clipboard on top of a box of supplies, then lifted it and walked toward the barn.

* * *

Holt waited for her on the steps outside the lab. Kira nodded acknowledgement to him as she went up the steps ahead of him and opened the door.

He followed, closing the door behind them, while Kira turned on the air-conditioning unit. She

129

normally left it on all day, but since she knew she'd be away for the four hours of Candace's picnic, thought it'd be better to save the electricity. Now she wished she hadn't been so frugal.

"I'm sorry it's so hot in here. I turned it off before lunch."

"That's okay. I've been accused of being overly tight with a dollar now and again, myself." He curled up the corners of his mouth at his joke. Kira kept herself from returning the grin, and busied herself by moving a couple stacks of books to clear a space for Holt to work.

She looked up to see Holt watching her, as usual. She cleared her throat and re-straightened the piles of books. Holt frowned, tossed his hat onto the love seat and sat on a stool beside her.

Kira pulled out her notebook. "Will you be ready to go back out to the corral soon to get that carcass out? I want to do an internal exam on it while we're there."

"Yeah. But we should leave now, though." He rubbed his chin and looked at the ceiling. "I'll take my lights. We'll only have a couple hours of daylight left once we get there."

Kira wrote the date at the top of a clean page then started a list of things to do. "Okay. What do I need to do to help?"

"Would you mind getting together some food and water for tonight? That'd make it easier for me to get the rest of our gear onto the horses."

Kira finished writing what they needed in her book. "Not at all."

Holt looked over her arm at her notes. "Do you always write everything down?"

"Everything. Always." She capped her pen and snapped her book shut. "That way, I don't have to remember so much, and it leaves a lot less room for error or questions later on." She stood and pushed the stool back with her thighs. "You should start taking notes, too." She walked over to her bookcase and ran her finger over several book bindings until she found an extra notebook, then pulled it out. "Here it is." Kira walked back over to Holt and handed it and an extra pen to him. "Meet you at the barn."

Holt stood and took the book and pen from her, looking uncomfortable holding the items.

Minutes later, Kira and Holt entered the barn from different doors. Kira noticed Holt's surprise at the overstuffed saddlebags on her shoulder. "Lupe packed them for me. I have no idea what's in them, but it feels like enough to last several days."

Holt looked at them again, doubtful. "I think we're in for something special. Dried foods are usually pretty flat."

Kira felt close to opening herself up to him again. Maybe she should just stop chatting with him. It would be so easy to forget herself, and she recognized she had a lot of work to do to stifle her feelings for him. She couldn't let herself fall for a man who might disappear for days when things got tough, and who couldn't handle raising Zoe with the kind of love she deserved.

Kira tied her doctor's bag, which was also overstuffed and heavy, onto her horse. She wanted to

131

be sure she had whatever she might need. After handing a filled canteen to Holt, she tied one onto her saddle. Then Kira noticed he had a bedroll tied to the back of his saddle.

"What's that for?" she asked, indicating the bedroll with her head.

Holt met her gaze. "Just in case. You never know when a blanket might come in handy."

It would be over her dead body that it would come in handy. "It's good to be prepared, I guess."

They rode out, and on the way, Holt tried to start up a conversation, but Kira gave short answers, trying not to be personable or friendly. Finally, he gave up.

She shook her head and smirked at the irony of the situation.

"What are you thinking?" he asked.

"I was thinking that we've come full circle. This ride is exactly like the first one we took out here, except our roles are reversed." Holt stared at her, and she saw he understood. She arched her eyebrows, shook her head again, and then looked forward.

They spent the rest of the ride in silence. It wasn't a comfortable silence, but Kira wouldn't characterize it as uncomfortable, either. It felt more like a truce, an appreciation for each other's position. She could live with that.

When they arrived, Kira felt Holt's anxiety increase. She felt a little tense, herself. They dismounted, both trying not to immediately look toward the large, brown mound inside the corral as they unpacked their gear and set up their work. Finally, there was no avoiding it.

They looked at each other. Kira tightened her lips, knowing how he must feel. "Ready?"

Holt looked away. "Yeah." They pulled on their latex gloves and masks as they walked over to the railing, then bent over and stepped through the rungs. The carcass was already stiff; the legs had straightened and were sticking up at forty-five degree angles. The other cows had instinctively migrated to the other side of the corral.

Holt started letting out lengths of rope from his coil. "I'll tie the rope around her midsection and head, then we can use our horses to pull her out."

"Okay." Kira helped him work the rope underneath the carcass, then watched as he tied a few knots and checked their stability.

Holt walked to the gate and swung it open. At his whistle, his mare trotted over, and he fastened a loop of rope around his saddle horn. Kira's horse wandered over to see what was going on, and Holt tied another end of the rope to that mare's saddle horn. The configuration looked like a triangle now, an animal at each point. "We need to do this from our saddles." They mounted their horses, and Holt continued. "Okay. When I say go, we spur the horses. But not too hard. This is going to take a while, and it'll be tough. We have to make sure the cow doesn't get caught on the posts coming out."

"Okay." Kira braced herself.

"Try to stay even with me. And, hang on. They may balk at first." He looked at her until she nodded that she got it. "Go."

They spurred their horses simultaneously, and the horses jerked against the ropes. Kira's horse fought it at first, raising her forelegs a foot off the ground. She settled down a second later, and Kira looked over at Holt. He'd been helping her control her horse back by reining his horse away at a sharper angle.

Finally, the carcass started to move across the ground. Once that happened, they were able to keep the horses moving at a steady pace, so although progress stayed slow, it became easier. It took fifteen minutes to drag the cow out to a place where Kira could work, but it felt like forever. Kira was covered with sweat and her muscles shook.

They dismounted, and Holt took his hat off and wiped his forehead with his sleeve. Kira saw him look her up and down as if appraising her condition.

"Why don't we take a break?" he asked her.

She nodded and unhooked the loop of rope from around her mare's saddle horn. He helped her unsaddle her horse, then slapped the animal's rump, sending her trotting. Next, Holt unsaddled and released his mare. After leaving their gloves and masks over the fence, they walked over to their gear.

"I brought some stuff to clean up with, disinfect our hands and faces at least." She knelt at her doctor's bag and pulled out some cloths and a bottle of cleanser.

"Good." Holt took a moistened cloth from Kira and wiped down his face and hands. He tossed the cloth over the railing with his gloves and mask, then kneeled at his pile of gear and pulled out his canteen.

While Holt drank, Kira disinfected herself with another cloth. "That was rough." She opened her canteen and drank deeply.

134

Holt capped his canteen, and hung it over a fence post. "Yep."

They rested under the overhang in the shade, which was only a bit cooler. Kira guessed it was about one hundred and five degrees today, which would put the temperature in the shade at around ninety or ninety-five. In another month, the heat was going to get really bad. She heard the men saying they started carrying several canteens with them, and doing the work farthest away from the ranch in the earliest hours of the day. That meant they were spending nights out in the desert so they could be up at dawn to get their work done before the hundred and fifteen degree heat sizzled the desert.

"Kira."

Kira looked up at him. Holt was leaning with his back against the horse-food container.

"Thank you for what you did at lunch today."

Kira looked away, at the corral, at anything other than him. "There's no need to thank me."

"I'm embarrassed about being caught in those lies, and--"

She shook her head and reached for her canteen, angry that he'd brought it up. "We'd better get to work. We only have about 45 minutes of daylight left." She capped her canteen and stood up to get her things. She heard him unwrap another toothpick.

She handed some new gloves and a new mask to him.

Holt took them without comment, and walked toward the carcass.

Kira stayed in the shade to put on her gloves and mask, to give them both some space.

Kira walked over to where he stood over the animal. He had become somber, looking at what she knew was his love. Her heart softened a little. She felt sorry for him, and tried to understand what he'd been going through. Kira knelt at the belly of the animal and drew out her scalpel.

"Would you take notes as I do this?" she asked, handing him his book.

He grabbed his notebook and pen, then opened it to the first blank page and poised the pen above it. Kira looked down at the cow's stomach, and mapped out in her mind how she would cut, envisioning where the major organs were located inside.

She leaned over and drew the blade lengthwise down the center, from the cow's sternum, toward its hind legs. She brought it back up and continued along the same cut, slicing through the other layers of flesh, until she'd entered the body cavity. For Kira, this was the kind of work that wiped her mind clean of anything else. She became totally focused, excited about what she might see. Kira began describing everything she saw.

"Slow down, slow down," Holt said, scribbling rapidly across the page.

"Sorry." Kira pushed some intestines out of the way, looking for the forestomachs. "Here's one," she mumbled.

Kira cut it open and described the lesions she saw there.

"That smells putrid."

"Digested food in a day-old carcass usually does. Be glad I'm not cutting open the intestines." She clipped a piece of the diseased stomach tissue and put it into a sterile container. Next, she took her cordless, circular bone saw and cut some samples, which she stored in another sterile container. Next, she started digging for the other stomachs, liver, heart, and lungs, all the while describing what she was finding.

"Kira?" Holt had kneeled at her side to watch.

"Yeah?" She continued working.

"I appreciate your agreeing to make me a part of this."

"What really happened, is you agreed to make *me* a part of this." After a moment she added, "I'm sure we'll get further this way."

"Yeah." He sighed. From the corner of her eye, Kira saw Holt's mask change shape as he rolled his toothpick from one side of his mouth to the other. She almost lost her stride, thinking about his mouth, his lips, remembering how his tongue once caressed hers. She blinked a couple times to remove the image and continued working.

"We're losing the sun."

"I'll flip the switch." Holt walked away, and Kira held her thoughts. A second later, halogen light bathed a ten-foot circumference around the work area.

He returned and squatted on the other side of the animal, facing her. She began rattling off details again.

"I think we should talk." He'd paused in his writing.

"Don't miss anything." She didn't want to lose any of her thoughts.

"I'm not."

137

"About what?" Kira grunted, lifting an organ into view.

"About last week."

Kira didn't answer, but kept working. As long as she kept talking science, she'd be okay, she thought.

"Kira."

Kira increased her volume and speed, hoping to keep Holt occupied. She didn't want to talk to him about anything other than this.

"Kira," he said above her voice.

Kira stopped moving, pushed out a loud breath, and glared at him. "Holt, I'm up to my elbows in cow guts right now. Even if I did want to talk about this-- which I don't--this definitely would not be the time."

Chapter Nine

Holt's stony stare met hers. She held it for a moment, and then resumed her work. Finally, Holt began writing again.

For the rest of the examination, Holt remained silent, for which Kira was grateful. When she finished, she peeled off her gloves and dropped them into the body cavity. Her mask followed. Holt did the same.

"What do we need to do with this now?" she asked, meaning the carcass. She didn't think they could just leave it like this, so close to the corral.

"We'll need to drag it away, so the scavengers don't get too close to the other animals." His hands were on his hips, and he looked down at it.

"It's a mess, I know." She shook her head.

"It looks like the scavengers have already been here."

"They have." Holt looked at her, and then nodded.

Kira looked into the darkness. It was completely black beyond the edge of light. They'd have a difficult time getting back tonight.

"Let's do it and get back home," she said, picking up her bag.

"We can't get it as far away as we need to, and still make the ride home tonight."

This was not what she wanted to hear. "Well, then, let's just leave it here."

"No way. It's too close to the corral still. Scavengers may prey on the cattle."

"Holt, why didn't you think of this before we left?" He just shrugged. She looked at him a moment more. "Fine. Let's do this thing."

They refastened the rope loops around their saddle horns and pulled the carcass out several hundred more yards. When they were finished, Kira was so tired she wouldn't have been able to ride back even in broad daylight.

They made their way back to the pool of light by the corral. Holt dismounted and pointed the light toward their gear. "There's our stuff. I'll keep the light on until we're ready."

"What? You mean...you're not going to leave the light on all night?" She wouldn't be able to see her hand in front of her face, and although she wouldn't admit it, the thought of predators unnerved her.

"Why would I do that? I wouldn't be able to see the stars."

Kira couldn't see him, but detected a slight hint of amusement in his voice. "We don't need to see the stars tonight. I really think we'd be safer with it on." She made it to their pile of gear and turned around, then looked straight into the light. "Okay?" She didn't hear anything. "Okay?" Still nothing. "Holt, it's not funny."

Holt stepped into the light from behind her. "Okay."

Kira screamed. "Damn it." She suddenly felt like crying, but struggled to look normal. "That wasn't funny."

His expression sobered. "I'm sorry. I didn't know you'd get upset."

"I'm not upset." She felt her cheeks burn at the defensiveness in her voice. Plus, she was too old to be afraid of the dark. "Turn it off. I don't care." She bent down and arranged her gear, then laid down in the dirt, her head on the pile.

He came and stood over her. "What are you doing?"

"Going to sleep." She crossed her arms and rolled to her side.

"Aren't you forgetting something?"

"I'm not hungry. Go ahead." Kira sat up, tossed the saddlebags at his feet, then laid back down, crossing her arms again.

"I'm not talking about food."

Kira kept her eyes closed and feigned sleep.

He continued standing there. "It's gonna get cold."

While desert temperatures soared during the day, they definitely dipped low at night, and she was beginning to feel a little chilled already. Now what?

Kira sat up and looked at the ground, feeling like a pouting child. She pulled her bottom lip back in line, then looked up. Holt held his bedroll, a challenge on his face.

"You planned this." She squinted at him.

"No." But he had been pretty sure they'd have to spend the night out here. He was guilty, though, of purposefully having only one bedroll. He didn't know why; it was stupid. Holt had decided before coming back to the ranch that he didn't want to get any further involved with Kira, but they'd be getting pretty close tonight.

"I didn't." He looked away, and holding an edge of the bedroll, threw it onto the ground under the overhang. The bedroll was a double, just right for two bodies if they stayed close. He stole a glance at her and saw her eyeing it.

"We're stuck here for the night, so let's just make the best of it, okay?"

Kira scowled at him, her crossed arms squeezing her body, her shoulders rising. She was obviously cold. But would she share the only source of warmth he could offer?

When she didn't reply, he said, "We should eat what Lupe packed. She'll kill us if we come back with those bags full."

"You might be dead before those bags make it back, if you try anything tonight, " she threw out. Holt looked at her, and she continued. "You came to me, asked me to work with you to save this ranch. To do that, I need to trust you, Holt. I thought you understood that, and now this." She motioned to the bedroll. "I gave you my trust in the beginning, and you blew it when..." Kira shifted her eyes away, then back. "When you left." She lifted her chin.

They stood there watching each other, then he placed his hand over his heart, hoping she'd believe him. "I swear on my mother's love that I will not try anything tonight." Kira squinted at him as he continued. "Our bodies are going to touch, Kira. That's just a fact, but nothing beyond that will happen."

Kira thought a moment, then nodded. She grabbed the saddlebags and plopped down onto the bedroll. Cautiously, Holt lowered himself onto the

142

bedroll, keeping a good two feet between them. He watched as she opened the bags and placed containers of food between them. The look on her face, and the words she'd spoken tonight told him he'd really hurt her, and it was going to take a lot to earn back her trust. Suddenly, he wanted that almost as much as he wanted to save the ranch.

He had done this, so he would just have to undo it.

Holt looked the food. "This is definitely not flat...or dried." He picked up a container, held it up to the light, and snorted. "Lupe has never sent me with Tupperware." He took something Kira handed him and realized it was silverware rolled into napkins. "And I never got something as civilized as this." Kira looked at him as if to say that it was because he wasn't civilized enough for silverware, let alone a napkin.

Kira scooped out the contents of several containers onto two plastic plates and handed one to him. Lupe had sent cubes of beef, cooked medium rare, just how he liked it. On his plate next to the beef were potato salad and three-bean salad. A large piece of cheesecake drew his eyes away from the rest of the food.

"How did this cheesecake make it?" He touched it with the back of his pinkie. "It's still cold."

"She froze it, then put it in this." Kira showed him a thermally insulated container, then began eating. Unless he pissed her off again, it was going to be a quiet night.

"So, what's next on the project?"

143

Kira looked up and finished chewing, then swallowed. "We do a lot of tests. That'll be my job, mostly."

"What will be my job, then?"

"Literature search."

"Oh." That was the problem with science -- so much could be said in so few words.

They finished their meal and put all of stuff back into the saddle bags. After they each took a quick break in the dark to relieve themselves, Kira took off her shoes and laid them by her gear, then pulled out her pistol from her bag, laid it down next to the bedroll, and crawled inside.

"That's not to use on me, is it?" Holt asked.

Without rolling over to look at him, she said, "Predators."

"I'm moving the light so it's not directly on us." No answer came, so he adjusted the light beam.

Holt pulled off his boots and went to the opening of the bag. He laid down his own pistol and started to get in, expecting Kira to move over, but she stopped him. "I want to sleep by the zipper."

Holt sighed, exasperated. "Fine, let me get on the inside."

Kira unzipped the bag and leaned forward to make room for him to crawl over her. Holt wriggled in, while Kira tried to avoid touching him, and once he was settled, she squeezed over to her side, her face against the zipper.

Holt rolled over the other way. "Goodnight." He got no answer, so he closed his eyes and went to sleep.

* * *

144

Holt awoke with a start. Something was wrong.

He cocked his head and listened to the unmistakable sound of some carnivorous animal eating the carcass. That must have been what woke him. It sounded like one lone animal, most likely a coyote, and one that would probably bring back several more later on. The horse nickered and he saw that they'd moved close by, into the light.

Holt leaned back, but then he heard another, more alarming sound. He rolled over toward Kira. She was crying, but when he gave her a slight shake, found that she was still asleep. She mumbled something, a short two-syllable word or phrase, over and over.

Holt leaned up on his elbow and watched her. He wasn't sure if he should wake her up or let her ride it out, but supposed that as long as she didn't start thrashing, he'd let her sleep through it. But he hated watching the pain on her face. Tears ran down her cheeks onto the sleeping bag. He caught one with his finger, then rubbed it between his finger and thumb, thinking.

What was it she kept repeating? Cl...something. Kira began to shake her head and move her arms. Without warning, she slammed her elbow into Holt's sternum, sat up, and screamed the word. The coyote yipped and trotted off.

Holt sat up and grabbed Kira's arms, turning her to face him. She looked at him with confusion, awake, but groggy. Her gaze went to her surroundings, then to his hands on her arms. Holt loosened his grip.

"You were having a dream."

Kira looked away and shook her head. "I was cold and...didn't know where I was."

Even if he didn't know the truth, Holt wouldn't have been convinced. The inside of the bedroll was roasting. This was obviously a very private part of Kira's life, so he wouldn't ask. Not tonight, anyway.

She trembled beneath his hands; he wanted to comfort her, protect her. "Let me help you get warm, then." He tried to wrap his arms around her.

"No." She pushed him away and laid back down, turning her back to him again.

Holt lay down, facing her. Kira burrowed into the bag, burying her head past the opening, even with his chest. She still trembled. And after listening carefully, Holt heard her crying again, so decided to take a chance.

"Kira, I'm not trying anything with you, I just want to help you get warm." He moved his arm over her.

"No." Her voice cracked. She tried to shrug off his arm, but he held it firm.

"Look, my hand isn't even touching you. I swore last night I wouldn't try anything and I won't. I promise." She stilled. "I promise."

She didn't say anything else, and Holt felt her breathing slow. He began to relax, and Kira surprised him by scooting into the curve of his body. She turned away from him even more, so she was almost on her stomach, but at least she was letting him comfort her.

Holt wasn't sure he should sleep. He was afraid he'd somehow change positions and end up with his hand somewhere it shouldn't be. So, he kept his eyes open and listened to her breathing and the other night sounds, letting his chin touch the top of her head. Strands of her hair tickled his nose.

It meant a lot that she'd let him comfort her like this. Kira said that her sister had died. Since Zoe was still a baby, then the death must have happened recently. What an idiot he'd been to not realize that before. Dealing with her grief over her sister's death, on top of the pressures of single-motherhood, was definitely heavy duty stuff. Not even the stresses of his own situation had plagued him this much.

In her sleep, Kira snuggled against him. He tried to move the lower half of his body away from her, hoping to prevent his unbidden arousal from becoming full-blown. Somehow, these tender thoughts about her and her closeness to him only increased his physical attraction for her. But Holt could not get this way around her. They'd made it abundantly clear to one another that there would be no relationship now. He thought about the cattle to take his mind off of Kira.

Finally, the sun began to rise. He loved the sunrise, how it started out just barely changing the black to navy, then to light blue. Then, the mountains would be awash with rose and magenta. Kira should see this.

"Kira," he whispered, close to her ear. "Kira." He had to force himself not to nibble that ear. This was more difficult than it should be. He'd never had trouble like this once he'd made up his mind he didn't want a particular woman, but he'd been painfully aroused almost all night.

147

She stirred and rolled over under his arm, then peeled open her eyes and blinked the sleep out. Holt leaned over her, in a position they'd been in before, when things between them were different, and she looked at his arm across her chest. He yanked it away.

"I wanted you to see the sunrise." He nodded toward the east.

Kira leaned up on her elbow. She watched without words, the minutes ticking by, and Holt felt an odd communion with this woman. He wondered if she felt it, too.

When the whole circle of sun rose above the horizon, Kira unzipped the bag and sat up, her back to him. "Thank you."

Holt heard tears in her voice. Still leaning on his elbow, he reached for her shoulder and turned her toward him. Kira met his eyes, and one large tear fell from her right eye. She squeezed her eyes shut and pulled her shoulder out of his grasp, turning her face away.

"What's wrong?" he asked in a gentle tone.

"Nothing." Kira wiped the tear away as if it were burning her skin, and sniffed. "It's nothing." She went to her gear, shook out her boots to remove any creatures that may have crawled inside during the night, then sat down and pulled them on.

Holt sat up and followed her with his eyes. "It's not nothing, Kira." She ignored him. "Does it have something to do with your dream?"

Kira flinched, but continued jamming gear into her saddlebags. "It's none of your business."

Holt got out of the sleeping bag and rolled it up. He couldn't stand to see her cry, and it was making him crazy. He tied the ropes around the bedroll, jerking them across the material, wishing he could break them just to release his tension. Finally, he just couldn't hold it in. "Tell me why you're crying, damn it."

"I'm not crying." She sniffed again.

"Don't lie." Holt tossed the bedroll to the side.

"You do."

That hurt. But she was right. "This has nothing to do with me." He looked at her. "Does it?" She continued working. "Answer me."

Kira twirled around on her heals. "No!" she growled at him. "It has nothing to do with you, or with you and me. There happens to be a lot more to me and my life." She nearly spat the words at him, and breathed as if she'd just run a three-minute mile.

"I know," he shot back. "Like Cleo."

Kira's face paled and she stared at him with wide eyes.

Holt knelt three feet away from her, in front of his own pile of gear. "What's going on?" Holt was afraid she would bolt, maybe just start running into the desert and never come back. Kira looked ready to spring away, but a resigned expression fill her eyes, and her shoulders drooped. She sighed and looked toward the sunrise, staring at it so long, Holt thought she wasn't going to speak.

"My sister. She loved the sunrise. She'd make me watch it with her whenever we were together." Half of Kira's mouth curled up in a sad smile. She sat down in the dirt, wrapped her arms around her knees, and seemed to be looking far away, remembering.

Holt didn't move. He held his breath and waited. The struggle he saw in her eyes, crossing her face, made his throat constrict and tears burn his own eyes. The depth of her emotion, and her attempt to control it, awed him.

"When we were kids she used to sneak into the kitchen a couple hours before sunrise and make homemade muffins and fresh orange juice for us. Then she'd sneak into my room and kiss my cheek to wake me."

Kira, still gazing at the horizon, brushed her right cheek with the backs of her fingers. Tears cascaded down her face, and all Holt could do was stare at this transformed woman. She was even more beautiful now, still strong, yet tragic.

Her hand slid from her cheek and became a fist at her heart. Kira closed her eyes, causing pooled tears to stream out. "She died on the way to my graduation." Kira lowered her face to her knees. She breathed in deeply, exhaled, then lifted her head and met his eyes. Her tears were gone.

"Your sister," he said, and she nodded. Holt felt as if he'd be punched in the stomach. Granted, he hadn't lost a brother or father to death, but when he was a kid and found out Ben and Treat weren't his by blood, it felt that way to him. The sick feeling returned, and he shook his head. "I am so sorry."

Kira lowered her head again to her knees. "Yeah."

Holt couldn't let her sit there alone. He needed to give something to her, wanted to help her through this. From his squatting position, Holt moved one of

150

his feet toward her and brought himself to her side. He kneeled, spreading his knees to either side of her, sat on his heals, and put his arms around her. Kira leaned into him, letting her face rest in his shoulder. He rocked her, leaning his cheek on top of her head.

Holt murmured to her. He realized Kira's graduation had only been about four or five months ago. Not long enough. "It's gonna take a long time, Kira. A long time." She nodded against his chest. "I'm sure she'd be proud of you." He paused, still rocking her. "You've graduated vet school, high honors, my father tells me; you're going to save our ranch. You're raising a baby on your own, and you're helping out Candace, too. You're accomplishing a lot."

Kira hugged him quickly, and then moved away. "Not enough, though."

He looked at her, confused, and watched as she stood and gathered up her bags. She walked to her horse grazing nearby and saddled her, then buckled on the bags. Holt got moving, too. They had a lot of work to do in the lab and he hoped it would be less than the couple of weeks Kira had promised his mother.

When they were both ready, Kira led her horse over to where Holt stood. He looked up from the cinch he was tightening, and saw her mount her horse and stare off into the distance. She looked uncomfortable by what had happened, so without another word, Holt mounted up and they rode away.

Chapter Ten

Tap, tap.

Cleo hammered a nail into Kira's birdhouse, showing her how not to hit her thumb, and Kira looked at her with admiration as Cleo's laughter tinkled in her ears.

Kira smiled and stirred, touching the surface of consciousness.

Tap, tap, tap.

She opened her eyes and rolled over, realizing the sound hadn't come from her dream. Through the blinds, she saw the shadow of a man illuminated by the moon behind him, wearing a cowboy hat, looking a lot like Holt. Kira threw back her thin sheet and blanket and got out of bed, feeling the usual depression after just dreaming about Cleo. She pulled her knee-length T- shirt down and tiptoed over, where she twisted the plastic rod on the blinds, changing their angle so she could see out. "Holt?" His face was still in shadow and the bright moon glowed into her eyes.

"Open the window." His voice was muffled through the glass.

Kira pulled the string, raising the blinds up a few feet and then dragged the window open. "What are you doing?" She still felt half asleep.

He grinned and held up a plastic cake holder. "Homemade muffins a la Lupe." He then held up his other hand, which contained two thermoses. "Fresh squeezed orange juice and just brewed coffee."

Kira stared at him. His smile was so endearing, her heart constricted. She felt those stupid tears start to fill her eyes, and she began to cry, dropping her head to her chest.

"Kira..."

She kept her head down, but felt him reach through the window and lift her hand from the windowsill. She squeezed his hand and he held it tightly.

"Kira."

She couldn't help it. She just kept on crying and tried to turn her head away. Holt leaned into the window and lifted her chin with the fingers of his other hand, turning her face toward his. His tender expression made her cry harder. "I miss her so much," she choked out.

"I know...I know." He opened his palm and she leaned her cheek into it.

"This...this was our tradition."

"Maybe it's time to start a new one. Come on." He pulled her closer to the window, making her lean toward him.

Kira looked at him, surprised that he wanted her to join him, and that she wanted to see the sunrise with him again. "Let me grab some shoes." She tried to pull away.

"No, you won't need them." He held her hand and pulled her back toward him.

"Holt--"

Holt reached into his back pocket and pulled out a sack, then held it out to her. Confused, she took it, opened the package and pulled out a pair of soft, beaded leather moccasins. The beads glinted in the moonlight.

She inhaled sharply. "Holt, they're beautiful." She held them to her heart.

"They're handmade from deer hide."

"Thank you." Kira bent to put them on. "They fit."

"I know."

"I'll be right out." Kira turned to leave the room, but Holt caught her hand again and pulled her back.

"This will be a new part of our tradition." He pulled her toward the window until she leaned out a bit.

"What will be?" A strange exhilaration washed over her.

"You have to come out the window each time." He chuckled low and soft.

"And how do you propose I do that?"

Holt grabbed her under her arms and lifted her up; she twisted her body and came to rest sitting on the sill. Then Holt slipped one arm under her knees and the other behind her back, picked her up, and lifted her the rest of the way out.

Without delay, he gently set her onto her feet, and dropped his arms, as if he were her brother and did this sort of thing all the time. He picked up a thick, woolen blanket and wrapped it around her shoulders, then picked up the other things he'd brought and walked into the desert, moonlight illuminating their path.

Kira followed, the leather moccasins hugging her feet. "Have you ever done this before?" she asked, already feeling protective of their new tradition.

"Never," he whispered.

154

Kira's heart swelled, knowing that this really was just theirs, that Holt had cared enough to think of her. They finished their journey in silence, until they were well away from all of the ranch buildings. The stars were beginning to fade with the first morning light.

"Here's our spot." Holt stopped and spread a blanket on the ground, then took Kira's hand and helped her to sit on one side. He joined her, setting the food down in front of them.

"The other night at the corral," he said, as he opened the plastic cake holder, "you served me." Holt took a clean handkerchief from his pocket and draped it over her lap. Then he took a muffin, steam rising from it in misty tendrils, and placed it on the hanky. "This time, I'll serve you."

Kira watched as he poured her a cup of orange juice from one thermos and a cup of coffee from the other, then placed them in front of her. She was speechless. His eyes held respect, reverence. Something changed inside her. She smiled at him, and they both looked up into the sky. Tears slid down her cheeks again, but still she smiled. "I think she knows, Holt."

He reached over and laid his hand over hers, resting on her knee. "I'm sure she does." Kira turned her hand over and wove her fingers between his, then clasped his hand.

They watched their second sunrise together in silence, hands clasped, but otherwise still. They shared the thermos cups to drink their juice and coffee and ate as many muffins as they could.

When the muffins were gone, Kira leaned over and kissed him on the cheek. "Thank you, Holt."

"You're welcome," he whispered.

"You know..." she tilted her head to peer at him. "...You're more special than you think."

* * *

"Thanks." Kira took the pages of notes from Holt and their hands touched. She pulled her hand back slowly, allowing the contact to last a few seconds longer. They'd been working together for five days, and since that morning when he took her to see the sunrise, she'd catch herself laughing at his jokes, even telling some of her own. She'd started looking forward to these little collisions of skin on skin, and their voices had taken on an intimacy when they spoke to each other.

They worked silently for several minutes, but Kira couldn't concentrate, so she raised her eyes and peered at him over her microscope.

Holt looked up and caught her, so Kira lifted her head. "That was quite a sunrise this morning."

"Yeah." They studied each other. "Holt--"

He looked back to his books so suddenly it jarred her train of thought. "I'll be able to give you some more notes on this stuff soon."

"Holt," she started again.

"I'll be on the range tomorrow, though. Gotta check on things." Holt pushed his nose closer to the page and ran his finger over the text. He looked back and forth from the book to his notebook, writing intently. "I'll be back the next day, though."

"That's fine." She was still eyeing him. She could see the emotion in his eyes, and wondered why he wouldn't speak of it.

"Holt."

Holt shut his book. "I think I'd better go." He started to rise.

"We need to talk." Kira rose and blocked his way to the door.

"What about?" he asked, not meeting her eyes.

"You know what about."

"No ..." He avoided her eyes for a moment, and then looked at her.

"Okay, let me enlighten you." She crossed her arms and leaned against the counter. "You haven't touched me or said anything improper to me in days."

"And this is a problem?" he asked, sounding incredulous, raising his open palms.

"It's become a problem. You want to."

"No-o-o-o." He drew out the word with what sounded to Kira like obvious faux-innocence.

Kira sighed sharply. "Why can't you just be honest? This is affecting our work." Holt shook his head and tightened his lips. He stood silently and Kira tensed. Finally, she gave up. "All right. If you can't be honest, I can. I--"

A knocking interrupted her. She looked at the door, and then back to Holt, who moved his gaze away, then back. They stared at each other a second more, and then she turned and opened it.

"Kira, I'm really sorry to do this to you," Candace blurted. She was holding Zoe, bouncing her in her arms.

"What's wrong?" Kira opened the door wider, letting Candace in.

"Hi, Holt." Holt nodded and Candace turned back to Kira. "I just received a notice in the mail. It's taken a while to catch up with us because of the move. But, well," she looked at Holt again, then back to Kira, "I won that contest with my Pineapple Peanutty Bomb!"

Kira inhaled, and then both women squealed and hugged each other, squeezing giggles out of Zoe, and turning around in a circle as they did so. "That's great! I told you you'd win." Kira held her friend back from her and smiled. "I'm so proud of you. This could be just what you need to get enough publicity to start your business."

"I think it will be, Kira, but that's my problem."

Kira took Zoe from Candace and balanced the baby on her hip, hugging her. "What's the problem?"

"Well, like I said, the notice got here late. I'm supposed to be in New York tomorrow morning. It came with a free airline ticket."

Kira's mind began to race about what this meant for her job, then felt guilty for thinking of herself.

Candace added in a rush, "I already asked Lupe if she could help, but she can't. I'd only be gone for four days, but I don't know what to do. I know this'll put you in a crunch with Zoe and your work, but I really want to go."

Now Kira really felt guilty. Candace deserved to go, but sounded so worried about leaving her in the lurch. "Candace, you have to go. Zoe is my responsibility, not yours. You have to think of yourself." She looked at Holt, then Zoe. Kira lifted

158

her face to Candace. "This is your big break, Candace." She squeezed her friend's arm. "Don't even think about us here. Just go."

Candace looked at her doubtfully, so Kira pushed her toward the door. "Go. Go pack." Kira herded her to the door and sent her out.

"Well, if you're sure..." She looked over her shoulder.

"I'm sure."

"I'll stay if you want me to." She wrung her hands.

Kira took a step out the door and turned her friend around. "Candace, don't ever sacrifice something that's important to you for me or anyone else."

Candace looked at her, and then her expression changed from unsure to determined. "Right. You're right." She nodded and laughed. "I'm outta here!"

"Good!" Kira leaned against the doorframe and stuck her head out to watch her skip toward the guesthouse. "Good luck! Congratulations!"

When Candace was out of sight, Kira came back in and shut the door. She looked at Zoe, but Zoe had begun to flirt with Holt again, and he stood stiffly, looking from the baby to her. Kira looked over at her work in progress and sighed. "Okay." She bit her lip, thinking. Like she'd said, Zoe was her responsibility, and that was that. "I'll just have to work when Zoe takes her naps, or when she's playing on her own. I'll have to move the crib to the lab." Kira looked at Holt. "Will you help me move some stuff over?"

"Sure. But I don't see how you're going to get anything done until Candace gets back." He leaned against the counter and studied her.

Truthfully, Kira wasn't sure either, but felt insulted that Holt should point that out. "I can work and take care of Zoe at the same time."

Holt chuckled. "Yeah. We'll see." He stood away from the counter. "Come on. Show me what you want me to bring over."

Later, Holt and Kira had arranged the crib and brought over some toys and diapers. Holt stood back with his hands on his hips, looking at the crib. "I just thought of something. Where is Zoe going to sleep at night?"

"Oh." Kira grinned. "I guess I can fix her up in my laundry basket. That ought to work."

Kira knelt next to the baby, and he listened to her sweet, hushed voice. She was a great mother. Although Kira was able to concentrate on Zoe exclusively when the baby needed her, the moment Kira got a chance to get back to her microscope and books, it appeared she had no concentration at all and he could tell she was getting frustrated. Kira came back to her work, giving Holt a tired smile, then put her face to the eyepieces of the microscope and adjusted the fine focus.

Holt looked at his book, but kept thinking about Kira. Over the past week, he'd grown so relaxed around her he'd had to keep reminding himself that she was hands-off. He'd set the course for their relationship when he'd run off, and Kira had made it perfectly clear as to where they stood. But she'd really surprised him when she'd held his hand during their second sunrise, and then kissed him. It had taken every ounce of strength he'd had not to take it further.

From the moment her tears moistened his palm at her window that morning, he was lost. He wanted her so much more than he ever thought he could want a woman, more so every day. Even now, knowing Zoe absorbed all her thoughts, he wanted her.

Holt looked over Kira's shoulder to the baby and his heart warmed. Then his gut clenched. He wasn't supposed to have feelings for any baby, especially not a baby who wasn't his own.

Until today, he'd always believed adoptions were a bad idea, unnatural, and doomed to failure. But Zoe was just a kid who needed love and support from a mommy *and* a daddy. Maybe he could be the one. He looked at Kira struggling, and it hit him. His attitude was different because he wanted Kira so badly. He leaned back in his chair, stunned.

Kira sighed and leaned her forehead into her palm. "I've been looking at the same things I've looked at all day, and trying to figure out what my last thought was." She looked at him. "You were right. I can't do this."

Holt stood. It was now or never. "Kira, let me take care of Zoe for a little while so you can work." She looked at him with a doubtful expression. "I'll stay right here and play with her," he added.

"Holt, I don't think..."

"Come on..." Holt put his hands on her shoulders as she began to rise. "Sit back down, and let me at least try."

161

Kira lowered herself back to her seat. "But what about the other ranch work you said you had to do?"

"That's only if you're progressing on this problem, which is still the priority." She twisted on her stool to face him. "And you're not progressing, right?" She looked down and frowned.

Holt felt a stab of guilt. "I'm not judging your efforts, Kira, I just want you to let me help you."

Again, she looked at him suspiciously. "Why?"

"Because we're a team, remember? You said it."

She couldn't argue with her own words. "That's true. But, what do you know about babies?"

"Nothing. But I'll be right here, and I can ask you if I have to."

Zoe started crying and they both looked over at her. "Oh..." Kira started to go to her.

Again, Holt pushed her back down. "Let me try."

She looked from Zoe to him, then back to the baby. "Okay, but hurry." She crinkled her brow and shook her hands in front of herself. "I can't stand to hear her cry."

Holt grinned. When he kneeled next to her, he felt that familiar uneasiness and fear. What was he doing? How was he going to do this? Zoe had tipped over from her sitting position and lay there, still crying.

"Hol-l-l-l-lt!"

"Okay, okay..." Holt looked at the baby one more second then leaned down, scooped one hand under her head, his other beneath her bottom, and lifted her up against his shoulder. She stopped crying immediately and leaned her head back to gaze at him,

162

then smiled and cooed. Holt met Kira's look of astonishment.

"Nothin' to it."

Kira curled up one side of her mouth and shook her head. "We'll see." Then she swiveled around on her stool and went to work.

Holt made funny faces, then stuck some of Zoe's toys on his head, and hooked them on his ears. Anything for a laugh, which Zoe gave him in abundance. She had dolls, and a couple large plastic cars. He took one of the cars and made a 'vroom' sound as he ran it up Zoe's leg, across her belly, over her shoulders, and down her arm. She squealed with delight.

Holt looked over at Kira. She seemed lost in her work, writing, reading, examining, and he felt proud to be able to give this to her. He knew she loved her work.

When Zoe started to fuss, Holt looked at his watch and thought she must be hungry, so he went to a cooler sitting by the door and found a few bottles of milk. He took one to the baby, hoping she liked it cold.

It took him a few minutes, but Holt finally got Zoe situated in his arms so she would stop wriggling and suck on her bottle. He sat cross-legged on the floor, watching her. Zoe stared at him and smiled around the nipple, breaking suction, milk dribbling down her neck.

"Come on," Holt said, wiggling the nipple in her mouth. "Eat up." He chuckled, and Zoe hummed, then started sucking again. They sat that way for only fifteen minutes, the time it took Zoe to demolish

163

eight ounces. She definitely had inherited Kira's appetite.

He picked her up and rocked her in his lap, thinking he was getting the hang of it. It almost felt natural.

"You do make it look easy."

Holt looked up, surprised. "How long have you been watching me?"

She shrugged, bringing to mind his response to her after he'd been watching her in the barn a few weeks ago. She smirked at him, and he grinned back.

"It's not too bad, really. I kind of like it." He looked back at Zoe and set the bottle on the carpet. Zoe began to cry a little and wriggle in his arms again.

"You're supposed to burp her now." Kira sat next to him.

"Oh, yeah." He lifted the baby to his shoulder and patted her back. "Like this?"

"That's usually how I do it." She tilted her head to the side. "But Candace rubs her back and seems to have a lot of luck."

Holt looked at Kira, then Zoe's back and started massaging the baby's back in an up and down motion.

Kira reached up and laid her hand over his, curling her fingers under his hand and changed his movement to a circular motion. Holt noticed the softness of her skin on his rough knuckles, and remembered the softness of other parts of her body. He wanted to feel those parts against his bare chest again.

"Like this."

Even though he'd begun moving his hand in the new pattern, Kira left her hand on his. He raised his gaze to Kira's face. She looked shocked, and Holt knew she'd felt the same jolt he'd felt every time they touched. The idea that it had taken her this long to accept that she wanted him niggled at his pride, but that couldn't dampen his pleasure. She withdrew her hand, but continued looking at him.

Chapter Eleven

"Like this?" he asked her softly.

She nodded.

Kira's eyes softened, and he knew something had changed, just as sure as he knew the difference between a bull and a cow. She stared at him with different emotions darkening her eyes, and it sent a powerful urge through him, an urge to bring her into his arms next to Zoe.

After a few minutes, Zoe rewarded them with a loud belch. "Oh," he said with a groan. "I feel something warm oozing down my back." Holt grimaced.

Kira laughed. "That's spit-up." She rose and brought back a wad of paper towel. "It happens sometimes. And formula stains." She began wiping Holt's shoulder. "Sorry. I forgot to warn you."

"It's okay. My shirts have been sullied by worse." Zoe still hung her head over his shoulder, and the feeling of Zoe and Kira touching him at once made him feel protective, like they belonged to him.

Then, a loud expulsion emanated from inside Zoe's diaper. Holt froze and looked at Kira, whose movements had also ceased. She looked at him and burst out laughing.

"I guess you're going to get a diaper changing lesson now." She was still laughing.

"Oh, God. Are you sure?"

"Oh, definitely." She went into the bathroom and brought out a changing pad, a diaper, and a tub of wipes, and arranged them in front of Holt. "Okay, lay her down." She pointed to the changing pad.

Holt did, and followed Kira's instructions through the whole process.

"Oh, come on." Kira nudged him. "You should see your face. You've done nastier things on this ranch. This couldn't possibly be worse than dehorning or castrating."

Holt tried to erase his look of distaste. "I guess not." But the smell was pretty bad. He wrapped up the dirty wipes inside the dirty diaper, just like Kira said, then tossed it into the trash. "However, dealing with poopy diapers and spit-up now ranks high on my list."

Holt realized that these finer details of parenting had not wiped out any sexual desires for Kira that he'd felt just moments ago. In fact, he wanted her even more.

"Your pooh-pooh list?" Kira laughed. She grinned at him and he smiled back, shaking his head at her bad joke.

"Do you need a break from work?"

"Maybe a little one. Do you need a break from Zoe?" The baby looked up at Kira when she heard her name, and Kira tickled her cheek.

"I'm fine. I could go for hours," he lied.

She laughed. "Yeah, right."

Kira pulled Zoe onto her lap, and then looked up at him, serious. "I really appreciate you doing this for me. I hate that I need so much help. I should be able to handle everything, but for some reason, I just can't."

She looked so precious with Zoe in her arms, and Holt had the strange desire again to wrap his arms around both of them. He settled for lightly laying one

167

arm across Kira's shoulders. "Don't be so hard on yourself. You've had a lot going on, remember? Besides, that's why kids usually have two parents."

She nodded and looked at him as if waiting for something else, so he kissed her.

He promised himself he'd only kiss her once, so he prolonged it. At first, Holt felt uncertainty in her lips, then she relaxed against him. She warmed to him, and Holt reveled in the strength that gave him. Zoe giggled and patted his chest, reminding Holt he couldn't show Kira his full feelings, so he finished the kiss and pulled apart from her just enough so their noses touched, then leaned his forehead against hers. Kira's eyes crinkled up in a smile.

"I've wanted to do that for a long time," he whispered.

Kira hesitated, and then Holt saw a decision in her eyes. "Me, too."

He gave her a quick peck. "Okay. So where were we? Are you taking a break from work?"

"Yeah. I think I'll see if I can get Zoe down for a nap." Kira rose and rocked the baby in her arms. It wasn't but a few minutes and Zoe fell asleep against Kira's chest, a little string of drool hanging from her lip. He and Zoe had something in common: drooling over Kira's chest.

"What are you smiling about?"

"Huh? Oh. Nothing." He stood up and gazed at Zoe. He stroked the top of her head, then watched Kira lay her down in the crib and pull a light blanket over her. "I was just thinking about you," he admitted.

"What about me?" she asked, with a teasing note to her voice. She turned around and surprised him by wrapping her arms around his waist and leaning back to look into his face. "I bet you can't tell me."

Holt took the dare and told her, then grinned as a rosy pink flushed the apples of her cheeks. "What do you think about that?" he goaded.

Kira smiled and released him. "I think it's going to be difficult for you to work while thinking about that." She turned toward the counters, but Holt grabbed her arm and turned her back.

"Who said we have to work right this very minute? We were having a conversation." He leaned toward her to kiss her again.

Kira leaned back in his arms and looked at him playfully. "While this is very interesting, it's not going to help us solve any problems." She tried to pull away again, and again Holt pulled her back.

"Wanna bet?" He kissed her hard this time, trying to get her to focus on just this kiss. Her body was still twisted away from him, but as the kiss lengthened, she turned toward him and wrapped her arms around his neck. Holt pulled her against him and slid his hand into her hair, cupping the back of her head. The inside of her mouth was warm, and she moved her tongue in a languid motion.

Holt loved the feel of her hair woven through his fingers and draped over the back of his hand. H deepened the kiss as he backed her toward the loveseat. Kira went limp in his arms, and without breaking the kiss, Holt laid her onto the couch and sat on the edge, pressing as much of himself onto her as he could.

She whispered a moan and pulled his shirttails from the waist of his jeans. Holt grunted into her mouth and moved to allow her greater access. She spread her hands on his chest and belly, and it was all Holt could do to not rip the buttons off her shirt as he tried to get it open.

Finally, he felt her bra under his hands and he caressed her breasts. Kira hugged him and broke the kiss. She began raining light, tender kisses along his neck and throat. Holt tucked a thumb underneath the top edge of one of her bra cups and stroked her nipple, feeling Kira press her pelvis into him in response, and noticing how quickly the nipple contracted. He squeezed her breast with his whole palm, then buried his face between her breasts, rubbing his mouth, nose, and cheeks against her skin to get as much of her scent within him as possible. Then, he moved his lips down toward her belly, kissing her skin.

"So soft," he murmured.

Kira groaned loudly, and shoved her hands into his hair, knocking his hat to the floor.

Holt heard a noise, and Kira froze. He lifted his head and looked into her face. "What was that?" he asked, realizing there was nothing worse than holding completely still while fully aroused.

"Zoe. I think we might have woken her up." Kira levered herself up, almost knocking Holt backward to the floor and peered over him to the crib. "Looks like she went back to sleep, though."

"Good." Holt tried to push her back down and kiss her but she was already distracted.

"We really should take advantage of her sleeping." She tried to get up.

"Absolutely." Again he tried to push her down.

"No." She pushed again. "I mean to work, silly." Kira smiled, a knowing look on her face, but Holt wondered if she really knew what stopping at this point was going to do to him.

"Okay." He struggled to keep the strain out of his voice, dreading the ache that would soon settle in his testicles. He stood up and pulled Kira to her feet. She looked at him and he gave her a quick peck, which she returned. "You're right. Let's get some stuff done, then tonight we'll finish what we started." Kira walked to her microscope and to her back, he asked, "Right?" He held his breath.

"Perhaps." Her lips curved playfully. She slid onto the stool and began focusing the scope on her sample.

Holt exhaled. It sounded promising.

"Perhaps we should talk, instead," she said.

Holt dropped his shoulders. "Dinner tonight, then?" He walked around to his side of the counter and sat down.

Kira looked up. "Dinner?"

"Yeah. I'll cook Mexican food."

She considered with her head tilted. "Okay." Kira put her face back to the scope and didn't look up the rest of the time Zoe slept.

Holt didn't know how she did it. He sat there trying to conquer his body and bring his mind away from visions of her lying naked beneath him, but she was as cool as a December night by a watering hole.

* * *

Kira opened the door and let Holt in. He smelled as if he'd just showered, and was wearing a light musky scent. He held two grocery bags, with packages of tortillas poking out and fresh peppers and tomatoes resting on top of other things. He stopped when he heard a voice coming from inside, mingled with a basketball game on the television.

He looked at her sharply. "What is he doing here?"

"Shh." She laid her hand on his arm, keeping him in the foyer. "He came by, pining away for Candace. He looked so sad, I said he could stay for a while."

"What's a while?" he asked, looking at her and then in the direction of the front room. "Am I going to have to cook for him?"

"Possibly." As he sighed, she pushed on. "Holt, I just don't have the heart to ask him to leave. You should have seen his face." When he just stood there with a stony look, she added, "Holt, he's your brother." He sighed again and shook his head. "Come on, it could be fun," she cajoled.

"Okay, but he better not stay too long. We have things to discuss, remember?"

"How could I forget?" She stood on her toes and gave him a quick kiss, which seemed to cool him off a bit. She smiled and led him into the family room.

Treat looked up from the game, a beer in his hand. "Holt," he greeted his brother, then glued his gaze back to the television screen. "Oh! Oh, man. He should have made that. Whatta loser."

"What game is it?" Holt asked him.

"The Suns."

Kira took the bags from Holt and went into the kitchen, and Zoe stood up in her playpen and cooed at Holt as Kira walked by. Kira brought back a beer for Holt and one for herself. She stood over the two men who had become engrossed in the game.

Kira cleared her throat. "Excuse me. Men?"

Holt looked up. "Huh? Oh. Sorry, Kira." He stood up and took the beer she offered.

"That's okay. I was just wondering if you would keep an eye on Zoe while I take a quick shower."

"You trust me to watch Zoe after only one baby-sitting lesson?"

Kira grinned with sarcasm at Holt's feigned shock. "Yes, but don't get so wrapped up in the game that you ignore her. Okay?"

Holt saluted. "Yes, Ma'am."

"I'll only be about ten minutes." She rolled her eyes before turning to go down the hall. "Then we can get started on dinner. " She waved at Zoe and the baby waved her whole arm in the air, smiling.

Ten minutes later, Kira walked back down the hall toward the front room, her wet hair slicked back. She wore a pair of cutoffs and an oversized red T-shirt with the sleeves rolled up.

"So, looks like you're breaking your rule," she heard Treat say over the television.

Kira stopped just out of sight, unsure whether she should go back to the bathroom or step out into the open. She listened for Holt's response, but there was none.

"Come on," Treat continued. "You can admit it."

173

"There's nothing to admit," she heard him say calmly. Against her better judgment, Kira decided to stay where she was. She couldn't resist listening, and would just bet this had something to do with her.

Treat guffawed. "Nothing to admit? Come on. You're the one who always said it was lower than low to get involved with any woman with a child. And here you are in the thick of it."

Kira's heart constricted. Holt said he would never date a woman with a child? She strained to hear something, anything, from Holt.

"Keep your voice down," he growled.

Kira almost stepped away from the corner of the hallway when she heard them speak more.

"Why? She's a woman. She said she'd be ten minutes, so she'll be twenty." He snorted. "That's how they all are."

"Kira is different," Holt said.

She leaned her back against the wall, listening, feeling her heart sink to the pit of her stomach.

"And I'm not breaking my rule. You didn't understand my rule clearly."

"Oh, yeah?" he asked.

"Yeah. My rule was that you shouldn't get involved with a woman who has a child unless you're serious about her."

Kira stood away from the wall, her hopes rising, holding her breath.

"And, you're not breaking your rule?" Treat asked with disbelief.

"Nope."

"Oh, come on. You mean to tell me--"

"I'm telling you I'm serious about Kira. And that's all I'm gonna say. It's none of your damn business."

Kira twirled around in a silent touchdown dance, mouthing the word 'yes' over and over again.

"Did you hear something?" Treat asked.

Kira froze, then turned and ran back down the hall to the bathroom on her tiptoes. When safely inside with the door shut, she smiled at herself in the mirror and sighed. Holt was serious about her. It was a good thing, she thought, since she was serious about him, too. As a matter of fact, she loved him. Kira held her cheeks, covering the bright red glow, looking at her reflection as if for the first time.

She'd never felt this way. "I'm in love." She sighed, then squealed softly and danced another jig. After a few minutes, Kira forced herself to look calm, then left the bathroom.

She entered the family room and stood there a second before they noticed her. Zoe straddled Holt's right thigh, and Holt had one arm wrapped around her. Zoe moaned and waved her arm at the television screen every time Holt did.

"Hi," Kira said, trying not to smile too hugely. Holt looked away from the screen and stood up abruptly. "Sorry it took me fifteen minutes instead of ten. I guess women are just like that." Treat looked away from the game to her, and both men gave her a quizzical look. She laughed inwardly. "Want to get started on dinner, Holt?"

"Uh, sure." He handed the baby to Kira, and she followed him into the kitchen.

Holt began laying out all the pieces to the meal. "You can go keep my pining brother company if you'd rather."

"No, I wouldn't rather." Kira felt her heart swell when Holt looked at her with pleasure. "I won't be much help to you because of Zoe, but I'd like to keep you company, if you don't mind."

Holt stopped unpacking the sacks and spread his hands onto the edge of the tiled counter top. He leaned across to get closer to Kira. "I'd love it."

Kira lowered her head and looked at him with raised eyes, a slow smirk growing on her face. Holt leaned over more, and Kira leaned across to meet him, then she let him kiss her. Although it was a short kiss, to Kira it held such tenderness and promise. Holt pulled away and smiled at her, then turned back to his task.

While Holt worked on dinner, Kira fed Zoe, then bathed her and put her to sleep, looking forward to eating with leisure and talking about something other than diseased bovines or award winning bulls with immense sperm counts. She deserved this little break, even if she would have to get back to work soon after dinner.

* * *

"Dinner was delicious," Kira said, leaning back in her chair with her glass of wine. "Thank you so much for making it."

Holt grinned. "Thank you, and you're welcome."

It seemed to Kira that she and Holt had had dinner in a bubble, talking, giving each other secret

176

looks, promises. Treat didn't engage in their conversation, but contented himself with shoveling into his mouth as much of Holt's hard work as possible, his loud gulping sounds punctuating the otherwise intimate silence.

Kira and Holt looked at Treat. "It's a compliment." She grinned.

Holt lifted his wineglass and sipped.

"Ah," Treat said, raising his face up and wiping his mouth once with the cloth napkin, then tossing it down on the table. "Now, if only we had one of Candace's desserts."

Kira set down her glass and raised her index finger. "As a matter of fact, I took something she made out of the freezer today, just for this occasion."

"All right," Treat cheered, patting his stomach roughly. "Bring it on."

Kira served dessert and coffee, and she and Holt continued to make small talk, waiting for Treat to leave. Kira could tell they were both thinking the same thing, and they began to smile knowingly at each other, while Treat served himself a second helping of dessert. Then, the telephone rang.

Kira answered it. "It's Candace," Kira said to them. Treat perked up.

"Kira! It's so awesome here!" Candace said.

"It's an exciting city," Kira said. "Have you checked into your hotel? What's your agenda for the next couple days?"

"Tomorrow all the winners and runners-up will cook their entry-recipe. That's in the morning. Then, in the afternoon, what we made will be on display for the public to see. Kind of like at the state fair."

"Mm-hmm." Kira stuck her finger in her other ear to hear better. Candace spoke rapidly when she got excited, and Kira didn't want to miss anything.

"Then the next day we're given some sight-seeing tours around the city, we have lunch, then the afternoon is the award ceremony!"

"It sounds great. Do you have a speech prepared?" Kira heard a huge inhalation on the other end of the line.

"I didn't even think of that, Kira. What am I going to do?"

"Calm down," Kira said, hearing Candace starting to get frantic.

"Well, here I am the grand prize winner, and I don't even know what to say."

"I'm sure you'll be fine. Just think of something simple to say that only takes about a minute."

"Oh gosh—hey--is that Treat I hear in the background?"

Treat had become noisy upon hearing that Candace was on the phone, and wanted to talk to her.

"Yeah. He and Holt are here. We had dinner and one of your desserts tonight."

"Oh, let me talk to him! He can help me figure out what to say."

Kira cocked her head and held the phone away from her ear in disbelief, then put it back to her ear again. "Okay. Just a second." Kira looked over at Treat who was already on his way over to her. "She wants to talk to you."

Treat snatched the phone away. "Candy? Oh, Candy, baby. I miss you."

Kira walked away, shaking her head. Holt met her halfway to the table and handed her a glass of wine, refilled. "Thanks."

"What's that all about?" he asked, nodding his head to the phone.

"Well, my friend Candace doesn't need me anymore." She sighed, shaking her head. They moved to the couch with the overstuffed cushions covered in thin, smooth white cotton and sank into their softness.

"No?" he asked, chuckling.

"Nope. She's asking for Treat's advice now." Kira sipped her wine and smiled at Holt.

"Well, then we'll probably be here all night."

"I hope not. I have a few things I'd like to say to you later."

But they ended up sitting there for forty-five minutes, getting more and more impatient to be alone. Holt looked at his watch when Treat finally hung up the telephone.

He came over and plunked down on the chair to the right of the couch, as Holt and Kira looked at him. "Well?" Holt asked.

"Well?" Treat repeated. He was grinning ear to ear, just like that first time Kira met him. He was very happy to have just spoken to Candace, and Kira suspected he was a lot more attached to her than he'd admit.

"Did you get everything squared away?" Holt prodded.

"Oh, yeah. She'll be great."

"Good."

Kira nodded and sipped her wine. She crossed her left leg over her right and swung her left foot in a short back and forth motion. She and Holt just quietly looked at Treat, willing him to leave.

Chapter Twelve

"Well," Treat said, rubbing his thighs and patting his knees.

"Well," Holt said, leaning forward as if getting ready to stand.

Kira was so impatient, all she could do was continue wagging her foot and sipping wine. She smiled tightly at Treat when he looked from Holt to her.

"Oh. I guess I better go then," Treat said, finally understanding.

Holt bounded up. "See you tomorrow."

Kira got up and helped Holt herd his brother to the door.

"Yeah. Thanks for dinner. I, uh, didn't know you could cook."

"Thanks." Holt leaned in front of Treat and opened the door for him. Kira had to stifle a laugh, because it looked like Holt was close to pushing Treat out the door. Treat moseyed out, and Kira barely had time to say good-bye over Holt's shoulder before Holt swung the door shut.

The sudden stillness was jarring. It seemed like slow motion to Kira as Holt turned around and smiled at her.

"Finally." He crossed his arms. "Now we can pick up where we left off." In two steps, he was pressed against her. Kira wrapped her arms around his neck and kissed him.

"Holt." She pulled her lips away. "We really should talk." She was having trouble concentrating.

"Mm, about what?" Holt moved his lips over her jaw line.

"About...mmm, that feels good...about Zoe." Kira leaned her head over as Holt reached his lips under her ear and to the nape of her neck. "I wanted to tell you...that...Zoe is -"

"Great. Zoe's great. I'm crazy about her and about you, so you don't have to worry. Okay?" He moved his mouth to hers, and pushed his tongue against her lips.

Kira smiled as his tongue entered her mouth, and she slid her hands to his shirt buttons. Then thoughts of her job intruded.

Holt stopped kissing her. "What is it?"

She sighed. "We should be working." Kira let her hands slide away from Holt's buttons, and she stepped back.

Holt moved forward to maintain their embrace. "Look." He slid two fingers under her chin, lifting her face so he could gaze into her eyes. "You've been working hard. I've been working hard." He lowered his lips to hers and kissed her. "We can take a break now and then. Right?"

"Right," she agreed, still unsure.

"Let me convince you." He reached under her shirt and unhooked her bra. Kira sighed into his mouth as he spread his hand over her bare back, then dragged his palm around to her left breast. She felt the jolt it sent through him, and Holt buried his hand in her hair to grasp her head and kiss her deeply, as he kneaded her breast.

"Maybe you're right." She arched her back and moaned, urging Holt to trail kisses from her chin to the collar of her shirt. His large hand was hot, and his calluses increased her arousal as they grazed her nipple.

Holt nudged the neck of Kira's T-shirt away with his mouth to get to her collarbone. "All you've got to do is focus on this." He kissed and nuzzled the crook of her neck. Suddenly, she found herself being carried in Holt's arms toward the bedrooms. She was in a delicious trance and wanted nothing more than to continue feeling this wondrous, escalating pleasure. She was convinced. And definitely focused.

"Which one's yours?" he asked, sounding desperate.

"There," she murmured.

The door was ajar, and Holt toed it open. Kira heard it tap the stopper, then felt a slight falling sensation and a small bounce as the mattress cushioned her beneath him. The weight of his body brought emotions she didn't know she had, and didn't know she'd ever want to feel. She belonged to this man, and Heaven help her, she wanted him to claim her, to make her his own. Kira felt as if Holt had owned her heart and body for millennia.

He kissed her again, and moved his hand to her other breast. Kira finally got his shirt completely unbuttoned and explored his chest with her palms. It was smooth and contoured, hard and wide, and Kira felt the ridges of his abdominal muscles as she flexed her pelvis into his, imagining what those muscles would feel and look like as he made love to her.

The sounds of their foreplay whirled through Kira's mind. Holt's rapid breaths warmed her ear, and her own breathing slowly built into pants and sighs. Kira's soft, high-pitched moans mixed with Holt's deeper tones, making her want to explode. Skin rubbed against skin, their chests, stomachs, and hands.

Kira unfastened Holt's jeans and slipped her hand inside. He was hot, so hot. And very hard. She rubbed her thumb over the tip of his shaft, smoothing the moisture there across the satiny head. Holt groaned.

"Oh, God, Kira." Holt moved his palm to her crotch, over her jeans, and Kira pressed herself into his hand. She had never felt in such need of any man's touch, and knew her jeans couldn't hide that fact from Holt. He worked at the button and zipper of her pants.

"Holt." Kira breathed heavily, arching her neck and closing her eyes. She wanted to tell him what she was feeling, to share more than this physical experience with him. "Holt," she said again. "Holt, it feels so good." She heard him moan in reply, as he devoured her neck and shoulders with kisses. "I never knew it could be like this."

"Mm." He continued moving over her, almost frantic. "Never."

"Holt, I want you. Touch me," she commanded, just as he'd opened her jeans. He pulled off her T-shirt, and Kira tossed aside her bra. She leaned on her elbow as Holt lifted himself up and worked her jeans and panties down, caressing her buttocks with his warm hand.

He looked at her and splayed his fingers across her pelvis. He lifted his gaze to hers and she saw reverence and wonder emanating from the most beautiful eyes she'd ever seen. She would never want to look into any other eyes as long as she lived.

Kira helped him get her pants off, and he threw them away without taking his eyes from her, then knelt between her raised knees.

"Beautiful." Holt slid his hands down the inside of her thighs. "You are so beautiful." He lowered himself to her and kissed her.

Kira grasped handfuls of his hair, holding him to her, abandoning herself to him. Never before had she felt so open to a man, so ready to give all she had. After several minutes of Holt's tongue and lips worshipping her most tender parts, she pulled his head up, wanting his face near hers. He kissed her thighs, her abdomen, her navel, as she dragged him to her. Finally, she brought his lips to hers and she kissed him deeply. He held himself above her on his hands, the tip of him stroking, feather-like, across her wetness. Kira ran her hands down his flexed and defined arms, then slid her hands to his shoulders and down his back, over his denim clad buttocks, to his slightly spread thighs between her legs. His taut quadriceps rose up under her palm, rock hard.

She had to have him. Now.

Something prehistoric arose in her spirit. She felt a thrill at the thought of giving herself to this large, powerful man, towering over her. A man who could bend a two-ton beast to his will, but who would never hurt her.

Kira let her hand roam to Holt's manhood, and she held it firmly, eliciting further moans from him. Then she hooked her thumbs under his loosened waistband and began to work his jeans off. Holt kept

185

his lips to hers while he helped her accomplish the task, but before Kira could drop the jeans off the edge of the bed, he reached into one of the front pockets and pulled out a condom.

"Thought I was going to have to get one from my drawer." She nodded toward her bedside stand, several feet away. "I'm prepared for you, too."

"That's too far away -- I'd have to let go of you." He tightened his grip.

Kira chuckled - a deep, throaty sound - and sat up halfway, taking the packet from him. She smirked at his surprise when she tore it open, pulled the condom out, and rolled it onto him. Then she looked into those eyes again, pulling him back onto the mattress with her.

Holt lifted his shirt off quickly, throwing it to the floor, and fell on her with a hunger, and when he entered her, they both moaned heavily and held themselves motionless for a moment, savoring, their eyes locked. They began to move in unison, still looking into each other's eyes, creating the friction and pleasure that had driven their species for eons. Kira felt as if she had lived only to be here, right now, with this man. She loved him.

Looking into his eyes and feeling him inside her enhanced her arousal a thousand-fold. She knew he could see every nuance of emotion and sensation in her gaze, as she saw the same in his. Holt nibbled her bottom lip and began thrusting against her.

"Holt." She moaned. Kira held him to her tightly with her arms and her legs, causing their bodies to writhe with their lovemaking. She wanted to hold him so tightly that their bodies would meld into one being.

They were one being, and Kira knew neither of them would be the same after tonight. She saw in his eyes an honesty she had only caught glimpses of before, and Kira was positive that this encounter embodied many firsts for both of them.

A thin sheen of sweat formed on their bodies. She tightened her legs around his hips, and he wrapped his arms around her body, lifting them both into a sitting position with Holt's legs crossed beneath her, her own legs still folded around him. Holt nuzzled her breasts as she began moving to a different rhythm, different sensations.

Kira held his head and neck in the stiff crook of her arm, her other arm squeezing his shoulder and chest to her body. His left arm strapped her waist firmly against his torso while his right hand cupped her buttocks, working them as her hips rocked over him.

The sheen of sweat became rivulets, beading up under her hands and arms, slicking her breasts against his face. Holt lifted his lips to her neck and flicked his tongue over her flesh, turning the heat between their bodies into an unbearable fire.

Kira heard her own moans begin to grow in her throat, alternating with gasps for air. She threw back her head, arching her breasts high, as shattering shards of light filled her vision. Holt thrust harder, more erratically, as he met her climax, biting her shoulder in his abandon, squeezing the breath out of her. His muscles trembled beneath her hands, against her body.

Their movements decreased in urgency, became subtle, languid.

Slowly, they recovered. Holt still moved once or twice within her, and Kira dragged lazy kisses over his temple and forehead.

Holt leaned her back, lay on top of her, and then rolled to his right side, bringing her with him. "You are the most wonderful lover I've ever had."

"Mm. How many have you had?" She loved teasing him.

"Only one."

Kira lifted her head and looked at him, confused.

"I've been with a few other women, but they could never be called lovers." He kissed her flushed lips. "Not after this." He grinned at her. "It must be all that stress you've been talking about."

Kira laughed, pressing her cheek against his chest. "Funny."

"Whew." He shuddered. "They say stress can kill." He began stroking her hair. "Luckily, I ended up here."

Kira lifted her head to look at him. "Now, come on. It *was* stress."

"Kira. Please tell me you don't think this --" he motioned to them and the clothes-strewn bedroom, "was to relieve stress."

Kira ran her palm across his chest, smiling slightly. "Well, no, not all...of this." At his triumphant grin she added, "I just meant it caused us to act on something we wouldn't have, that's all."

"Uh-huh." He sighed and chuckled. "Okay."

Kira pressed her face against his warm skin again. From the moment she met him, Kira knew there was

188

something different about Holt. From his standoffish attitude when she was hired, to his passionate response to the animals and even his brother, Holt was always a man to be reckoned with. He'd been a main player in her life on the ranch, and now, he was in her heart.

He'd helped her speak of Cleo's death, releasing her trapped feelings. He helped her take her first tentative emotional steps forward. And she trusted him. She hadn't believed for a moment that he wouldn't be all over her that night they'd slept in his sleeping bag at the holding corral. But he'd kept his word.

Kira snuggled closer, hugging him tightly. He returned her squeeze and stroked her bare back with the pads of his fingers. Kira's heart swelled and she had to tell him how she felt. "Holt?" Kira curved her hand around the back of his shoulder.

"Hmm?"

"You don't have to say anything..." She lifted her face to his and met his gaze. "I love you." He met her gaze and she held it, afraid of what she might see there. She didn't see laughter, or embarrassment, but acceptance. He nodded.

Holt cradled her head with his hand and brought her toward his, then kissed her with tenderness, a caring that could only come from a man who held his woman in great esteem. His woman. That's what she was now. Not just in her mind, but in Holt's, too.

When his kiss ended, Kira smiled at him, and they laid their heads next to each other's, examining each other's face.

"I wish I could've seen you dancing in the hallway tonight," Holt said, then kissed her nose.

Kira jerked her head up. "What?" Kira tried to hide her surprise, but felt her face flush.

"I almost believed Treat when he said you'd be late." He laughed. "But then I heard you stomping around and running back to the bathroom." Holt laughed more and shook his head at the picture he must have painted in his mind.

"You couldn't have heard that," she said, incriminating herself.

"Treat couldn't have heard it, but I could have." He smiled softly. "I've grown sensitive to your presence lately."

"Oh, have you? What is my presence saying to your sensitivity right now?" Kira flicked her tongue over his left nipple and slid her hand to his groin, cupping him. "Getting anything?" She grinned, feeling wicked.

"Oh..." He rolled on top of her. "I think I might be getting something ..."

* * *

"How's it going?" Holt slipped his arms around her from behind and nuzzled the side of her neck. Kira sat on her stool, pouring over a reference manual on all bovine illnesses ever found in the United States. Holt had just come back from the range. He'd had to put down about fifty animals today, and needed to empty his mind of the death, and his heart of the pain.

190

Candace had come back last night, and Kira was making better progress. He was eager for her to figure out this mess so they could take care of it and put the ranch back in the black. Of course, he was also glad to be alone with her again, especially now that she belonged to him.

He liked the sound of that idea in his mind. His woman. He did care for her, and he loved making love to her. And, he reminded himself, she said she loved him. A man could do a whole lot worse.

"Pretty good." Covering his hands with her own, she leaned back into his embrace. "I think I might find something out today."

"Yeah?"

"Yeah." She bent back over her book and pointed to some bold-faced words on the page. "I figure that if it's not BVD, then it's obviously something that looks like it."

"Okay."

"So, I'm reading through everything to find something similar."

Holt nodded. "Good idea."

Kira leaned back into him again and sighed. "I'm glad you're done shooting. It was killing me to have to listen to that."

"It was killing me to have to do it." He hugged her and she squeezed his arms to her.

"I know. I'm sorry you had to. I wish you would use injections."

"It was just faster and cheaper, Kira, and unfortunately, money is a huge concern right now."

"I know, I know." She knew it was true but hated it.

191

"Well, things should be quiet now, so maybe that'll help." He rested his chin on her head and rocked her gently.

"I hope so. I'm feeling so tense today. Restless."

Kira laced her fingers between his and Holt held her hands tightly. He needed to make love to her, replace the images of the morning with her beautiful body, with the expressions of pleasure he would see on her face. Kira had turned out to be a wild lover, but he should have figured that, since she threw herself into everything with such emotional intensity. He loved it that she didn't expect to use the bed every time, that she accepted him into her body wherever they were in the house at the moment he wanted her. Hell, at the moment she wanted him. She initiated sex at least as often as he did.

Holt became aroused. "Want to take a break?" He raised his right palm to her left breast and massaged it through her T-shirt. Kira's hand still held the back of his, and moved with his caresses, filling his head with erotic images. He'd have to take a cold shower if she turned him down.

"I don't know," she murmured, obviously enjoying what he was doing to her, but needing some convincing. Again.

"Maybe if I can help you relax, it'll come to you more quickly." Holt bit her neck and then kissed the same spot.

"Think so?"

"Sure." He rolled her nipple between his thumb and forefinger. Kira had said she hated bras and had stopped wearing them when she spent her days in the lab. He loved it.

192

She craned her neck and kissed his jaw slowly, moaning softly, moving her lips toward his ear lobe, where she pulled it between her teeth. "It'd be irresponsible..."

"We'll make it fast..." Holt slid his left hand between her legs. The heat there slammed through his brain, and his groin tightened. He turned her toward him only half way and kissed her deeply. Kira reached one arm around the back of his neck and the other to his hardness pressed into her lower back. She grabbed his length through his jeans and Holt moaned with her.

He worked his hand against her and felt her, wanting to touch her flesh. He quickly unbuttoned and unzipped her jeans, then slid his fingers beneath her panties. Simultaneously, Kira leaned back further and spread her legs to give him better access while she worked on opening his jeans behind her back. Kira's actions matched Holt's urgency. Touching her wasn't enough. He held his right arm tightly around her midsection, lifted her up and worked her jeans and panties from her hips.

Kira held fast to Holt's neck, but used her other hand to remove her jeans the rest of the way. She sat on the stool, naked from the waist down, but Holt had to see the rest of her. He quickly slipped her T-shirt over her head, dropping it behind him, then wrapped his arms back around her, placing his left hand between her legs again, moaning as his fingers slipped into her warm, wet folds. Kira grabbed the back of his hand, pressing him further, lifting her hips into his grasp.

"I always manage to let you distract me from my work." Kira had managed to unfasten Holt's jeans with one hand, and worked them down an inch, but couldn't get them further. "Isn't there something unethical about this?"

Holt reluctantly took his hands away from Kira's body just long enough to remove his own clothes and boots, then was back against her in an instant, kissing her neck and shoulders, nibbling her ear. "I'm aiding your progress," he said behind her ear. "Nothing wrong about that."

With his right hand, he put upward pressure on Kira's buttocks, and she stood on the chair rails, raising herself from the seat. Holt moved over the stool, taking her place, and then with one swift, fluid motion brought Kira onto his lap, planting himself inside of her. They gasped and began the rocking motions that would bring them to climax. Kira leaned forward and held on to the edge of the counter-top, pushing against his groin. Her muscled thighs covered his own, and she wrapped her feet around his calves to the inside of his ankles.

Holt kneaded her right breast with his left hand, and moved his right hand to their joining. She circled her hips in his lap, then threw her body back into his, almost knocking him off the stool.

He heard his own growl-like chuckle come from the back of his throat, and stood, leaning Kira forward over the counter top, her upper body covering her notes and papers. He grasped her hips and moved inside of her, loving the sound of her feminine sighs and moans. She felt so good, but something was missing.

194

He wanted to see her face, look into her eyes as he made love to her, and this was suddenly too impersonal. Holt leaned over her and kissed her right shoulder, slowing his thrusts. "Turn around."

He pulled himself out of her and she faced him. Holt pressed his erection against her belly and pulled Kira into his arms, kissing her deeply and feeling himself throb against her. Bending slightly, he lifted her into his arms, carried her to the loveseat, and placed her onto it in a sitting position on the edge of the cushions. She leaned back and smiled at him lazily, opening her arms to him. Holt held himself above her and pressed himself against her opening. Just as he was about to enter her again, he remembered he wasn't using a condom.

"Uh...we're forgetting something." He took himself away from her, away from where he desperately wanted to be.

She groaned. "You made me forget." She got up and pushed on his chest. "I guess that's that, then."

"Wait!" Holt gently nudged her backward with his lips and hands. "I have one with me somewhere." He looked around for his jeans.

"I was kidding." Kira laughed. "Hurry up."

Holt located his pants and rummaged through the pockets, hoping he hadn't lost it, or worse yet, damaged it while working. It would be too ironic to have it but not be able to use it. Finally, he found it. He turned back to her as he tore the wrapping from the condom. She laughed again, that deep, sultry sound that made him want to devour her with his body.

In less than two seconds, he had it on and was back where he belonged. Ah, yes, he thought, where he belonged.

Thirty minutes later, Kira bent to retrieve her T-shirt. She looked so much better now, ready to tackle her work again. That was all she needed, Holt thought, letting his male ego swell as he watched her from the couch.

He was good for her. Not only did he keep her on her toes, but he gave her what she needed, when she needed it. Kira looked at him as he sat up and pulled on his boots. He smiled at her. "You're gorgeous."

She smirked at him and pulled her hair out from under the loose collar of her T-shirt. "Going to stay and help out this afternoon?" she asked him.

"Do you need me to?" He stood and stomped his feet, bringing his jeans hems down further.

"I can find something for you to do." Kira plopped onto her stool and swiveled toward the counter. She nudged her reference manual to the side and looked through the microscope lenses. Holt found his hat in the corner by the bathroom and bent to pick it up.

"Have you checked on the animals you treated in the holding corral?"

"I'm planning on going today."

"Oh, my God."

"What?" Holt strode to her side in three long steps, placing his hat onto his head with one hand.

She looked up from the scope and then to the reference manual, then back to the scope. After a few seconds, she looked up at him. A beam of sunlight coming through a crack above the door lit her eyes.

Damn, she was some kind of beautiful. "What?" he asked again. She looked at him, her eyes as wide as her smile.

"I think I've found it." She shook her head and pushed a stray lock of hair out of her face, then grabbed a tote bag and began putting samples and books into it.

"What are you doing?"

"We have to see a foreign disease diagnostician." She stopped, then set the bag onto the counter and moved toward the door, keeping her notebook under her left arm.

Holt grabbed her other arm. "What are you talking about?"

"Let me tell you on the way to the phone." She tried to pull her arm away, but he held fast.

"Come on, Holt. We need to call the government."

That shocked him into releasing her. She was out the door before he knew it and he bounded out to catch up with her.

Chapter Thirteen

Kira set the receiver down and braced herself, gripping the arms of the big chair at the desk in the office, and then raised her eyes to Holt.

He'd begun pacing during her conversation with the Department of Agriculture.

"Are you going to tell me what the hell Rinderpest is, now? You're killing me with suspense and I need to know what to do about this thing."

Kira took a deep breath. "Rinderpest is a foreign disease still existing in places like Mexico and Japan."

"Well, if it's foreign, what the hell is it doing here?"

She shrugged. "That's what I intend to find out." Kira wanted to look away, but held his gaze. Her chagrin warred with elation that she was finally on the right track. At least, she thought, they would now soon be done with this.

Holt eyed her for a moment, increasing Kira's discomfort. "I assume there's a test for this?"

Kira nodded. "We'll have it tested by the foreign disease diagnostician from the U.S. Department of Agriculture."

"How long?"

"Only days." She hadn't told him the worst part. "Holt, there's more--"

He looked at her and shook his head. "I know. We're quarantined."

"And quarantine means not even the well animals can go to market until this thing is handled. The agency is going to send some people over to monitor our actions."

Holt exhaled and turned away, his arms crossed and head down.

"We also can't salvage the meat." Kira expected him to turn around, but he didn't. "I'm sorry."

He turned then. "Kira, there's nothing for you to apologize for." He propped his hands on his hips. "I don't think any of us could have anticipated this." He looked down at her, still in the big chair, then sat back down in the chair facing her. He sighed. "Okay. What do we do now? What's the prognosis?"

"Most of the sick animals will die, but some can recover with rest and fluids." Kira could hardly stand to utter her next words, but had to forced them out. "We have to put down the sickest animals and concentrate on trying to save the others." Her stomach churned at the thought. "That's what the agency will want to monitor. Our slaughter and disposal of the animals."

He looked bewildered. It would be a daunting task, and Kira would never wish anything like this on a ranch owner or the livestock. She looked for some sign of acceptance or understanding from Holt.

Finally, he drew in a long, deep breath, and then let it out slowly. Kira watched as he patted his shirt pockets, looking for a toothpick. He found one, put it into his mouth, then leaned his elbows onto his knees. He hung his head, looking at the carpet between his feet.

"When are those agency people coming?" he asked, raising his head.

"We need to tell them when we're ready to do it," she said softly.

199

"Tell them to come tomorrow. I'll have the men start rounding up any strays. We might as well start with the holding corral."

Kira winced. The holding corral had been Holt's own testing grounds. Those animals were like a symbol to him, and frankly, to her, too. To Kira, the fact that Holt was starting there meant he'd given up. His voice and the droop of his shoulders, combined with the almost lifeless look in his eyes told her he was defeated. Kira tried not to feel responsible for that, but just couldn't help it.

"I'll try to make the resolution of this mess go as smoothly as possible."

He nodded.

"And I'll find out how the disease was introduced into the herd, to prevent it from ever happening again."

"Will the agency want to know that?"

"Yes, but they'll also want to know that the disease has been removed completely, meaning they'll most likely test all the animals and any possible sources, like feed, dirt, manure piles, insects. We'll definitely feel their presence for a while." Kira picked up a pencil and wove it between her fingers. "The only good thing is that we'll get some financial aid from the government, so the ranch won't go broke."

Holt nodded again, then stood. "Well, let's get going."

"To the corral?"

"Yeah, I just want to take a look at them before tomorrow."

"Okay. Let me make the call and we'll go."

"I'll find Dad and tell him. Meet you outside."

Kira picked up the telephone receiver and watched Holt walk out of the office, slapping his hat against his thigh.

* * *

On the ride out to the corral, they were dealing with the turn of events. She knew she'd get her ten percent now, and the job, --a huge relief-- but couldn't feel completely happy, until she had the Crockett ranch back on track. She felt like she'd benefited from someone else's misfortune.

If she weren't emotionally involved with Holt, his unhappiness wouldn't affect her as strongly. She felt his depression like waves pushing her down. Kira didn't want to feel depressed, and she didn't want Holt to feel that way either. But, there was nothing she could do for him. She couldn't cure the illness, and even if she had discovered it sooner, the fatality rate probably would have been the same. And, she might not have had a relationship with Holt at all. He wouldn't have been forced to work with her, accept her as a necessity to the ranch.

Kira looked over at him, moving with the horse's lazy gait. His usually relaxed posture was strained, matching the tension in his face. His forehead was wrinkled, his mouth turned down. Even though he said he didn't blame her, she worried that he might. He must have sensed her gaze, because he first flicked his eyes at her, then turned his head.

It looked like a struggle, but he managed a slight smile. "Don't worry. Things'll be okay."

"I think that's supposed to be my line."

"Well, you look as worried as I feel, so I thought I'd try it out."

Kira smiled. "Thanks."

Holt grinned back, halfheartedly, then looked forward again.

When they made it to the corral, Kira expected most of the animals to look worse than the last time she'd seen them, but they didn't. "Look." She dismounted and went to the fence for a closer look.

"What?" Holt seemed almost apathetic and looked at the group of animals as if not seeing them.

"Look at them, Holt. They don't look half-bad. Don't you see?"

He perked up a bit and looked over his horse's head at the cows. "They're not dead, anyway." He dismounted and joined her.

Kira leaned her elbows on the top rung of the fence. "Well, Holt, you may have discovered the best way to treat the possible survivors." She smiled at him, feeling for the first time that day that Holt would have something to smile about, too. He didn't reply, but slowly let his eyes wander over each animal. A couple were still in bad shape, but a few were also very likely going to make it. This was wonderful news.

Still not seeing any change in his disposition, she added, "Holt, this is major." He looked at her. "Don't you get it? You may have just given something to the entire veterinary community with this discovery. Maybe you'll be famous."

He furrowed his brow and looked back over his animals, as if seeing them differently. "Famous may be pushing it."

"Come on." Kira grabbed his arm and tugged him toward their horses. "You've got some concoctions to concoct.

She jabbed her foot into the stirrup on her mare and swung herself into the saddle. In just a few days, she and Holt could concentrate on rebuilding the ranch and exploring their new relationship. And in a couple of weeks, Kira could tie up her child-custody battle once and for all. Things would finally settle down.

* * *

Again, the gunshots. Kira could barely concentrate with the guns in the background and the intrusion of the agency people milling about her lab and the ranch. The Department of Agriculture agents had been here for two weeks now, going over her notes, examining her samples, and taking tons more of their own samples and notes. They commended her on her work, but she had to choke out insincere 'thank-yous'.

The reality of all the dying animals was really getting to her. She felt sick constantly and just couldn't think with all the noise and movement. Hopefully, they'd all be gone in a few more days. She hadn't been able to even talk to Holt, he'd been so busy overseeing, and being overseen, working with the agents. He was everywhere at once, making sure his ranch and animals were being taken care of properly.

It was so like him. She smiled, remembering the way he didn't back down from some of the pushy D

203

of A people, not letting them boss him around in front of his men, or showing him up with their knowledge. He'd made sure to read everything he could get his hands on regarding Rinderpest before they'd arrived.

And it'd paid off. After matching their knowledge during their first conversation, they'd finally backed down and began treating him as an equal. Ben and Catherine watched from the sidelines, letting Holt run things with the agency, and Treat really had no choice but to either do as he was told, or disappear.

"Okay, wrap it up," she heard one of the agents say behind her. She turned and watched them putting their samples and copies of her notes into their brief cases. Henderson, the man in charge approached her.

"We're done with your lab and samples, Ms. McGovern."

"Thank you," was all she could say.

He nodded briefly. "We'll be helping the rest of the team in the field and be out of everyone's hair in about two days."

"Let me know what I can do to help."

"We will." Looking around the confines of her shed-turned-laboratory, a bit of disbelief tinged his expression. "You've done good work here."

Kira resisted a smirk. "Thank you, Mr. Henderson." She slid off her stool and walked him and his team to the door. If they didn't request her presence in the field, Kira had plans to get started searching for the origin of the disease right away. She wanted answers.

Henderson turned back to her before leaving the lab. "We'll be working on getting some answers from

204

our end, but please let us know if you find out anything else."

"You can be sure I will." She smiled, wishing he'd hurry up and get out. She didn't feel guilty for having such uncharitable thoughts. She'd already been quite hospitable, and even though she knew they were only doing their job and they were helping her and the Crocketts, she just wanted them gone. This was her sanctuary and she wanted peace.

And maybe with them gone, she would be able to squeeze in more time with Zoe and Holt. Since they'd been here, she'd worked from six in the morning to midnight every night. It was all lab work, nothing physical, but she was still beat. She'd timed every meal at the guesthouse with Zoe's schedule, so she could see her rapidly growing baby as much as possible. Zoe was sitting up pretty well now, and would actually hold her doll and try to play with it. It was fascinating to Kira to watch the changes every day, but Zoe wasn't the only one changing.

Holt had worked in the field from very early until dark, and then he'd come help out Kira in the lab until midnight. They'd had no energy for love-making, although they would give each other 'the look' and make hot promises that when this was all over, they'd make it up to each other. Holt and Kira's work relationship seemed to be more synergistic than ever. They fed off each other, kept each other going. Holt respected her opinions, and she loved that solid, stable feeling she got from working with the perfect partner.

* * *

"So, Ms. McGovern," Holt said, slipping his arm around her shoulders. "They're finally gone, along with most of my herd." He bent and kissed her upturned face, square on the lips. "What say we put this behind us once and for all, and take a little break?"

Kira spread her open hand and fingers along the side of his rib cage and pulled him to her. The early evening sunlight scattered through the settling dust and the crickets chirped their good-byes to the departing agents as their caravan of trucks and vans snaked off into the desert. Most of the smoke from the disposal fires had dissipated, along with most of the odor. They'd had to burn many of the carcasses, because it would have been impossible to gather them all from the range and into an area where they could be loaded up and hauled away. Kira felt immense relief that this part of their ordeal was over.

She smiled, feeling as if she'd experienced Holt's kiss for the first time. "You're sounding awfully magnanimous in the face of things."

"How else can I be? All I can do is move on." Holt squeezed her to him.

"True. And you hardly yelled at anyone the entire week."

Holt ignored the comment and nuzzled her neck. He muffled a growl and stood away from her. "I think we should get out of the public eye." He grabbed her hand in his, the size of it making her feel as if she were a child holding a grown-up's hand, and started dragging her toward the ranch house.

"Where are we going? You're not taking me to your house." Kira started to pull on her hand in vain.

"We're just going there to get a few things."

In minutes, Holt had gathered whatever those few things were and re-entered the living room, motioning to Kira that he was ready. He had a large set of bulging saddlebags draped over his shoulder, igniting Kira's curiosity. Then, he took her to the stables and directed her to saddle her horse while he got his mare ready for a ride.

"Where are we going?" she asked again.

"For a ride," he said. She looked over her mare's back and caught the look he gave her. He left no question as to what they were going to do once they got there. The anticipation aroused Kira's senses. Holt's kiss tonight was almost the only physical contact they'd had in a week, and she was ready to share herself with him again.

An hour later, they were still on horseback. "How much further? You are planning on having us back sometime tonight, aren't you?" They were moving single-file between walls of orange and tan rock, the deep blue sky just a strip above their heads. The skittering of pebbles beneath the horses' feet echoed around the hollow sound of their voices.

Holt turned around to answer her. "We're almost there. I'll definitely have you back to Zoe tonight, I just wanted to have a few hours with you, and show you something."

"What is it?"

"Patience," he chided.

He turned around and Kira was left staring at his broad back and his hips as they heaved in the saddle. It was driving her crazy. She felt a fine sweat break out all over her skin.

"I don't have much more patience, Holt. I haven't touched you for a week and I need you now."

He only looked back at her with a devious smirk, apparently not as desperate or hungry for her as she was for him. He was pretending. He'd better be. She stuck her tongue out at him and his smile broadened before he turned back around.

Holt stopped his horse before going around a long finger of rock blocking their path. "Close your eyes." He took her reins from her hand.

Kira rolled her eyes at him before doing as he said, then let Holt lead her mare around the rocks.

"Don't look until I tell you to. I'm taking you to a place I don't think anybody else knows about. It's my personal hide-out."

When her horse missed a step on the slippery rocks, Kira grabbed onto the saddle horn. The sounds changed. She heard water, maybe a fall or a creek, and birds chirping. The air became cooler and just a little damp, and shadows fell across her closed eyelids. It was all she could do to keep her eyes shut, waiting for Holt to tell her to open them.

"Okay."

Slowly, Kira opened her eyes. She was sitting in the middle of an impossibility. To her right, a waterfall ran into a creek that cleaved two green banks covered in cottonwood trees.

She quickly dismounted and Holt followed, dropping their reins. She heard him follow her to the edge of the creek, where she knelt and dipped her hand into the water. It was cool and soft on her skin. She sat down, arms looped around her knees, then looked up at him.

"I am amazed. This is beautiful." Kira's eyes followed him as he crouched down next to her, one knee on the ground.

Holt lay down on his side, propping himself up on his elbow, and pulled Kira down next to him. He immediately started kissing her. She tilted her head to give him better access to her neck and jaw, reveling in his touch.

"Finally," he mumbled in her ear, as he took the lobe between his teeth and stole her self-control. She circled her arms around his neck and pulled him on top of her.

Later, they lay naked on the grass, the last warmth of the sun on their skin as it dipped below the tops of the cliffs. Kira, on her back, cradled her head in the crook of Holt's arm, who lay on his side again.

"What stress?" she slurred, her eyes barely open.

Holt kissed her forehead. "I have something for you." He whistled for his mare and she came running with Kira's horse following, as usual. He jumped up and went to one of the saddlebags. Kira sat up to better admire his lithe, naked form.

He came back with something wrapped in a bundle of soft white flannel. "I wanted to give this to you while it was still light outside, so I could see how it looks." He handed her the bundle and she pulled back the corners of the cloth to reveal his gift.

"Oh, Holt." She took a quick breath and looked up at him, opening her eyes wide. "This is beautiful." She looked back down at the sand-cast silver and hand-polished turquoise squash blossom necklace. She stroked the large silver beads and bugles, connected by half-dollar sized medallions of

209

intricately set blue stone, all meeting at the bottom center at the symbolic squash blossom--an upside down horse-shoe shape of silver inlaid with rows of turquoise. The crevices had turned black with age, giving the necklace an antique look.

Solemn tones laced his voice. "My grandmother gave it to me and it's been in my family for generations. I want you to wear it." He took it from her hands and hooked it around her neck, then lifted and held the heavy piece in his palm, the back of his hand filling the space between her breasts, his rough knuckles against her tender skin. He stroked the back of his hand over the inside curve of her right breast, before laying the necklace back down against her.

Kira sat frozen, stuck on Holt's last sentence. "If this necklace has been in your family for generations, then what does this mean?" she asked, fingering the heavy pendant and barely breathing.

"It means...." He cupped her hand that held the necklace. "We belong together. You're my woman, and there are no other men in your life from this point forward." He took her hand from the necklace, brought it to his lips and kissed her knuckles.

Even though he gave voice to her own thoughts, she bristled. Had she expected more? "So, what your saying, is that this necklace serves as notice to others around me that I'm yours now?" He nodded and she crossed her arms. "And what about you? Does it serve the same notice to others about you?"

He seemed taken aback. "Well, yeah. Of course."

Kira cocked her head. "You don't sound as sure now."

"I just hadn't thought about it, but--"

210

"But you thought about how things in my life were going to change." She was breathing heavily now, scowling. The nerve of him!

Holt grabbed her upper arms and brought his face to hers. "What I was trying to say is that you're absolutely right."

"What?"

"I said, you're right. It means the same thing for me."

Well, that was better. Her ire began to smooth. "Well, good."

Holt breathed a sigh, shaking his head, looking relieved.

"Now let's get something else straight."

Chapter Fourteen

"Kira ..."

"You're putting this necklace on me like you're a dog marking your territory." He looked incredulous. Good. "I don't like that connotation, but if that's what you want to do, then maybe you should let me mark you somehow."

Holt shook his head and opened his hands, beseeching. "Kira, that's not the way things work. The man has to mark out his territory. It's expected. The woman knows how the man feels."

"I don't know how you feel." Her arms stayed crossed and she felt impudent, damn him. "Not really. I know you want us to be exclusive with each other, but that doesn't tell me anything except you're territorial. Which I already knew."

He draped his right arm over his raised right knee and dropped his head, letting it hang for a moment, before raising it to meet her gaze. "You want me to tell you how I feel about you?"

"Yeah. And Zoe."

"I think Zoe is great. I like being around her, and I want to be an influence in her life." He stopped and looked at her. Kira quirked an eyebrow.

"And...." Taking both her hands, he forced her to uncross her arms. "And I think you are wonderful. I want to be with you all the time, and when I'm not with you, I'm thinking about you." He brought both of her hands to his lips and kissed them.

Kira watched as he let his eyes drop to her breasts. What he said had been a good start, and seeing his eyes burn into her made her breasts ache for his touch. He kissed the inside of her left palm and up the inside of her arm. Kira's head dipped back an inch, and her eyelids closed halfway. She was losing control again.

"Anything else?" Her breath came out in short bursts.

"Yes. You have no other choice." His breath, the sounds of his kisses, and his beard-stubble on her passion-sensitive skin drove her crazy with wanting. She pulled her arm away, reflexively, but Holt held it fast and moved with a sureness that multiplied her desire.

"Just so we know where we stand," she murmured.

His mouth had reached the inside of her biceps and Holt moved to her nipple, taking it completely into his mouth. She crumpled in his arms at the sensations from his tongue. He pushed her back onto the grass, then rolled on top of her. His arousal grew against her thigh, and she became impatient. For a man who couldn't describe his feelings well, he had done a pretty good job. And he was expressing them quite well right now, too.

She let herself accept his explanation. It wasn't exactly what she'd hoped for--this was not a marriage proposal--but he was honest. *A woman could do worse*, she thought, abandoning herself to Holt's loving.

Holt nudged her knees apart and pressed his erection between them. "So, are you satisfied?" he asked, looking completely serious.

"Not quite." She pulled him into her.

* * *

213

"I think we should call it a night." Holt stretched, closing his notebook. He'd come to check on her at eight, and sat down to help her. Now it was one in the morning. Holt yawned. "We'll get more done if we get some sleep." He looked at Kira over the books and equipment. She was bent over a book, her pen poised above the paper, and he could see her eyelids drooping from four feet away. "Hey." He moved around the counter to shake her gently. "Did you hear me?"

"What?"

"Kira, you look like death eating a cracker."

"Thanks so much," she slurred. Kira wobbled on her stool and Holt steadied her.

"See? When you're over-tired, you get sarcastic." Holt took the pen from her hand and swiveled her around, then straddled her legs. He wrapped his arms around her, pulling her against himself.

"You deserved it. You insulted me," she mumbled into his chest.

She'd been overdoing it, trying to find the origin of the disease, wanting to take care of every detail. But it wasn't even her responsibility now. The Agency could take care of it. So he didn't understand why she was pushing herself, except that she was a perfectionist. That he could understand. And, he knew she was making sure she'd get her ten percent, which she didn't have to worry about anymore. Kira had met the requirements of the contract. So, he'd make her slow down and relax.

Holt pulled her off the chair. "Come on, let's go to bed."

Kira pushed against him. "No, not just yet. I'm so close now. I may have the answer in just a few minutes." She tried to swivel back, but Holt held her immobile between his legs. "Really, I wouldn't be able to sleep if I stopped now."

He was sure she'd slept a few seconds on his chest, but resisted the urge to contradict her. "All right. I'll stay here on the couch and give you thirty more minutes. Then, we're going to bed. We, not just me."

"Your territorialism is cute, Holt. Thanks." She'd said it with a straight face, probably because she couldn't muster up the energy to smile. He stepped back and she picked up her pen and bent over some papers again as he bent over her and kissed her cheek. She leaned heavily into his kiss and managed a very slight smile.

His eyes slid down to the squash blossom necklace he'd given her. She'd worn it every day since. He felt proud and satisfied that she'd seen reason. Holt squeezed her right shoulder before going to the couch to wait.

He looked at his watch before tucking both his hands behind his head. It was one-fifteen. He'd give her until one forty-five, then take her to bed and hopefully muster up just enough energy to make slow, warm love to her. Then, he'd make her stay in bed until noon. Holt wouldn't allow her to do anything except play with Zoe, and eat things he'd make for her. As he watched her work, her eyes drooped lower, her pen moved erratically across the page.

She was safer with everyone knowing she was his. Besides, the men acted differently around her, and his mother's eyes sparkled when she saw Kira wearing the necklace. His father seemed to treat him as if he could handle more responsibility, and Treat became a little surly when he saw it, probably feeling as if Holt shouldn't own any family heirlooms since he wasn't a full-blooded Crockett.

But Treat also owned a share of family trinkets. As a matter of fact, Treat had their grandmother's wedding ring, which contained a diamond chip set in filigreed yellow and white gold. Its main worth was sentimental and historical, but he knew if he were full-blooded, he would have received that ring. Holt closed his eyes to clear the negative thoughts and willed himself to stay awake for Kira.

Later, he found himself opening his eyes, and pushed the light button on his watch. The digital LCD told him it was three in the morning. He sat up, rubbing his face and looked over at Kira, blinking his eyes so he could see more clearly. She was asleep on her notebook, pen hanging loosely between her fingers. Holt walked silently to where she was spread across the counter and leaned his face closely to hers. Her mouth was slightly open and she sighed daintily as she breathed out. So beautiful, he thought, as he pressed his lips to her cheek.

He peeked at her notes beneath her hand. She had fallen asleep in the middle of a sentence and the last character had turned into a long blue line that drifted off the page onto the counter-top.

He took the pen out of her hand, laid it to the side, and then pressed his whiskered face against

216

hers. He wrapped his arms around her waist, squeezed her, breathed in her scent. When she didn't stir, Holt began kissing her cheek and neck. "Sweetheart," he murmured in her ear, then nibbled her ear lobe. "Come on, honey, it's time to go to bed."

Kira groaned and tried to push him away.

Holt helped her to her feet. "We're still in the lab, Kira. Let me help you get to bed."

Kira put her arm around his waist and her head on his chest as he walked her to the guesthouse. When he got her into bed, he stripped her naked, admiring her body, then undressed and crawled into bed. Holt pulled her back against his chest, curving her body to his, then fell asleep.

Kira awoke to the sounds of Zoe laughing and Candace singing. Her toe was touching something hairy, and she realized it was Holt's leg. She turned her head, watched him sleeping, listened to his even breathing. He faced her, his arm folded under his pillow. Morning sunshine lit up the stubble along his jaw making it glow golden-red against the dark brown stubble that was in shadow. Kira placed her open palm on the corded bulge of his bare chest. It felt hard and woke a slow burning in her sex. A raised, blue vein snaked across his left bicep, and still more veins roped his forearm. Holt truly was a beautiful man; no doubt about it. She'd never taken the time to examine him fully.

Her eyes traveled back up Holt's arm and chest to his face and open eyes. She gasped. A knowing grin curving his lips. "Good morning, Sunshine."

"Good morning." She smiled. "I don't remember getting here."

Holt raised her hand from his chest and kissed it. He was doing that a lot lately, and she loved it. She felt as if she was his queen and he was paying homage to her. Just as things should be, she thought with a grin.

"I guess I worked late last night, but I think I remember where I left off."

He pulled her to him, pressing his morning desire against her abdomen. They smiled at each other. "You left off on the counter-top." He chuckled.

Kira exhaled a throaty laugh. "Oh. Well, I guess I might remember just before that, then."

Holt rolled on top of her and insinuated himself between her legs, rolling his hips against her with a wicked grin.

She wrapped her legs and arms around him "But I guess I can think about that later."

The morning was glorious. After making love in a sure, unhurried pace, they showered and joined Candace and Zoe in the kitchen.

"Good morning. What are you making?" Kira asked Candace as she kissed and hugged the baby.

"Hi, Kira, Holt. I'm making chocolate-chocolate chip pancakes covered in chocolate syrup and chocolate whipped cream." Candace turned around holding a plate of the stuff. "Want some?" All that chocolate, combined with her devastating smile...something special had happened.

Kira smiled at Holt, who moaned at the sight, then accepted the plate from Candace. "I'd love some, thanks." Kira sat down at the table. Holt joined her after pouring them two cups of coffee.

"So, what are you celebrating?" she asked her friend. Holt looked at her questioningly, then shifted his gaze to Candace.

"Oh, Kira." She laughed. "I never could fool you." She brought two more plates of food and set one down in front of Holt, then sat at the table with the other plate.

"Well, come on." Kira motioned to their breakfast. "I've seen you make chocolate things before, but never to this degree." She smiled at her friend, and watched as she tried to act nonchalant. "Tell me."

Candace giggled and shot out her left hand, palm down, for Kira to see. Kira gasped, and heard Holt's grunt of disbelief. She held Candace's long fingers and turned her hand to catch the light through the kitchen windows. Candace was wearing the most beautiful antique ring Kira had ever seen. It fit her finger perfectly, the delicate swirls of gold matching the look of her slender fingers.

"Treat asked me to marry him." She was happier than Kira had ever seen her.

Kira sighed as tingles spread across her chest. "It's so beautiful, Candace." She met her friend's eyes, feeling tears pool in her own. "Congratulations. I'm so happy for you."

"Congratulations, Candace," Holt said.

It sounded like Holt was choking. Kira didn't know what was bothering him, but she was worried about Candace. Kira remembered exactly where she had left off last night -- with a discovery that would affect her best friend's happiness.

* * *

"Treat." She came up on him in the barn. "We have to talk."

Treat stood up from picking his horse's hooves and propped his hands on his hips. "Did you see the ring I gave Candace?"

He puffed out his chest. Kira's necklace felt heavy against her chest, reminding her of her own recent designation as a woman belonging to a Crockett man. The only difference, of course, was that Candace was engaged to be married, and Kira was just...well, marked.

She shook her head to get herself back on track. "It's not about that." She looked around at the other men busy with their work. "Let's go someplace where we can talk privately."

Treat looked around also. "You're not going to try to talk me out of it, are you? You had your chance." There was that Cheshire grin again.

Oh, God. What she was about to tell him would probably tone down that ego. She sighed. "No, that's not it. It's business. Meet me at the branding corral." She turned and walked out of the barn, hoping to get a few minutes to build herself up to the task. She'd thought she had already done that, but facing him, knowing what the possible consequences were, and how it would probably hurt Candace, made the words clog her throat.

When she made it to the corral, Treat was still a good ways behind her. She leaned her elbows and one foot on the railings and looked out at the vast desert. It was so beautiful and desolate. The mountains rose up and the plants and animals seemed so insignificant against the enormity of the rocky peaks, so small compared to the entire desert spreading further than any eye could see. It was already dusk. Kira had put this off as long as she could.

"So?" he said, sounding impatient.

Kira figured he was insulted that she hadn't cooed to him about his conquest and generous offer of marriage to Candace, or that she hadn't seemed jealous. She turned to him, leaving one elbow still on the rail.

"I have to tell you something I've discovered in the lab. Something I want you to know about before I give my report to Ben."

"Kira, I don't care about cells and atoms." He backed off a step. "Go tell Holt about that science stuff, he'll listen." He turned to go.

"It's about you," she shot out.

He stopped and looked back. "What do you mean?"

Kira took a deep breath and looked him in the eye. "I discovered the origin of the disease." She didn't see any recognition in his eyes, which was good, because she had hoped he hadn't known. "The cattle you purchased last February were infected with it."

Now he understood. She could see him remembering when he shopped the auctions, chose

221

those animals, made the deal. Then his face hardened. He stood motionless.

"You know Mexican beef is illegal in the United States. I have to report it to Ben, of course, but I also have to report it to the agency." Still, he said nothing. "I just wanted you to have a little notice so you wouldn't be surprised." She waited for a tirade, but he just looked at her, bitterness growing on his face. He lifted his top lip into a snarl. "I'm sorry," she said, walking past him. She would talk to Candace now, give her some warning.

"It'll never work." He growled behind her.

She stopped and turned to face him. "What won't?"

"You think you're still getting a part of this ranch?"

"I've fulfilled my obligation, so, yes."

"And Holt helped. That wasn't in the contract. You were supposed to diagnose and treat the cattle, not you and Holt. I doubt you'll get what you came for. And Holt had it planned that way the whole time, to look like he'd done most of the work." He barked out a laugh.

Kira stomped away. She wanted to defend Holt to him, but her words would fall on deaf ears.

She couldn't go talk to Candace right now. She was too mad. Kira changed course and headed toward the lab. Maybe while she cooled down, she could finish copying her notes from her field notebook to another identical but cleaner book. Kira always kept both books for reference, in case she was ever questioned in the future, or her notes were ever subpoenaed, but she liked to have the rewritten ones because she could make them neater, easier to read, and more organized. Just thinking about it began to calm her. Yes, that's what she'd do. She'd finish that up tonight, and then would write the official reports to Ben and the agency tomorrow morning. But she would still talk to Ben tonight.

And she would tell Holt before that, too. She could really use his support right now, she thought, clomping up the wooden stairs to her lab. One of his bone-crushing hugs would make everything okay.

* * *

Holt cleaned and rearranged all of his lab glassware in his room, getting ready to distill more of his treatment. He needed this solitary confinement, as he thought of it, to clear his head. Treat had given their grandmother's ring to Candace. He'd asked her to marry him. He didn't know why, but it made him mad. It felt like Treat had beaten him to something, some important finish line.

Holt should have been the first Crockett son to get engaged and married. After all, what did Treat know about commitment? He'd been running around with anything in a skirt the past few years. But, damn it, Holt hadn't felt ready to get married. He cared for Kira, sure, but spend the rest of his life with her? How could anybody possibly decide something like that on such short notice?

The thought of Kira made him smile. They were sleeping together every night. Hell, they were practically living together, and right next door to his own house, his parents. Neither of them had said anything to him, but he figured his mother might have his father talk to him about it. She was a traditionalist, through and through, and wouldn't feel comfortable with this arrangement for very long.

Which made Holt wonder if that was why Treat had asked Candace to marry him. Maybe he was trying to show Hold up, be the one to 'do the right thing'. He shook his head and placed the last piece of Pyrex tubing into his distiller.

Holt heard his door open, and he turned and saw Treat leaning against the door jamb.

"What?" Would the boy ever learn to knock?

"Just thought I'd do you a favor and let you in on something, brother."

Holt quirked his eyebrow, waiting.

"Kira found out how the disease was introduced into our herd."

Holt picked up on the 'our' term, and wondered at Treat's sudden team-spirit. "And?"

"And she means to implicate you as the idiot who screwed up the family business."

"You're full of it." Folding a towel he'd used to dry his Pyrex, he laid it onto his desk with a deliberate motion. "She hasn't said anything about it, and she wouldn't do something like that."

"Oh, yeah she would." Treat stood there, apparently waiting for Holt to beg him for the information.

Holt glared at him. "Treat, say what you've come to say and get the hell out," he growled, growing dangerously impatient with him.

"Why do you think she needs this job so badly, huh?" He paused. "She needs it so she can keep

224

custody of that kid. It's not hers, you know. It's her dead sister's, and the kid's grandparents are fighting for custody. She has to have a job and be in court to prove it in two weeks."

Now Holt was listening, but he played it straight-faced all the way. Whether what Treat was saying was true or not, he wouldn't give his brother the satisfaction of knowing his reactions or feelings.

"She hasn't told you?" Treat laughed. "And I thought you guys were so cozy."

"Leave, before I crush you," Holt said, in a low, steady tone. He paced toward Treat, to shove him out, but Treat backed out of the doorway on his own.

He chuckled. "I'll leave. But you'll find out. She's been using you this whole time, and she's believed the only way to get what she wants is to get rid of you. And she's gonna do it, buddy."

Holt did shove him this time, all the way down the tiled hall, then grabbed Treat's shirt and rammed him up against the wall. "If you repeat what you've just said about Kira, I will crush you. You'll be so broken by the time I'm done with you, you'll think that last fight of ours was a dance." Holt jerked his brother away from him like he was a piece of rotten meat, then walked into the office and shut the door.

He had to think. He began pacing. Holt knew Zoe was Kira's niece, but she hadn't mentioned a custody battle. If it were true, would that be a strong enough driving force for her to...to what?

He didn't even want to think about the rest of Treat's tale. Kira would never attempt to hurt his future on the ranch. Even if he did somehow bring

225

the disease into the herd, it would have been an accident, and Kira would present it as such. And she certainly wouldn't go to Ben without discussing it with him first. Holt looked in the direction of Kira's lab, imagining he could see her through the walls, hunched over her books.

No. Treat had to be lying, and he'd go find out. Holt left the house, determined to set Treat straight. He'd make him apologize to Kira if he'd spread this nonsense to anyone else's ears, and then he'd give him his best right hook. Unconsciously, Holt clenched his fist.

He entered immediately after knocking, not waiting for Kira's response. She was sitting at the desk, two lab notebooks in front of her, obviously in the middle of recopying her notes.

She looked up in surprise. "Hi." She sounded pleased to see him.

Chapter Fifteen

"Hi." He closed the door behind him. "What'cha doing?" More worked up about this than he should be, he tried to play it cool.

"I'm recopying some of my notes." She left the books open and came to him, wrapping her arms around his neck. "I'm glad you're here, I need to talk to you. And I could use a hug."

Holt hugged her quickly, then reached up and pulled her arms down. She looked at him, obviously noticing his edginess, so he kissed her briefly on the lips. That seemed to appease her, and she took his hand and led him back to the counters.

"I need to talk to you about something, too."

"What about?" Turning, she lifted herself back onto her stool. She looked at him expectantly and smiled.

Holt leaned against the counter and put one foot up on the bottom rung of her stool. "Treat told me something today," he began, and noticed her expression darkening. "And I don't know why he would know something like this and I wouldn't."

Kira sighed and closed her eyes for a second, then looked back up to him. "I was going to talk to you tonight, Holt, that's why I--"

"Wait a minute." He held up his hands to stop her. "Let's just make sure we're riding the same mule here." Holt decided to start off slowly and ask about Zoe first. Then, maybe he'd be able to discuss the cattle purchase that brought the disease into the herd.

She waited for him to speak.

"Is it true that there's a custody battle over Zoe?" The surprised look on Kira's face shocked him. How could she hide this from him? "Well?"

Kira opened her hands. "Yes, but--"

"Why are you with me?" he asked. And wasn't he supposed to be a part of Zoe's life? A full part?

"What?"

"Getting this job was more necessary for you than I thought. Did you hook up with me so I could help you diagnose the cattle? Or because that'd make it easier to figure out how to get rid of me?"

Kira exhaled sharply and held her hand to the side of her head. "What are you talking about? You know how I feel about you. I can't believe...." She turned her back and wiped her eyes.

Holt took advantage of her turned back to peer into her notebook. And there it was, the phrase stating the disease had been introduced into the herd through a February cattle purchase. And next to it was the line of ink trailing from the last word and off the page. It was that page he'd looked at, but not read, when he was helping her to bed the other night.

His stomach clenched and his throat felt choked with mud. He made all the cattle purchases for the ranch. If it were true that he'd carelessly infected his own herd, what would his father say? What would Ben do? Disinherit him? Let control go to Treat? Holt would have nothing then.

"I meant to tell you," she said, facing him.

He glared at her, despising her duplicity.

"Why are you looking at me that way?"

Holt tried to shutter his feelings from her. "You've spent enough time on this thing." He

228

motioned to her stacks of notes, books, and petri dishes. "I think you should move on to something else, get into the day-to-day workings of the ranch now." He would turn her away from her plans and soften the blow of the truth to his father on his own. Jeez, would he go to jail?

She furrowed her brow, looking confused. "I'm not done yet, Holt, and I am into the day-to-day workings of the ranch. Remember?"

"What do you mean you're not done? You've diagnosed the disease. You've got your ten percent. Why don't you leave the rest of it to the Agency?"

Kira uncrossed her arms. "What are you saying? What is this?" She walked back toward him, slowly.

"I'm trying to get you to stop obsessing about this thing and get you to help me rebuild our business."

She shook her head. "Holt, why? It's part of my job." Her gaze was intense, as if she were trying to read his thoughts.

He hid himself from her, and it was the toughest thing he'd ever done. "I just want us to move on."

"I hope you're not thinking I won't get the ten percent if you can keep me from doing this."

So, there it was. The ten percent she was so desperate to get. Treat, for once, was right. Holt would have to leave the lab soon. He felt as sick as he did the day he learned that Ben was not his biological father.

"I just said you've got your ten percent. I just want you to stop."

"I can't. I won't." Her voice sounded as deadly as he knew his own did.

How did they get to this place? Why had he allowed himself to be so blinded by her body, her eyes, and her smile? "So that's it?"

"I guess so."

"You'll regret this." He left the lab, slamming the door behind him. At the bottom of the stairs, he patted his front shirt pocket, looking for a toothpick. There were none. He felt all of his other shirt and pants pockets, but he only found his one emergency cigarette and match. He pulled them out, looked at them in the moonlight, ran the cigarette under his nose and breathed in, long and deep. It smelled so good.

He shouldn't smoke it. He looked back at the lab. To hell with it. He deserved it. Holt ignited the match with his thumbnail and lit the one and only cigarette he had allowed himself in over three months. He held the burning match in one hand as he drew smoke through the unfiltered end. God, it was good. He felt his control coming back already, felt his raw nerves begin to calm. Holt shook the match once, tossed it to the ground, then stomped away.

Kira stared at the closed door, confused. That was out of left field. She paced the lab in circles. She thought he knew her better than to think she'd use him. And to try to stop her work--that was wrong. She had needed his support and understanding, and he'd blown it.

Kira started to feel closed in. There was no way she could continue working right now, even if she was just copying notes from one book to the other. Not after this. She had to get out of here.

230

She slammed shut the notebook she was copying from and stared at its cover, laying her hand on it like it were her bible. Inside this book was so much work. No less than her body and soul had gone into it. Nobody could possibly expect her to just end it before it was over. There was a beginning and an end to everything, and she wasn't finished yet. Of course, if he had let her speak, he'd know that it basically was over, and she just had her report to write. Kira decided to take a walk around the ranch, clear her head. Maybe then, she'd be ready to come back and write that report. Then she'd tell Holt a thing or two.

She looked down at the necklace, heavy against her sternum. She wasn't ready to call it quits with him, but he had to be receptive to some serious conversation tonight. There was no way she was going to live with a man who couldn't be straight with her, she thought, as she made her way across the grounds toward the corrals. And if there was one thing Kira knew about what had just happened, it was that he wasn't being forthright.

She walked and walked, mostly in circles around the populated areas of the ranch. She tried to review her conversation with Holt in her mind, to find some key to what was in his head. When he first entered the lab, she remembered him seeming a little uptight. He had asked her about something Treat had told him, and she'd thought for sure that he meant the diseased cattle Treat had purchased in February. But instead, he had asked her about Zoe.

And he'd gotten so angry over the custody battle.

Kira stopped, hands on hips, and looked up at the stars. As usual, they made her and her problems

231

seem so meaningless. But they weren't. They were real, and she had to deal with them. What was so odd about their encounter tonight was when he jumped right into what she was doing on the job. Instead of pursuing the Zoe thing, he got on her about work. Why?

She had already made one pass around the perimeter and decided to do another. Holt, more than anyone else, should understand her desire to do things completely, get every detail right. What was it Treat had told her tonight? He'd said Holt wasn't going to let her get her ten percent of the ranch. She hadn't believed him at the time, but Holt had brought it up almost immediately. As a matter of fact, it was one of his main reasons for wanting her to stop her work on the project. He'd told her she'd already won it.

Everyone had been so busy lately; she hadn't had time to finalize things with Ben. Heck, she hadn't even seen him in a week. Kira didn't know what to believe, and now, who to believe. She had thought she could trust Holt. She loved him.

But maybe she'd been wrong.

* * *

She wasn't going to get away with this. From his position behind a corner of the barn, he saw her leave the lab and head out toward the corrals, away from the ranch house and guesthouse. It looked like she'd be gone for a little while, but he only needed a few minutes, anyway. He just couldn't let her mess him up like this.

He made it to the lab door in shadows the whole way, avoiding the beams from the spotlights that kept most of the living areas lit. He looked around, and then slipped inside and closed the door. The light was on, and on the counter he found what he wanted.

There it was, lying open, with the phrase that could ruin it all for him, staring up at him, incriminating. He grinned and took the book to the sink in the bathroom. He tore out that page and several others before it, just to be certain he'd get everything about himself out of it, then wadded up the first one, threw it into the toilet and flushed it, watching it disappear. He decided to burn some at the same time he was flushing the others, then thought, hell, why not just light up the whole damn book?

He stood it up in the sink, its covers spread wide, the pages undulating between them. Standing up like that, it'd burn fast.

He searched all of his pockets until he found a lighter, and felt a flicker of excitement run through him. In a few seconds, it'd all be over. He flicked the metal wheel with the gas valve down, then turned the flame up all the way. It stood three inches tall. Beautiful. He touched the flame to several places between the spread pages of the book, and made sure to catch the cardboard covers on fire, too.

He was right. It went fast. So fast, he worried he might lose control of it and get caught. He'd batted at a few sparks swirling about, and hurt his hip on the bathroom counter. But, then, it finished burning. He opened the little bathroom window and waved out the smoke, then rinsed the ashes down the sink drain. He wiped his hands on his jeans. He was safe, now.

He closed the bathroom door to keep any lingering smell from entering Kira's work area, then slipped through the lab door and slinked back through the shadows the way he'd come.

* * *

Kira stopped short. She thought she saw something moving by the lab door. There it was again. Kira saw the silhouette of a man who looked like Holt leaving her lab, and she figured he'd probably come to hash it out with her again, but found her gone. Well, she wouldn't call after him. She felt much better after her walk, but wasn't ready to talk to him yet. Once he was out of sight, she returned to the lab.

Before sitting down to her copying, she went to the little refrigerator, pulled out a soda, and then swung the door shut. She headed toward her notes, but changed her mind and went back, deciding she wanted a candy bar, too. Kira opened the door again, and stuck her head inside.

She reached in and grabbed one of her favorites, hoping she'd be able to stop at just one tonight, then cocked her head. It smelled like overheated electrical wires.

She kneeled down and peered behind the refrigerator, crammed against the wall. Maybe it wasn't getting enough airflow to take the heat away. She pulled it away from the wall, but didn't see anything. It was probably nothing.

She finally got back to her work area and slid onto the stool, then cracked open her soda and took a sip. Then, she ripped open her candy bar wrapping and took a small bite, picked up her pen and looked down.

One of her notebooks was missing.

She looked around the counter-top, thinking she might have shoved it away, but it wasn't there. She looked under the counter, bending down and sticking her head beneath it. Not there, either.

Kira remembered closing it before she left, so maybe she'd put it on the shelf without thinking. With a sigh, she made her way to the bookshelves by the couch. And that's when she really smelled it. Something was burning. She noticed the closed bathroom door, which she thought she had left open. Then her eyes were drawn to the bottom, by the smoke creeping from underneath it.

Kira took the two steps to the door and swung it open, which sucked smoke right into her face. She coughed and waved her hand, trying to clear her view and the air she was breathing. She could barely see into the tiny room, but did see the flames.

The whole bathroom was on fire! She backed out quickly and closed the door. She headed toward the lab door, but turned instead and ran to gather her notes. She grabbed the book, and then thought she should take some other things, too - important papers, reports. When her arms were full she turned and stopped.

Fire dripped from the ceiling above the lab door, onto the wooden slats of the floor. The slats caught quickly and in the time it took her to blink her eyes once, her way out was blocked. Still holding her papers, Kira turned around in circles, looking for another way out.

There was no other way out. This was a refurbished tool shed, and there had only been one door. Kira knew fires consumed entire houses within minutes, but she was frozen. She hugged her papers to her chest, feeling the silver and turquoise necklace pressing into her skin.

Holt.

She had seen Holt leaving the lab. One of her lab books was missing. And now she was trapped in this burning building.

Kira dropped all her papers onto the counter-top and unbuttoned the first few buttons at the top of her shirt. She was going to get out of here, but not without her notebook. She stuffed the book into her shirt, re-buttoned it, then ran to a part of the wall that had no furniture against it and threw herself into it, hoping it would give way.

It held fast. She slammed her shoulder against it again, still with no affect, then grabbed one of the stools. She stood back, jostled the chair in her hands to get a good grip, and put her shoulder against the seat with the stool legs sticking out in front of her like a bull's horns. She was not going to die and leave Zoe.

With all her might, Kira ran, ducking her head into her shoulder behind the stool seat. The percussion of the stool legs hitting the wall sent her reeling backward, but the stool hadn't made a dent in the wall.

236

The fire had consumed over half of the room. Think, she told herself, looking around. Her eyes passed over her doctor's bag, then jerked back to it. She grabbed it, tore it open, and rummaged through its contents, throwing things out. The heat was getting to her, and the smoke hovered from the ceiling like an inverted ocean, its waves caressing her shoulders, choking her lungs. Smoke tides boiled toward the floor.

Kira dropped to her hands and knees and crawled to the part of the wall she'd tried to break through, dragging the bag with her. I will not panic, she told herself, as she felt her heart rise up in her throat. Tears streamed from her eyes, trying to rinse away the sting of the smoke. The fire roared in her ears and a beam creaked and gave way by the bathroom. She didn't take time to look over her shoulder, but re-opened her bag and dug through it until she found her motorized round-blade saw. It was designed for cutting only delicate bone and cartilage, but it would have to do. She only hoped it had a charge left in its batteries.

Although the blade wasn't wide enough to make it through the whole thickness of wood, her plan was to try to cut through at least a partial layer, outlining a shape large enough to crawl through, then to kick it through the rest of the way.

She mapped out the shape of the hole in her mind, then began cutting. She couldn't hear the whine of the saw above the growing, crackling flames, and her own coughs, but could see her progress as the blade made a very fine slice into the wood. The blade was dulling fast, catching in the groove, and she wasn't even a quarter of the way around the circumference she needed. She pressed her body against her arms, trying to help the cutting with pressure.

Kira grew frantic and saw Zoe's face in her mind...then Cleo's. Kira pushed her face into her shoulder, trying to use her shirt to filter her air, then decided she had to scream for help. It would use up precious amounts of oxygen, but it might be her only chance now.

Terror filled her eyes with more tears, while choking sobs racked her body. She screamed for help, barely recognizing the high-pitched shriek as her own voice. She coughed more, realized she wasn't getting enough air. She was going to pass out.

She brought her right foot up and pounded it against the area she'd already sawed. Anything might work, she kept telling herself. She couldn't give up. Not yet, not ever. Kira vowed right then and there that she'd continue sawing, screaming, and kicking, until she died.

Muffled shouts reached her through the wall. "I'm in here!" she screamed, not pausing in her efforts for escape. "I'm in here! Help me! Help!"

She couldn't breathe. The smoke was only three inches above the floor. She laid down in a fetal position, facing the wall, to allow herself to still kick the wall and cut the last part of the opening, while keeping her head as far away from the encroaching flames and smoke as possible. She couldn't get as much leverage, but managed to finish the outline of her opening.

Cleo's face appeared again and looked troubled. She told Kira to try harder. For Zoe. Kira decided to risk putting her head closer to the flames so she could put more force behind her kicks. She braced herself on her arms behind herself, her legs poised in front of the sawed outline, and kicked. The thud of her feet as she repeated the motion over and over began to fade as she became weak and dizzy. Moisture sizzled out of her skin, and she smelled her hair begin to singe.

She smiled at the vision of her sister. Maybe being with Cleo would be better. She was so tired; she closed her eyes.

"Move faster, harder!" Holt yelled at his men. "I can't hear her anymore!"

The entire ranch had come running when they'd seen the fire. They had been outside for over a minute now, chopping at the only wall not covered in flames, using axes, picks, shovels, hoes, anything they could get their hands on. From the moment they'd discovered Kira was inside, not one of their faces held anything but heart-pounding fear and determination.

Catherine, her nightgown billowing in the air currents created by the blaze, sprayed the building with a feeble drizzle from a garden hose. Holt and Treat fought side by side, wielding axes against the wall while Ben ordered some of the men to affix a large pump and fire hose to the underground water tank nearby. They lived so far out into the desert that the fire department wouldn't arrive until it was over.

Finally, they split the wall open and black and gray smoke boiled out, forcing the men to step back.

Holt ran inside, unable to see through the smoke. He figured she'd try for the door, so he blindly headed that direction. He stumbled over her immediately and his heart wrenched when he discovered she was unconscious.

The flames licked at the floorboard, just inches from her head. The flesh on his hands burned when he lifted her body into his arms. He cradled her head under his chin, protecting her body with his own, then ran back out and continued running until he was at least a couple hundred yards away from the burning shed.

Then he kneeled on the ground, laid her down, and checked for her pulse and breathing. When he found her heartbeat, tears stung his eyes. Catherine ran up with a wet cloth. He took it from her and carefully wiped the smoke from Kira's face, avoiding several burns on her skin.

Slowly, she woke, then rolled to her side, coughing violently. Holt tried to help her lean over, holding onto her arm with one hand, his other arm wrapped around her shoulders. "No!" she screamed, breathy and hoarse. She struggled in his arms.

"It's okay, it's okay." He soothed her, holding her tightly. "You're safe, Kira. I've got you. You're safe." She still fought against him, and he thought she might be delirious, confused. She struggled to get up, and Holt couldn't hold her.

"Let me go, damn it!" she yelled angrily. The look he saw in her eyes stopped him dead. She hated him and was afraid of him at the same time. And then it hit him: she thought he was responsible for this. Stunned, he released her.

Kira rose to one knee, put her other foot on the ground and got up, then walked a few steps toward the blaze. Holt could see her body heaving for air as she stared at the collapsing building, and wondered where she found the strength to even stand. She looked back at him, and he saw that she had closed him out. It almost killed him.

Kira glanced at the fire once more, then she wobbled away. Holt got up to go to her, thinking she wouldn't make it another step, when Candace ran up with Zoe screaming in her arms.

Kira stopped, and slowly collapsed, just as the walls of the shed fell in with a loud clap.

Chapter Sixteen

Holt waited a whole thirty-six hours before going to see her, because the doctor said she'd be in bed at least that long. He was desperate to talk to her, touch her. He'd been angry with her that night, but not enough to want to hurt her, let alone kill her. Hell, he hadn't even known she was in the lab. He had gone there to talk with her more. She wasn't there, so he'd left. Still, he felt terrible.

Holt glanced at the charred, blackened ruins that were once the shed, and Kira's lab, visible from the open barn doors. He was trying to keep himself busy, but close by. Two fire investigators crouched in the remains. He found himself wondering how something like this small, burnt building could keep two investigators so busy. Then, he hoped they wouldn't find out he'd started it.

It had to be the match he'd used to light his cigarette. He had only shaken it once to put it out before tossing it on the ground, right next to the shed's foundation. He closed his eyes, willing it not to be true, and shook his head. He hadn't even looked to make sure the flame was out. But Holt hadn't told any of this to the fire marshal when he'd been questioned.

When he'd heard the shouts and then seen the burning shed, at first, he was relieved that he knew Kira was away from it. Then, he'd heard noises from inside, and her desperate screams mingled with the crackling flames. It had scared the holy hell out of him. He'd grabbed an ax and fought for his life.

242

At that moment, he had realized what an idiot he'd been. He was going to tear that wall open with his bare hands if he'd had to, because he loved Kira, and he knew he would die if she perished in that blaze. So he was fighting for his very existence. Even now, nothing else mattered but Kira.

Holt wound up some new rope he'd just stretched and placed the coils on nails lined up along the barn walls. He rolled his eyes, remembering the necklace. What a dolt. He gave Kira that family heirloom necklace, but told her he wasn't marrying her. How could he even have thought something so ridiculous? Of course he was going to marry her! He'd be absolutely crazy not to.

It didn't matter that he'd infected the herd. It was an accident. He had always bought what he thought were the best animals for the ranch, and if some of them were sick, then he didn't know it and couldn't have seen it during his inspection of them. Either his father would see it that way, or he wouldn't.

Holt hung up the last loop of rope. He'd waited long enough. He dusted off his hands and made his way toward the guesthouse.

Candace opened the door after he knocked, and he could tell something was wrong by the look on her face. She just stood there, looking strangely sympathetic, silent. He brushed past her and tore down the hall to Kira's room.

"Kira?" he called, pushing open her door.

She wasn't there. Her room still looked lived in, but the bed was stripped, the sheets and blankets were on the floor. It felt dead.

"She's not here, Holt," Candace said in a small voice behind him. He continued looking around the room, and felt Candace slip past him.

"She said to give you this." Candace held out a cotton dishtowel in both hands, and he took it. Without unwrapping it, he knew it was the necklace.

He forced his eyes to leave the symbol of pain in his hands, and move to Candace's remorseful face. "When?" he croaked, not trusting his voice to say anything more. How did she do it without him knowing?

"Last night. After dark." Candace expelled a little puff of disbelief. "She'd insisted that she and Zoe had to leave. She--"

He grabbed Candace's forearm, startling her.

"She's left, Holt. Moved off the ranch. Quit her job."

The news hit him harder than Treat had that day in the field, just after that bull had almost mowed Kira down. He released his grip on Candace's arm and saw her rub it. "Sorry," he mumbled, grimacing. "Where is she?"

Candace hesitated. "She told me not to tell you."

With a nod, he accepted it. He'd find out where she was. Surely his parents knew, and if they wouldn't tell him, he'd just hunt for her. He left Kira's bedroom and ran into Treat in the hallway, but Holt didn't stop. Something about his brother struck him as different. He didn't seem as flashy. The recent events had probably affected him like everyone else.

He went straight to the office, where he knew his father was poring over insurance papers.

"Where is she?" he boomed, throwing open the office door, causing Ben's eyes to jerk up.

Ben looked back down at his papers and appeared to be engrossed in them when he answered Holt. "Holt. Sit down."

Holt was caught off guard. He'd expected his father to yell or lecture. Holt stepped toward the chairs.

"Shut the door," Ben said, sounding disinterested.

Holt walked back, grabbed the doorknob and silently shut the door. Then, he turned and sat down, stiff with expectancy. He sat without a word, looking at Ben, waiting to be addressed. Ben's blase tone didn't fool Holt, or lull him into a relaxed state. It was because it was so out of character that Holt's senses peaked. Maybe this was it--the moment he'd dreaded--when he had to look into his father's eyes, and see the disgust and disappointment.

Ben looked at him over his reading glasses, and then laid the papers down. "You know Kira's left."

"Yes, sir. And I want to know where she is."

Ben eyed him several seconds. "Where she is doesn't matter. I'm not sure specifically why, but she asked me not to tell you where she went." Ben stopped and examined him again, as if waiting for some telltale sign from him. Holt concentrated on remaining expressionless.

"Of course, you understand," he continued, "that she's quit her job."

Holt nodded.

"And that means she's forfeited her ten percent share."

Now Ben looked at him almost accusingly. He deserved it. A month ago, he would have been ecstatic. But not today. It hadn't even dawned on him until his father said it. Kira had felt so strongly about the fire, and probably their argument, that she gave up what she had fought so hard for, and won.

"Finally, a reaction." Holt looked up and realized he'd let his eyes drop to the ground. "But you're not as happy as I thought you'd be." Ben took off his glasses and dangled them from the first finger and thumb of his right hand. He again appeared to be waiting for some kind of explanation, but Holt had no intention of giving him one.

Ben shrugged slowly, once, then set his glasses down on the pages. "It's no matter, I guess. She's gone and we have to move on. At least she's promised not to sue us because of the fire."

Holt felt a surge of anger that his father would say that about Kira. She had almost died!

"Yeah." Ben rubbed his jaw. "It could have been bad for us, but she just seemed anxious to leave. Could have been expensive for us." He rubbed his hands over his eyes in a deliberate motion, seemingly unaffected by the whole thing.

How could he be so callous? "You know, you shouldn't--" he began.

"You wanted to see me?" Treat interrupted, standing at the door he'd just opened. Holt had been so intent on Ben's words that he hadn't even heard the latch tumble.

"Come in, Treat. Take a seat." Ben waited until his other son had settled into the chair next to Holt before speaking again. "I wanted you both here because the fire investigators, as you know, have been combing through the debris, trying to find the cause of the fire."

Holt shifted in his chair, and noticed Treat doing the same thing.

"At first, the investigators thought it was some of the wiring that was done to convert the building to a lab."

Ben then pointedly looked at Holt and he cringed inside. He hadn't thought of that. What if his work had caused it? That would be another major screw-up to add to his growing list. Holt held his father's gaze, willing him to get on with it.

"Anyway, they said they've found some things we'd all like to see and they'll be here in a few minutes."

Holt and Treat nodded at their father. Ben nodded back, then returned to his paperwork, replacing the glasses onto his nose.

The silence became almost unbearable. The only sound in the room was Treat's strumming of his fingers on his left boot that he'd crossed over his right knee. Holt looked at his brother, and Treat just shrugged at him.

Holt attempted to prepare himself to be ruined and shamed. He was sure Ben would announce that Holt had not only sickened the herd, but also started the fire. It was the end of his life and career as he knew it, and he'd be lucky if his father let him shovel manure when this was over.

Sweat ran down his sides, but he ignored it and threw all his mental energies into just looking and acting calm, and figuring out what he was going to

247

say. He'd have to think of something that might lessen his father's anger and the consequences Ben would enforce upon him.

Finally, they heard a knock on the door, and one of the investigators entered. "Mr. Crockett?"

"Mr. Fritz." Ben motioned to the man. "Come on in. Tell us what you've found." Ben indicated he should sit in one of several extra chairs placed to the side of the desk, and the man took a seat.

Holt saw Fritz look at him and then his brother as he set a manila envelope and his briefcase on the desk. He cleared his throat.

He must have been in his fifties, and Holt knew he'd spent the last thirty years doing fire investigations. The guy seemed a little prissy, with his immaculate dress slacks and tie. One of the fire fighters told him Fritz actually wore these things underneath his coveralls so he could look authoritative after rummaging through filthy investigation sites. In addition, the man was perfectly groomed. His handlebar mustache looked freshly waxed and his posture was steel-rod straight.

Keeping his eyes on Fritz, Holt rubbed his sweaty palms down his thighs. This was it. Stay cool. Holt swallowed, and the sides of his throat felt like sandpaper scraping together.

"Mr. Fritz, have you met my two sons?" Ben motioned first to Holt, then Treat, and made the introductions. Fritz gave each of their hands a brief shake, and then returned to his manila folder.

"I have our report, Mr. Crockett." He pulled out a stapled stack of papers. Holt leaned forward to try to make out some of the words as Fritz handed it to

Ben. "This is your copy, and I've also given a copy to the police."

"So you found something that would indicate this wasn't an accident?" Ben asked.

"We did, sir."

There was a pause, and Holt almost blurted out that it really had been an accident, but he took in a slow breath, and then exhaled even more slowly, counting the number of seconds he could draw it out.

"Well, out with it, man. What did you find?" Ben was now back to his usual gruff self, and even though Holt felt his future crumbling around him, he also felt a slight sense of comfort in his father's return to familiar ways.

"We've found that the fire started in the bathroom."

The bathroom? Holt tried to reason out how his match could have possibly started the fire on the outside, and moved to the bathroom. He knew he wasn't hiding his surprise well, and shifted his eyes, under furrowed brows, between his father and Fritz.

"Yes." Fritz' voice brought Holt back from his thoughts. "We found that some paper had been burned in the sink. We found the ashes in the drain."

Holt leaned forward, thinking he might have misunderstood the man. What was he talking about? Why would Kira have been burning anything at all? He pushed those questions aside, and tried to concentrate on what Fritz was saying.

"And why do you think it was deliberate? Isn't it possible Ms. McGovern had burned something?"

249

"No, sir." Fritz crossed his left leg over his right. "We interviewed Ms. McGovern before she left your employ, and since then, too. She said she did not burn anything, but was away from the lab for a while. She also said she saw someone leaving the lab just as she returned. She was trapped by the fire shortly thereafter."

Ben took the news well, Holt thought. He nodded, accepting what Fritz said as the truth, then glanced at Holt, then Treat. Holt felt truly sunk. Kira must have seen him leaving the lab. "Go on."

"Well, sir, we know that sparks from this fire made it up into the ceiling from the sink, and we've found some evidence that we believe tells us who started the fire." Fritz dug into the manila envelope and pulled out his hand, closed into a fist. He opened his hand toward Ben, but Holt could see what lay on his palm. He gave his brother a deadly stare, and gripped the arms of his chair.

In Fritz's hand lay a very large ruby. Although blackened with smoke and grime, it was still, quite obviously, one of the stones from Treat's rodeo award buckle. Treat had a look of innocence on his face, apparently pretending not to know what the stone was.

Holt wanted to kill him. Ben looked at Treat, growing rage tinged with disbelief coloring his face, but Holt was sure his father felt nothing close to what he himself felt.

"As you can see," Fritz said, "this is a stone from a rodeo buckle. Mr. Treat Crockett is the only person on this ranch who owns one. We're confident that this stone was knocked out of the buckle when he

250

started the fire in the lab sink, and if we look at the buckle, we suspect we'll find a stone of exact dimension missing from it."

Fritz turned his attention to Treat, and moved his hand into Treat's line of vision for his examination.

"You can't prove a damn thing." Treat chuckled like he thought they were idiots. "Besides, what would have been my motive? There would have been no reason for me to do this. I liked Ms. McGovern. Hell, I wanted to sleep with her."

Holt rose half way up from his seat, imagining his hands around Treat's scrawny neck.

"Sit down," his father ordered, without taking his eyes off his youngest son. Fritz put the stone back into his envelope and laid the packet on the desk. "As I said earlier, we've interviewed Ms. McGovern since she's left. She informed us that you brought infected foreign cattle into your herd."

Holt frowned at Fritz. Had Kira made a mistake? He always bought the cattle, not Treat. He was the cow man; Treat just rode horses. Holt fought with himself on whether he should speak up, or wait it out.

"That's a lie," Treat said with a humorless smirk. "It's my word against hers."

"No it's not, son," Ben said. He sounded defeated, his voice low, tired. Holt saw Treat look at his father, surprised, and Holt then looked to Ben also. "Kira made her final report, and she has all her documentation--"

"That's impossible!"

"Why?" Holt asked. "Because you tried to destroy her records?" It had hit him suddenly when Ben was

251

speaking. Why had he allowed himself to believe what his brother had told him that night?

Clearly, Treat had somehow found out about the contents of Kira's report, and had tried to get rid of the evidence. He probably threw in that bit about Zoe because he knew Holt would ask Kira about it, and assume everything Treat had said was true, if half of it proved out.

Treat narrowed his eyes at Holt, an intense look of hatred on his face. Fritz crossed his legs, looking satisfied and prepared to wait.

"Treat." Ben waited until his son looked at him. "Kira told me she warned you about her report before coming to me. She wanted you to be prepared. Her report says it was a mistake; we both know that's not likely."

Treat shook his head. "All right. I bought the cattle. I knew it was a shady deal, but I got them cheap, and they looked fine." He paused. "Hell, it should've been Holt. It wasn't even my job, but you sent me anyway. So it's your own damn fault this happened."

Holt looked at his father. Ben's gaze remained steady on Treat, and Holt returned his attention to his brother, expending so much energy on holding his aggression in check. He remembered now.

Ben had sent Treat on that cattle buying expedition and it had really rankled Holt. Ben said it was because Treat needed more experience, but Holt thought Ben was grooming Treat to take over.

"And the fire's your fault, too. You expect so damn much all the time. I *had* to burn her book."

252

"Are you ready, officers?" Holt heard Fritz ask. The man was looking toward the door, and Holt noticed two uniformed police officers standing by. Again, Holt was astounded that he had not heard their entrance. The officers nodded and moved forward. Treat looked back at them, then at Ben, with a look of alarm. One officer stood behind Treat's chair, and the other began reading Treat his Miranda Rights.

"You have a right to remain silent..."

"Dad!" Treat yelled, rising from his seat. The officer standing behind Treat placed his hand on Treat's shoulder in warning. Holt stared at Treat, but Ben affected a look of disinterest as he watched Treat's desperate moves to save himself.

"It was an accident. I didn't start the fire on purpose! I only wanted to burn her book." He emphasized each word. The officers took Treat by his arms and raised him to a standing position. The officer who had read Treat his rights patted him down, removing his firearm from his holster and a knife from his boot. The other officer brought Treat's arms behind him and fastened one handcuff to his right wrist. Treat jerked his arms away, and the officers struggled with him, got him under control, and finished cuffing his hands behind him.

"Aw, come on, Dad," he cried. "This isn't necessary."

Ben nodded to Fritz who picked up his briefcase and the envelope and left the office. The two officers turned Treat around and dragged him toward the door.

"Son, this is one I can't help you out of," Ben said.

Holt watched his father replace his glasses and bring the insurance papers up to his face.

Holt did feel a little bit of sympathy for his brother. After all, he grew up protected from all consequences of any actions he ever took. He never learned the concept of cause and effect, so why would he have done anything differently? Treat's voice echoed in the foyer, still begging Ben for help, as the front door opened, then shut.

When the house fell quiet, Holt waited for Ben to do or say something.

Ben sighed, laid the papers down, and took off his glasses. He looked up at Holt. "If what Treat says is true, he'll get off relatively easy. Not completely, but he won't get an attempted murder charge."

Holt nodded. He would tell Candace, and let her stay on the ranch for as long as she needed. She was engaged to his buffoon brother, after all.

"Holt. Son."

Holt raised his eyebrows to indicate he was listening.

"I owe you an apology."

Holt furrowed his brow and gave his father a questioning look. He just couldn't find his words just yet.

"I realized just a few minutes ago that I'd been way too lenient with Treat, and that's why he got himself into this mess." He looked into the distance, past Holt's head. "I couldn't let it go on. I can't do what he's expecting this time." Ben shook his head, and then looked back to Holt. "He almost killed someone."

Holt nodded, feeling that unrequited urge to kill Treat stick in his craw.

"And I realized, too, that I'd expected more out of you because of my leniency with him." He waited for Holt to nod once more. "It wasn't fair to you, and I'm sorry, son." Ben looked at Holt.

Holt paused, letting his father's words sink in. Ben had no idea what Holt had been through all these years, but it was a sincere apology, which went a long way toward repairing the damage of the past.

"Hell, Dad. I accept."

Ben's eyes teared up.

* * *

"Kira!" Candace cried when Kira opened the door.

"Candace? What's wrong?" Candace didn't answer but went straight into Kira's arms. Kira held her and listened to Candace's dainty sniffles and cries. "What's happened, honey? I didn't expect you until tomorrow." She led Candace to the couch, next to Zoe, who sat on the floor playing with a doll, and they sat down. Kira left one arm around her friend's shoulders and peered into her face.

"Oh, Kira, it was terrible. They've arrested Halloween." Candace unwadded a tissue she'd been holding in her hand and sobbed into it.

"Arrested him? Why?"

"For starting the fire that almost killed you."

"Halloween started the fire? Are they sure?"

255

She nodded miserably. "They found a stone from his buckle in the rubble, and he's admitted it. He said he had to burn your book." Candace hiccupped and dabbed at her eyes. "Oh, Kira. I gave the ring back to Holt and asked him to tell Halloween I couldn't marry him. I knew he was a little irresponsible." She cried more. "But, I didn't know he was capable of such...such...Ohhhh..."

Kira pulled Candace back into her arms and rocked her. "I'm so, so sorry."

"I just can't marry him now, can I?" she asked into Kira's neck.

"No, I guess not." Kira wanted to smack him for hurting her best friend. It seemed worse to her than starting the fire and deliberately trying to wipe out her evidence. Kira's thoughts led to Holt but she stopped them. Candace needed her. "You made the right decision."

"I know. It just hurts so bad."

"Shh ... I know. I know." And she did. It had only been four days since she had left Holt and her heart had a long way to go before it recovered. She'd felt like a coward, leaving in the night, but she couldn't face him, not thinking he may have started the fire, and that he was still against her owning a share of the ranch. Well, he didn't start the fire, but she couldn't trust him, just like Candace couldn't trust Treat. At least, they could console each other.

As if Candace had read her thoughts, she said, "Oh, and listen to me going on when you're hurting just as much. Aren't you?" Candace sat up and hugged her friend.

Kira smiled wanly. "It didn't turn out well for either of us. I thought it would have worked out for you," she said trying to steer the conversation back to Candace.

"Me, too." Candace held Kira's hands in hers. "You deserve to be loved. I'm sorry, Kira."

"Thanks." She fought the tears she still had refused to shed over him. "I thought he did, but I was wrong. He made me think he wanted me to win my share of the ranch, but he never did. I think he was deceiving me the whole time."

"Oh, Kira, no," Candace said.

"Oh, yes."

"No, Kira. I know you said this before when you left, but I know Holt loved you. He still does. I don't know about the ranch thing, but I do know this."

"How can you be sure? Didn't you just say you thought Halloween loved you and you can't marry him?"

"I can't marry him, but not because he doesn't love me. He loves me, but there were parts of him that were off limits to me." Kira shook her head at her friend, and Candace nodded. "I know, I know. I did it again." Fresh tears streamed down her face and her body shook.

"Oh," Kira crooned, then brought Candace back under her arm. "Don't be so hard on yourself. We've both learned a lot, and now we just have to try to go forward, okay?"

Candace sniffled again, and put on a brave face. "Okay. You're right." Candace gave Kira a strong hug. "Thanks for being my friend. You're always here when I need you, and I appreciate it."

"I know you do." She forced a slight smile. Boy, were they a pair.

"But I was serious about Holt loving you, Kira. Maybe you should talk to him. He's desperate to see you."

"I don't think so. He made his position clear the last time we spoke." Kira got up and made her way to the kitchen to get both of them something to drink. "Maybe you're right about him loving me, but that doesn't change the fact that he couldn't bring himself to accept my winning ten percent. So." she held two glasses, "is that really love?"

She brought out the ice tray from the freezer and began dumping the cubes into the two glasses. Her traitorous mind kept telling her that there could have been another explanation, especially since he had told her she'd won her share of the ranch. But if that were true, then why hadn't he just come out with the truth? She thought they had an honest relationship.

"Well, if I tell you something, will you promise not to get mad at me?" Candace asked.

Kira frowned at her friend and handed her a glass of ice water. "Since when have I ever gotten mad at you? Of course I promise." Kira sat next to her and waited.

"Before I left, Holt asked me to give you a letter. I didn't want to take it, but he begged me. You don't have to take it." Candace pulled out a crinkled envelope from her big drawstring purse and laid it on the coffee table.

Kira looked down at it, and didn't even want to touch it. Holt had touched it, and if she did, too, she might not be able to keep herself from ripping it open to devour his words.

"I probably won't read it. But thanks. I'm not mad." Well, she was, kind of. At Holt. Who could resist him when he was determined?

Candace sighed. "Oh, good. Now, at least if I ever see him again and he asks, I can tell him I delivered it."

"You won't ever see him again."

Chapter Seventeen

That night, after Candace and Zoe were asleep, Kira stared at the ceiling. She had stuffed Holt's letter in the back of the little box of bills she kept on the kitchen counter. In her mind, she could see its corner sticking up, beckoning her to come and open it, read it. She closed her eyes and lay in bed a while longer, still unable to sleep. Finally, she threw off the covers and went to the kitchen, disgusted with herself.

She turned on the light over the stove and stared at the little corner of Holt's letter, leaning against the counter with her arms crossed trying to explain to herself why she should just throw it away.

Damn it. She grabbed the envelope and tore it open. She unfolded the one sheet of paper, then ran her fingers over Holt's signature before reading his words:

Dearest Kira,

> *I need to see you. To erase that look in your eyes.*
> *It was Treat. It's always Treat. I should have believed in you.*
> *I'm begging you - Please see me.*

Holt

He wasn't the only one who didn't give the other the benefit of the doubt that night, and she regretted it. But, she couldn't see him; not yet. Too much had happened. She felt confused. Besides, he hadn't said anything about getting back together, or that he loved her.

No, she wouldn't run back to him with any hopes of that. Her feelings were too raw; she needed time to think. She folded and slipped the letter back into its envelope, then slid it underneath the cutting-board on the counter, to keep until...whenever she felt ready.

* * *

Holt sat at the desk in the office, looking at the manila envelope from Fritz. It had been sent to them after the police removed all the evidence they required. Ben told Holt to take care of it, since he was in charge now. He finally had what he'd always wanted: complete control of the ranch. But it was a hollow victory. For one, it wasn't a victory, as in a win. And two, something, someone else, had taken first priority in his life.

Kira.

If Candace had given his letter to her, then she got it over a week ago. He knew she had read the letter. Her curiosity would have gotten the better of her. After thinking about things more, though, he'd decided it wouldn't be right for him to chase after her. He didn't want her to feel threatened and he wanted her to make her own choice. And, it seemed that she'd made it. So that left nothing but to shove on, to throw himself into the running of the ranch.

Holt opened the envelope and pulled out a sheaf of papers. There was a letter on top from the court, saying basically, 'here are copies of the police reports you requested'. Holt figured his father wasn't leaving anything to chance and wanted to be up on things, should a lawsuit arise. Holt shook his head, knowing Kira wouldn't do that, still thinking his dad was being callous.

He paged through the report slowly until he came to Kira's, then read through her statements, which was torture for him. It brought back the fear of losing her in the fire, the look in her eyes after she'd regained consciousness, and mountains of regret. He found the part where she had told Fritz about someone leaving her lab that night. But, she hadn't mentioned who she thought it was.

Holt tossed the papers onto the desk. She had thought he'd done it, yet she didn't turn him in. Kira wasn't a stupid woman, so that could only mean she loved him. She'd told him she loved him before, but only people with crazy love protected someone they believed to be guilty of some crime.

Nasty hope wheedled its way into his brain. Holt was crazy in love with Kira, and now he knew she was crazy in love with him. Did that mean he might have a chance of convincing her to come back to him?

No, damn it. He wouldn't pressure her.

Holt slid down a few inches in the chair, looking at the reports. His eyes wandered to the envelope and he noticed a little bulge at one of the bottom corners.

He stretched his arm across the desk and caught the edge of it with his fingers, then slid it toward himself. He picked it up and reached inside, grabbing something round with a chain.

Kira's necklace. He held it in his stiff, open palm. Seeing it this closely, he realized it wasn't just a ball of metal like he'd thought. It had a claw-like clasp on either side of it, but one of them was broken at the hinge. The silver was blackened, like Treat's ruby had been.

Holt unfastened the other clasp and the silver ball fell open like an accordion. It was a locket holding six tiny pictures. He swallowed a dry lump in his throat, feeling like he was invading Kira's privacy, but he couldn't help himself. This was a part of Kira, something he knew had been, and was important to her. He felt closer to her just holding it.

The first picture was of a woman who looked incredibly like Kira. It had to be Kira's sister, Cleo. The next was a wedding picture of Cleo and her husband. Holt examined the pictures, one by one, and realized they depicted the progression of Cleo's life, including Zoe's first baby picture, and then a couple pictures of the threesome. Holt refolded the locket and refastened the clasp, then squeezed it in his fist. This was precious to Kira. She had to have it back.

Holt drew a deep breath and exhaled it quickly. Zoe was so lucky to have Kira as a mother. It was a relief that such a wonderful woman was willing to love and raise Zoe as her own.

Holt paused and ran those thoughts through his head again. Suddenly, he knew he was the world's biggest fool. Kira had accepted Zoe into her life and was doing a great job parenting her. Kira had also accepted him into hers and Zoe's lives, believing he could be a good parent to a child that was not his by blood. Kira had believed in him more than he had believed in himself.

He had allowed the knowledge that Ben was not his real father to taint his entire life, assuming that Ben couldn't love him enough or want to raise him as his own. Holt had quite possibly altered his relationship with Ben all on his own, and he wondered if maybe that might have even had an effect on Treat and Ben's relationship.

He had wasted so many years feeling bad about himself, and it was all for nothing.

Holt jumped up, dropped Kira's locket into his front shirt pocket, and began pacing the office floor. This cast a whole new light on everything: his relationships with Kira, his parents, his crew.

And himself.

Holt stopped and stared at a package sitting on the sofa table. It held a gift he'd ordered for Kira days before the fire. The past week and a half, since she'd left, he had wondered what the hell to do with it.

Well, he knew what he was going to do with it, now. He was going to find her, give it to her, and bring her home. His father knew where she was. He strode past the couch, swung open the door, and went in search of his dad.

Holt rounded the corner of the hall on his way toward the kitchen, knowing Ben liked to jaw with his mother over coffee, and ran right into him. Surprised, he grabbed Ben's forearms to steady his father. Ben looked much older today than he did just yesterday. "I'm sorry, Dad. Are you okay?" Ben was as tall as Holt was, but he seemed to have shrunk a couple inches.

"I'm fine, son. I was looking for you."

"Me, too, I need to talk to you."

Ben turned around and walked back the way he'd come. "Well, come on into the kitchen. Your mother and I need to talk to you first."

Holt followed, wondering about his father's serious tone. It wasn't the business-like, serious tone he'd used in the office when he had called Holt and Treat in to talk to the fire investigator and the police. It was much more personal.

They made it into the kitchen, and Holt saw Catherine sitting primly, expectantly, with her cow-print coffee cup in front of her. He smiled and leaned down to kiss her cheek as Ben walked around his wife and returned to his seat.

"Sit down, Son."

Holt sat at the round table, facing his parents, their positions forming the points of a triangle. "What is it?"

Ben sighed. "Son, Treat used his one telephone call last week to try to convince me to bail him out and make his problems go away."

"And you said?" Holt knew this was an important issue, but he really just wanted to get his information about Kira and be gone.

"We told him no, of course, but that's not why we need to talk to you."

Holt looked from Ben to Catherine, then back to his father and frowned.

Ben leaned forward on his forearms, holding his soup-bowl sized, cowboy print coffee mug. Holt

265

couldn't help but notice the contrast between the cups in his parents' hands and their facial expressions.

Ben sighed and hesitated. "Holt, part of Treat's argument for the necessity of me bailing him out was that he's our only full-blooded son." He motioned to Catherine, and she looked into her coffee.

"Yes, sir?" He swallowed. This was going to be painful. He hoped he could've just put it behind him without mention.

"Holt, Treat told me where you two got that notion, and I'm here to tell you, it's a bunch of bull." Ben emphasized the last words, surprising Holt that he'd speak like that in front of his mother. Holt looked at her and she nodded.

"We heard the rumors ourselves, back when we got married and had you. But, we knew what the truth was and just figured it'd blow over."

"Well, it didn't," Holt said, stunned.

"When did you hear?" Ben asked.

Holt leaned his elbow on the table and pressed his forehead into his hand, eyes closed. "About twenty years ago."

"Holt." Catherine laid her palm on his shoulder.

Holt looked at Ben. "Why didn't you ever say anything?" He sighed and shook his head. "All these years ..."

"Son ..."

"Why did you favor Treat over me?" He saw the shocked looks on their faces, but continued. "And did you really think it would just die out over time? Here?" The ranching community was old and everyone knew everyone's business for generations-back, and miles around. "You always held me back, yet eased Treat's way, encouraged him."

Ben's shoulders drooped but he didn't take his eyes from Holt's face. Holt turned to Catherine. "Mother." He took her hand from his shoulder and held it gently in his. "Didn't you see it?" Her face strained and tears glazed her eyes. Holt looked sadly at them both. "I'm not trying to blame you." He paused when Catherine sniffled. "But you've got to see how all of these things would add up to a thirteen year old kid." Holt shook is head again. "Twenty years ..."

Catherine released his hand, pulled a tissue from the sleeve of her housecoat and held it to her eyes. Ben palmed his mug, rolling it between his hands, studying his cold coffee.

"Son," he began. He looked at Catherine and she nodded at him. Ben sighed deeply. "Before I married your mother, she'd had some trouble."

"With Hiram Bogie?" he asked, quietly.

"Yes." Ben looked at Catherine and she squeezed his hand, and then continued the story for him.

"Holt, Hiram raped me when I was twenty." She reached out and touched Holt's forearm, stopping him from speaking. "Things were different back then. Some body else might have been strung up to the nearest saguaro, or dealt with in the courts." Her lips formed a grim line. "But not Joshua Bogie's son. He was untouchable, and, after that, so was I. As far as decent society was concerned."

"That's when your mother's father came to me," Ben said. "I had been a bachelor forever, and old Mac Grittman and I had been friends for just as

267

long." He paused and looked out the window as if remembering. "I never told him, but somehow he knew I had fallen in love with his daughter, who was young enough to be my own daughter." At that, Ben and Catherine smiled at each other. "He told me what had happened. And he wanted her protected. So, I married her."

"But who am I?" Holt asked.

"You're our son, Holt," Catherine said.

"Holt, when your mother got pregnant, we were pretty sure I was the father, but we didn't care."

Holt studied him, intently.

"But I can tell you without a doubt that you are my full-blooded son." Ben shook his head and chuckled. "You are just as mule-headed and serious as I ever was."

Holt began to deny it, but Ben cut him off.

"And whether you can see it or not, you are the spitting image of me. Well, when I was your age."

Holt sat silently for a moment. "But what about Treat?" he asked, still not totally convinced. "Why did you make it so easy for him, so different?"

"Holt, look at him." Ben held up his right palm. "He seems to have been born irresponsible." He sighed. "I don't know, maybe I made him worse, but I knew I didn't have to worry about you. I had to worry about him." Ben leaned back in his chair. "Would he succeed? And at what? I just wanted him to choose something other than women and booze. The rodeo, the ranch, whatever." Ben's smile was resigned when he looked at Catherine again. "She tried to tell me, but I wouldn't listen."

"Just like before," Catherine said.

"Before what?" Holt asked.

Ben looked as if he were deciding whether to tell him or not. "Well, she tried to convince me to marry her at least a year before she dated that snake Bogie. Said we belonged together." He sighed again. "But I wouldn't hear of it. She was my best friend's kid, for chrissakes." He took his wife's hand between his and grew more serious. "But, the point is, Son, I've hurt you and I'm sorry. I didn't see. I just didn't. I hope you can forgive me."

Holt breathed slowly and examined his father, then smiled at his mother. "I already have."

"Good." They smiled at him and exhaled.

"And, I hope you'll learn more quickly than I did, to listen to your woman more carefully. They know." He shook his finger at no one in particular.

"Dad, I already have," Holt said, laughing. They stood and exchanged hugs and Holt kissed his mother's cheek. "And that brings me to why I was looking for you this morning."

* * *

Holt pulled up to a small house with a 'for sale' sign in front, which had a 'sold' sign stuck on top of it. Kira had moved fast. She had bought a house and gotten another job, in just a few days. He admired her grit, but he would not allow his woman to work for any other rancher. Quitting that job would be the first thing she did, after taking him back.

He knocked on the door, and after a moment, it swung open. "Holt," Candace said with surprise.

"Kira said I'd never see you again." She smiled. "But I'm glad I have."

"You're gonna be seeing a lot more of me from here on out, Candace. Where is she?" He put the tip of his right boot on the threshold.

"She's in court today. She's going to find out if she gets to keep Zoe or not, and it all depends on this house and her new job."

"Damn." Holt knew these decisions depended upon not just having a house and job, but that both were stable and steady. It wasn't going to look good for Kira that she'd changed jobs and homes in such a short time. "When is she scheduled to go before the judge?"

"In half an hour. She went early to meet with her attorney, and Zoe and I are going to catch up with her. As a matter of fact..." Turning around, she picked up the car seat with Zoe strapped inside. "We're leaving right now."

Holt took the baby from her and waited while Candace locked the door. She turned and looked at him. "Are you coming?"

"Damn right," he said.

"Good for you. Want to follow me or come with us?"

"I'll follow."

On the way, Candace drove too slowly. Then she got too far ahead of him, and crossed over the train tracks just before the warning lights started blinking and the barriers came down. He was stuck and would be for ten minutes, because this was the long, afternoon train.

Holt waited, as patiently as possible, tapping his thumbs on the steering wheel, and bouncing his knee up and down. He looked over at the package on the seat, nervous about seeing Kira again. Would she take him back? Even though his parents' news had been a bombshell, it just didn't affect his life like it would have before he loved Kira.

He had to get to her. Holt stared at the train, willing it to go faster, or be shorter. Finally, the caboose chugged by and the blockades lifted. Holt sped to the courthouse, and by the time he'd arrived, Holt was sure Kira's hearing had already begun. Still, he hung back in the parking lot for a few minutes to prepare himself to face her. Maybe a walk around the building would calm his nerves.

* * *

"All rise for the honorable Judge Colby," the bailiff called.

Everyone stood and Kira's tension rose like bile in her throat. In just a few moments, she would hear the words that would alter her life forever. She crossed her fingers beside her thighs, glanced at Candace and Zoe, then turned and watched Judge Colby climb the stairs to the bench and sit down. He looked stoic, unreadable.

"Be seated," the judge said, banging his gavel.

Everyone sat, and Kira interlaced her fingers on the table.

"I've read several documents attesting to Ms. McGovern's employment and residential history over the past months. In the court's eyes, she's fulfilled the

271

necessary criteria, proving she is a fit parent. Let the record show Ms. McGovern has full custody of Zoe Phelps." The judge banged his gavel and asked for the next case to be brought before the court, while the Phelps' made sounds of outrage to their attorney.

Kira hugged her attorney, then hugged Candace and Zoe over the railing. "I'll file the adoption papers right now, Kira," her attorney said, snapping shut his briefcase.

"Thank you."

He smiled at her and nodded. "Congratulations."

"Let's go celebrate," Kira said to Candace and Zoe.

"All right!" Candace cheered.

Kira began to walk away, then and heard a strange but familiar sound behind her. She turned and looked toward the window, open to the morning air. She saw a cowboy hat, and below that, Holt's eyes, peering above the ledge.

"Kira," he whispered.

"It's Blockhead!" Candace squealed, grabbing Kira's arm.

Some people milling around that area stopped and watched as Kira went to the window and leaned out.

Holt stood there, his head a few feet lower than hers, a very serious expression on his face. She glanced behind her, noticing the few people watching, and blushed. "What are you doing here?" she whispered, trying to keep her voice from carrying.

"What was the verdict?" he asked, looking past her and around the courtroom.

"Zoe belongs to me, now." She lifted her chin proudly.

"Congratulations, Kira. You're the best mother she could ever ask for."

His candor surprised her. "Thank you."

"It's the truth. And that's why I'm here. To give you the truth."

Kira noticed he held a long, narrow box in his hands and assumed it was a bouquet of her favorite long-stemmed roses. But, she was not going to let flowers sway her. She looked at him, trying to reflect Judge Colby's poker face.

He chuckled. "I'd expected you'd make it hard on me, and you should." Holt cleared his throat. "Listen, Kira. I have some things to say to you, and I'm going to say them right now."

Kira crossed her arms. "I'm listening." Kira had hoped she would never lay eyes on him again, so she could some day wipe his face and memory from her heart. So far, she had had no luck. She had dreamt of him every night, and now here he was, in the flesh.

"Kira." He fidgeted. "I've been an ass. I was wrong in the way I approached you that last night. I believed in you up to that point, but I have no excuse for my lapse. All I can say is I was wrong, and beg you to forgive me."

Kira blinked back a stray tear, but kept her face hard.

"You've taught me that complete love and acceptance is possible, by giving that to me, and by showing me I could love a baby I didn't create." He paused, and Kira heard whispers behind her.

273

"I thought I was man enough to handle the gift of a woman like you, but I was wrong about that, too." He shrugged and looked down a moment, then brought his eyes back to hers.

Kira heard a few chuckles behind her, and she let a faint smile touch her lips. She wanted him back in her life, her arms.

"Well, I'm here to tell you I'm a man now. Nothing matters to me but you and Zoe. Not the ranch, not who my father is, nor what others think. Just you. And Zoe."

Kira choked back a sob.

"I love you, Kira McGovern. I have loved you. I want you to share everything of mine, to be mine, for ever." Holt knelt on one knee and looked up at her, his clear caramel eyes wide and sincere. "I would be humbled and honored, if you would marry me. Let me be your husband and Zoe's father. I promise, you'll never regret it." He offered up the long box. Kira leaned out of the window and lifted it up, setting it on the windowsill.

Her vision seemed to sharpen, as did all of her senses, and she knew Holt watched her, examining every nuance of her reactions.

She loved Holt with a wildness, an intensity, that would never let her go. She would never be complete without him. Tears ran freely down her cheeks. Holt stood up slowly, moving near her as she opened his gift.

She lifted the lid and spread back the tissue paper. Surprised, she laughed, short and quick. Kira pulled from the box a solid silver branding iron, the handle inlaid with the most beautiful turquoise, coral, and jet she'd ever seen. She turned the iron around to see the brand.

It was the Crockett brand, a 'Cr' in block letters, interlaced with a scrolled 'Mc.' She looked into Holt's adoring eyes.

"Everything I own will belong to both of us, and I wanted to prove it. To you and the world."

Candace sighed and sniffled, while Kira laughed and cried.

"So?" he asked, taking one of her hands from the windowsill into his, caressing the top of it with his thumb. "What's your answer?"

When Kira handed the iron back to him, he looked confused. But when she sat on the windowsill and slid out of it backwards, he caught her into his arms, laughing. Their kiss was interrupted by a smattering of applause. A small group had gathered outside and near the window inside, curious about the obviously romantic situation that was occurring. Embarrassed, Kira smiled and tucked her head under Holt's chin.

"Kiss her again," called an older woman in a long denim skirt and colorful western shirt. Holt obliged, and there were a few chuckles as the group dispersed.

"That's a relief." His voice was raspy when he came up for air. "I've ordered twenty-five real irons, just like this, and I had no idea what I was going to do with them if you turned me down."

Kira was delirious with love and happiness. This was right. It felt right, and she would follow her heart.

* * *

275

The wedding had been huge and wonderful, with all the hands and neighbors from miles around in attendance. Kira had changed into her riding clothes while Holt changed and got their gear together. They'd decided to honeymoon at Holt's secret spot in the dessert, and Kira couldn't wait to be alone with him. Her life and heart were complete.

They saddled up under a shower of birdseed and rode out, while Kira waved and yelled good-bye to Zoe and Candace, then the hands: Shorty, Grisly, Stretch, Slim, and all the others.

"You know," he said, after they'd ridden a ways and were alone.

"Yes?"

"You've come up with nicknames for every single one of my men, including Treat."

"Uh huh ..." She looked at him and smiled as sweetly as she could.

"Well, I was just wondering...did you ever come up with one for me?"

Kira grinned wickedly at him and he narrowed his eyes, teasing her back.

"Sweetheart ..." She sighed. "I love you."

"And?"

"And...you don't want to know." She laughed, then spurred her horse into a gallop.

Holt followed.

The End

ABOUT THE AUTHOR

An unemployed engineer by choice, Charlotte claims to be a full-time homemaker. In reality, she home schools her daughters, writes for and produces the newsletter for the Boulder Creek Watershed Initiative in Boulder, Colorado, and writes fiction. She's had one novel and three short stories published. Charlotte is an expert seamstress (she once owned a formal-wear alterations business) and loves to make bread and cheese, embroider, play the flute, and kiss her husband.

Visit Charlotte's website: www.charlotteraby.com

E-mail the author at: charlotteraby@hotmal.com

Charlotte's author page is:

http://www.readerseden.com/manufacturers.php?manufacturerid=105

Other Books from Writer's Exchange That You Might Enjoy:

Heart of the Wild by Rita Hestand (Contemporary Romance)

Kidnapped! And the day before her wedding too! But that wasn't the worst of it. Her kidnapper was none other than her ex-fiancee.

Trapped in a blizzard on a mountaintop with the sexiest man alive, Kasie Moore must struggle with her heart's desire and the independence she has always sought. How can she survive knowing she might lose...the heart of the wild!

In print at Amazon.com, or at:

http://www.readerseden.com/product.php?producti
d=215&cat=0&page=1

A Safe And Welcome Nest by Judith B. Glad (Contemporary Romance)

When loner Jake Borglund comes to Burns, Oregon, all he wants is a home for his son and the solitude to do his snowy plover mating behavior studies. He reckons without Delilah Grey, a contradictory, independent woman who is a combination of Earth Mother and Motorcycle Mama.

So she offers Jake a room and the warmth of family life, something he's never really experienced. Jake's son, Matthew, takes to Delilah immediately. Jake's feelings are more ambivalent--he desires her but he also fears being drawn into the town's social life, for he's never really learned to relate well to people.

Available in print at Amazon.com, and at:
http://www.readerseden.com/product.php?producti
d=179&cat=13&page=1

Travers Brothers Book 1: Chief Cook and Bottlewasher by Rita Hestand (Contemporary Romance)

Trapped in her own lies and uncertainties, Emma Smith was running in fear of losing her baby.

Deke Travers, oldest son on the 4 Bar None Ranch, needed one thing to make his life more peaceful, his brothers to settle down and get with the business of ranching. There was only one solution, marry them off to a country gal!

Then Emma crashed into Deke's life and Deke had found the answer to his problems--he thought! Emma was sweet and beautiful, and when she looked at him with those whiskey brown eyes he was a goner. Deke could tolerate almost anything but a liar! And The Chief Cook and Bottle Washer was lying! Available in print at Amazon.com, and at: http://www.readerseden.com/product.php?producti d=247&cat=13&page=11

Gracie's Holiday Hero by Betty Jo Schuler (Contemporary Christmas Romance)

It's the first day of December, snow is in the air, and Gracie Singleton Saylor's shopping for a Christmas tree when she runs smack into Merett Bradmoore, her high school hero. She can tell at once he's not the happy-go-lucky guy he used to be.

Fifteen years ago, Gracie's family faced a holiday without food or gifts and the handsome high school senior came to their rescue. Gracie, a freshman, fell a little in love with Merett that night and she's believed ever since that dreams do come true. Seeing that Merett, widowed with a seven-year-old daughter, has changed, Gracie is determined to return his gift of optimism. But can she return his hope without losing her own? Available at Amazon.com, and at: http://www.readerseden.com/product.php?producti d=420&cat=13&page=5

Made in the USA